THE DAWN-BREAKERS Novel

by

James J Keene

Preface

A movie screenplay is often based on a novel. However, this novel is based on the film script by the author, recently published as a book in "THE DAWN-BREAKERS Movie".

Some may prefer to read the novel version of the story. The screenplay version might provide a different experience. What if the reader is handed the script and asked to be the Director of the production, "What do you see, hear and feel?"

This is the question that readers of either the movie or novel versions may answer. Those answers suggest a variety of experiences of the story linked to the imagination of each reader.

The objective of the author is that the experience based on either the movie script or this novel version may enrich the lives of readers.

The working title of the movie is "The Dawn-Breakers". This title has become well known among Baha'is from the important historical account presented by Shoghi Effendi, Guardian of the Baha'i Faith from 1921 to 1957.

In about 1986, the author and a prospective investor in the film production were invited to meet with Ruhiyyih Khanum (1910-2000), the widow of the late Guardian, in her suite while at the Theater Hotel, Vienna, Austria. The investor argued to Ms. Khanum that the movie should not have the same title as the Guardian's book. Her response was simple and brief, with a few words to the effect that she did not see any problem at all concerning the movie title.

At that time, the author had sent hundreds of pages including the script and supporting documents to the international administrative body of the Baha'i Faith, known as The Universal House of Justice, in Haifa, Israel. In a written reply, The House advised that the author should maintain control of the project and that they were praying for its success.

In the 1980s before "The Dawn-Breakers" screenplay was written, a detailed chronology of the story did not exist. Yes, many were familiar with the broad outline of the story based on various books that described its key episodes. So to write the film script, the author had to create a time-line of events in the story. This chronology was published in "THE DAWN-BREAKERS Movie", 2021, 30 pages in Appendices A and B.

After the author sent the script and related documents to The Universal House of Justice, one of the members began correspondence with the author. In one of these letters, he noted that he had shared the chronology with persons in the Baha'i community interested in Babi history. This may or may not have been appropriate since the documents at that time had been marked as proprietary materials of Keene Productions. Whatever the case, it appeared that there may have been some public release of the documents, perhaps mainly to Baha'i scholars.

Fast forward to the present writing of the novel version of the screenplay over three decades later. The internet was searched for illustrations for this book. Happily, it was noted that many sources now featured Babi history in chronology tabulations of events and dates, Wiki articles, videos and books, all closely following the chronology created by the author. Is this all original research or did the author's chronology play a role in some of these developments? In any case, the outcome is welcome.

In much of these works, historical figures are portrayed mostly in a one-dimensional, even zero-dimensional, manner. That is, the people are treated as if they were just cardboard cutouts or perfect saints. This can be both unrealistic and boring. In contrast, the movie script and this novel pose the question: what if these figures were real human beings? People who laugh, scream, cry, tell jokes, bleed, shout, smile, dream, get muddy. People with both weak and strong moments.

Finally, some housekeeping items may be helpful.

The dialogue in a screenplay might not include the name of a particular character. Hence, the script might invent descriptive names, like, say, "Waitress" or "Cop #1". This practice is continued in the novel version. Examples: A bread vender is "Bread". A wool vender is "Wool".

Many of the real names of characters are long and unfamiliar to many readers. Thus, many characters are identified with short names. Examples: Mulla Husayn is "Husayn", Abbas Quli-Khan is "General".

Scholarly accounts may carefully include accents on vowels in names of people, places and things. Sorry, folks. No vowel accents here. Technically, there is no ambiguity since each name, whether with or without accents, refers to the same person, place or thing.

The lights are dimming.
THE DAWN-BREAKERS is about to begin.

James J Keene PhD
July 9, 2021

Contents

Anticipation of the Mission of the Bab

This is the true story
of a youth from Shiraz known as the Bab

HAIFA, PALESTINE, 1843

At the Mediterranean shore of the small port of Haifa, Palestine, the sun is about to rise over Mt. Carmel, a barren mass rising right from the shoreline. Austin Wright and Captain move with the gentle sway of a fifty-foot cargo boat, where they sit on the stern rail. Three Arab locals are unloading sacks of grain: one in the hold, one on deck and one stacking the sacks on a cart on the small pier to which the boat is moored.

"A long way from America," says Captain.

"I can't believe I'm here," replies Wright.

"Don't start on that again."

A rooster crows at dawn. A few voices and a baby crying come from the few modest houses lining the street leading up the mountain. Each off-loaded sack thuds on the cart.

Wright: 32, an American Christian missionary, earnest, clean-shaven with moustache, a talker, seeks an audience.

Captain: unkempt beard, middle-aged British adventurer.

The Arab on deck throws a fifty-pound sack to the pier. As it leaves his hands, he hears the sound of wood and rope under suddenly increased tension.

The line attaching the bow to the pier has no slack and the bow rises slightly increasing its tension as each sack is off-loaded.

"People are buying white robes in London ... to climb a mountain like that," Wright says, gesturing toward Mt. Carmel.

Captain is a skeptic. "These people are insane."

The Arab on deck listens to the conversation as he works.

"They're coming here. You'll see!"

Wright gazes up at Mt. Carmel, "It began in 1755 with the great earthquake of Lisbon, Portugal."

A sea swell begins a slow roll of the boat as the Arab tosses another sack off the boat.

The bowline is about to give way. The rope unravels and slips. The deck and pier cleats strain and wood creaks. Cargo shifts below deck. A couple having an argument scream in one of the nearby shacks. It sounds like an earthquake.

The bowline is so tight that the boat can no longer move. Wright continues, "This one ranks first among all recorded earthquakes, killing 60,000 people in six minutes."

The bow-pier attachment gives way. The pier plank with the mooring cleat at the bow breaks loose. The boat bobs up and down. Wright almost goes overboard. Captain grips the stern rail.

"Jesus," Captain says, as he shakes his head in resignation while the Arabs hasten to refasten the bow. A small swell from the sea slams the boat into the pier.

"Are we sinking?" Wright asks with an impish smile.

Captain replies with playful sarcasm, "Just an earthquake."

2

"Ah. Then in 1780 there was the Dark Day. Imagine."

The picture in Wright's mind is a New York street with people looking up, circa 1780. The mid-day sun begins to darken.

"An eclipse?" asks Captain.

"No, the cause was not known," replies Wright. His imagined flashback to the event continues. The sun and sky darken. Star constellations become visible. New York people and animals react, run and look. The moon becomes visible in the darkening sky. Wright continues, "but in the day-time darkness the moon appeared red as blood."

A few seagulls fly by. Dogs are barking in the distance.

Wright looks for a reaction. But Captain just glances up at Mt. Carmel.

The sun has now arisen above the horizon. The sacks keep thumping their way from boat hold to pier cart. The Arab at mid-ship still listens to Wright's description,

"The third thing. The historic shooting star displays of 1799 and 1833. I tell you. All around the world, serious people are preparing for the sudden appearance of Christ next year."

Hearing this, the Arab drops a sack of grain on the deck as if it had become electrified and steps forward crying out in Arabic, "Shi'ihs are waiting for the prophet in Karbala!"

Wright looks to Captain for the English translation, "The Muslims also are waiting for their prophet to return in Karbala."

The Arab can speak a little English and barks out, "Next year. Big trouble," before resuming his work.

Closing his eyes Captain says, "Descend from the clouds, eh?"

Captain recalls having a drink ten years ago with Lt. Francis Farrant and Lt. Justin Sheil in the countryside near Hamadan, Persia. They are in a military tent. They see dancing light from camp fires and hear depraved partying of Persian soldiers in the night.

"Ten years ago in '33, Farrant, Sheil and I were training the Persian cavalry forces of Fath-'Ali Shah. Suddenly there was silence. We looked outside."

They look up at the cloudless sky of Nov 13, 1833. Against the constellations of fixed stars, with that of Leo seen prominently, hundreds of shooting stars appear as flying sparks. This is the famous "Leonid" meteor shower. The dramatic burning of each entering meteor is heard. The breaking of several meteors into pieces is even louder. Fireballs created by large meteorites are breathtaking, followed by thunderclaps. This shooting star display is said to be the biggest recorded in history.

Fath-'Ali Shah, 1834

QAZVIN

Two women walk briskly down a narrow street in the noon sun. We suppose they are women by their voices, since they are completely covered in black veils and the only opening is a cloth grid of a few square inches for them to see out. Their black forms contrast the light brown mud walls along the dusty street. They are Tahirih and Mardiyyih.

Tahirih: 26, is beautiful, a "man's woman", a child prodigy, known as the most educated woman in Persia, a renowned poetess. At age 13, Tahirih had been forced to marry her cousin, now about 35, the son of a Mulla who is a brother of her father. Thus, Tahirih was related as wife-cousin, niece and daughter respectively to three powerful clerics in Qazvin.

Her sister, **Mardiyyih**, 20, is her attractive and faithful companion.

TAHIRIH
Babi Poetess

Others are on the street, as Tahirih's husband passes them.
"That was my husband. Now I've had it."
"If he knew it was us," Mardiyyih replies.
They both laugh. The other women on the street are covered in identical head-to-toe veils which are indistinguishable.

Tahirih's Husband: 35, is cruel and arrogant, but unable to subdue her free spirit and outstanding intellect.

The two women stop at a door along the walled narrow street. It opens just enough to see a man inside. It's Tahirih's uncle, mid-40s, open mind and heart.
Tahirih's eyes are barely visible behind the cloth grid opening in the full body veil. It appears that nothing is happening in this very brief encounter. However, Tahirih discretely passes a letter to her uncle. She pulls it from her sleeve handing it to her uncle, who then disappears behind the door. Not a word is spoken. The women scurry off.
As her uncle, his eyes not yet adjusted to the outdoor, mid-day sun brightness, is about to close the door, he notices a small disturbance down the street. A vendor points to the sky as he hawks copperware vessels from a street cart to potential customers. High in the sky, strange circles or halos appear around the sun. Tahirih's uncle glances upward as he closes the door.

7

It is dark inside the front door hall. He blinks with watered eyes.

He sees a long darkened hall, much like a tunnel, opening into a bright inner courtyard.

He squeezes his eyes shut again.

The light at the end of the passageway is replaced with that of the sun with halos in negative image. It is the after-image still tingling in his visual system. Words cannot describe the beautiful bursts of swirling colors that his vivid imagination freely adds to this unusual image. Blinking several times, in a stroboscopic series of images, he sees his hand rise into the passageway holding the letter from Tahirih. The letter is bound with a ribbon with its wax seal and addressed in Persian calligraphy. The letter rises to match the position of the sun after-image and mix with it. Tahirih's uncle whispers, "Karbala."

Tahirih's room has no windows and the subdued lighting comes from roof ports and the doorway, which opens as she and Mardiyyih romp in. The room is not big, but by the time they reach the other side, they have quickly shed their veils down to simple dresses. They dislike the veil, the discomfort associated with it and waste no time in getting it off now that they have arrived in their own women's quarters. Even though it is a cool day, they are covered with sweat, from the excessive clothing, the vigorous walk and the excitement of their mission. It almost looks like they had been swimming. Tahirih's face is particularly enticing. They embrace. Both are filled with emotion.

Mardiyyih says, "Now you can teach us again tonight."

"Um-hum. Tell the women."

Behind them, Tahirih's desk is filled with papers and books. Mardiyyih, then Tahirih, notice something on the floor behind a chair.

A closer look reveals bits of shredded manuscripts. Furthermore, some books have been torn apart and the ink well had been emptied over precious documents. They sigh at the view of this destruction.

Good thing the women had not yet fully released their embrace, so they can grab each other in sudden fear as a voice booms, "Women should not read and your 'poetry' is disgraceful ... Give it up ... and you can see my children again."

Tahirih's Husband had not yet left the room when the two women entered. He makes his statement and leaves. This is closer to the last, than to the first, altercation between Tahirih and her husband. Tears flow. He is gone but she calls out, "Our children ... my children."

Mardiyyih, speechless, tries to comfort her older sister.

The Shaykhi Movement in Karbala

KARBALA

Mysterious halos appear around the sun quite different in pattern than before. They are seen above the Shi'ih holy city of Karbala in Ottoman Turkish territory (now Iraq), near the provincial capital of Baghdad.

Tens of thousands of Persians flock to this city for its holy shrine of Imam Husayn, a sacred figure in Shi'ih Islam history. And they come to the city, at times, simply to get out of Persia for a while.

Karbala: Imam Hussein Holy Shrine

S G W Benjamin, Persia and the Persians, 1887

RESIDENCE OF SIYYID KAZIM, KARBALA

Siyyid Kazim has paused and is about to finish a talk to a group of some thirty men in a shady porch-like enclosure opening into the courtyard of his ample residence.

Siyyid Kazim, 59, is a Persian spiritual leader of the Shaykhi movement and perhaps the most prominent and respected resident of Karbala. As a measure of his stature, when Turkish troops sacked the city a few months ago (January, 1943) to put down an uprising of a rival Persian faction, the residence of Siyyid Kazim was hardly touched.

As Siyyid Kazim thumbs to a page in the Qur'an, some listeners are seen, including Javad, Sadiq, Mamaqani, Mulla and Karim.

And there is Shaykh seated at the periphery.

SHAYKH, 20 young Babi

Shaykh and a friend, Eyes, late teens, are slightly apart from the group.

There is an empty spot between Shaykh and Eyes on which a ray of light seems to dance on the tiles. The ray shines through a hole in an awning, flapping in the breeze.

Siyyid Kazim speaks, "I am spellbound by the vision. I am mute with wonder ... I am powerless to divulge the mystery and find the people incapable of bearing its weight." He closes the Qur'an and retires through a door to an inner parlor. His listeners begin to disperse.

In the center of Siyyid Kazim's parlor, Farrant sits, cross-legged, at the head of a Persian rug near a tea set. When Siyyid Kazim enters. Farrant, now 35, stands immediately showing deference.

"I heard your statement." says Farrant.

"You're a Christian. You know that the 2,000 year period of Daniel is about to elapse."

"There is discussion."

"Questions?"

"If you permit it, sir," Farrant replies. "The British Ambassador at Istanbul..."

Farrant and Siyyid Kazim plunge into a discussion of the affairs of the day.

FARRANT, 36
British Charge d'Affairs

Back in the courtyard, Eyes begins to move closer, but is detained by a gesture from Shaykh who then places his hand on the spot between them, where the ray of sunlight dances. The dancing of this illuminated spot seems magical.

Shaykh is older than Eyes, sort of the difference between college graduate and high school age.

Shaykh says, "Let me tell you about this spot. A few years ago an intimate of Siyyid Kazim awoke me at dawn." Bingo, just the inside story Eyes wanted.

Shaykh recalls how he, Siyyid Kazim and an intimate associate of Siyyid Kazim walked a Karbala street. Vendors are opening their shops. A man, putting on his turban, eyes them. The intimate associate of Siyyid Kazim is easily into his forties. Clearly, the younger Shaykh, tagging behind the two men, is thrilled to be part of whatever these illustrious gentlemen are about to do. Shaykh narrates, "The morning light had just broken. I followed them through the streets of Karbala. We reached a house. In the open door stood a youth."

Eyes is captivated as Shaykh continues, "He had an expression of kindliness I can never describe. He embraced each of us."

Eyes is leaning forward and has to be reminded not to block the light ray on the spot between them as Shaykh speaks.

"At the upper floor, we entered a chamber bedecked with flowers ... the loveliest perfumes. We sat. At the center ... a silver cup. The youth said, 'A drink of a pure beverage shall their Lord give them'."

Eyes says, "Words from the Qur'an."

Shaykh continues, "Siyyid Kazim drank from the silver cup, forbidden by Islam."

By now, Shaykh and Eyes are alone in the courtyard. Shaykh jumps up to better dramatize the end of his story.

"Three days later, the same youth arrived and sat right there."

The light ray dances on the tiles as Shaykh points. Eyes gives the spot a little more room.

"Siyyid Kazim was speaking to an assembly."

Now Shaykh has stepped up to the spot where Siyyid Kazim speaks some twenty-five feet away and acts out his description, "As soon as his eyes fell upon that young man, he said, 'What more shall I say? Lo, the Truth is more manifest than the ray of light that has fallen upon that lap!'"

Of course, Shaykh has puffed up his posture to his idea of the dignity with which Siyyid Kazim presents himself. He swings his arm around to emphasize how Siyyid Kazim had pointed to the spot where "the youth" had been.

"Some of Siyyid Kazim's listeners, Husayn, Quddus, Mulla, Sadiq, Javad and finally Mamaqani, turned their heads toward him. They all looked curiously. But the mean-looking, one-eyed Mamaqani, an ugly scare over the bad eye, looked disdainfully."

Shaykh surveys the courtyard to see if it is still empty. It is. They are alone.

"O.K. Ask me ... Ask me who this youth is."

Eyes grins, jumps up, raising his hand to be recognized as Siyyid Kazim's students would do and asks, "Can you reveal his name?"

Slitting his throat with his finger, acting Siyyid Kazim's role, Shaykh answers grimly, "If I divulge his name, we both would be put to death instantly."

After a journey from Qazvin, Persia, over the mountains to Karbala, Tahirih's uncle has delivered her letter to Siyyid Kazim one summer night in his parlor.

The opened letter from Tahirih is centered on Siyyid Kazim's writing table. Siyyid Kazim holds another letter, his reply, and speaks to Tahirih's uncle, "Your niece. The most educated woman in Persia. A renowned poetess. Now this."

The uncle asks, with his eyes, "Now this, what?"

Siyyid Kazim hands to him his sealed letter, with these words, "In my reply, I address her as Qurratu'l-'Ayn, 'Solace of the Eyes.' She has already stepped beyond poetry."

CHRISTIAN MISSION, URUMIYYIH

The Christian Mission at Urumiyyih is a handsome stone structure in the northwest of Persia, near the Russian and Turkish borders. This building still stands today. Urumiyyih is now called Rizaiyyih, Iran.

In the front parlor, the American Wright is speaking with a visiting British Bishop, near retirement, who does not share Wright's expectations. Bishop reads the religious newspaper, "Midnight Cry." Not lifting his eyes from the paper, he pays only minimal attention to Wright.

Wright is enthused, "In America, William Miller and Joseph Smith say the coming is imminent."

Bishop replies, "Here it says that British and American societies are spreading the Gospel in every part of the world."

"Just so! Everything is in place."

In his own low key manner, Bishop is skeptical, "With Mt. Ararat not far away and all the cloudiness lately, it might seem so."

Wright has found a listener, "The Sunnis and Shi'ihs say that..."

For the first time, Bishop looks at Wright with more than a glance, "Nothing simple can cross the bridge between us and Islam."

Sensing that he was not getting anywhere, Wright steps outside while Bishop continues relaxing and reading.

In the May-June night air, Wright strolls the crest of a slope with distant mountains barely visible. He looks back at the mission building, thinking, "We say 1844. They say 1260. In our calendar, 1844."

Swiftly, clouds part. Wright beholds the appearance of a stunning sight, the Great Comet of 1843. It was not called "The Great Comet" for nothing. It was so astounding that it was first seen during bright sunlight.

Wright begins to romp, jump and run away from the mission into the darkness. As he dashes off like a child, he screams as if the rocky empty slopes are lined with listeners. Wright always seeks an audience, "Their 1260 is our 1844."

Seated in the mission parlor, Bishop looks up momentarily from his paper. Perhaps the voice (of Wright) he hears in the distance is a whirling dervish. Not to worry. It is not uncommon that human voices in the distance interrupt the night silence.

As Wright's exclamations are now quite loud, a dervish peers at Wright from among some large rocks.

DERVISH, 50s rogue, Sufi mystic

Dervish is a sight rivaling that of the Great Comet. In his 50s, he has long stringy hair and mustache, an unusual outfit accented by his leopard's skin cloak and little round spectacles about to slide down his nose. His face has sharp but pleasant features. With wandering dervishes of this type, one may be dealing with a con-man or simply a bum or a genuine mystic spiritualist of the Sufi tradition.

The moving clouds reveal a fuller view of the Great Comet. Wright shouts, "That's it! It's happening!"

Wright is now dancing, twirling, his arms out-stretched and vocalizing loudly something not quite understandable. The mountains seem crowned by the giant comet glowing above.

Dervish inspects the ecstatic trance of Wright. He fingers his prayer beads and scratches his chin with the curved-blade hatchet commonly carried by such individuals. He seems to be considering several unspoken theories: "This Westerner has seen me here and is making fun of me" or "This Westerner is really with it, whatever it is."

www.ifa.hawaii.edu

Suddenly, Wright freezes as his twirl throws him eye to eye with Dervish. A bit dizzy, Wright notices the sharp, curved hatchet blade. Dervish howls, tosses the hatchet aside, jumping up to twirl in his own reverie. His spectacles fall at Wright's feet. Wide-eyed, exhausted, Wright sighs and dashes after him.

Now two "whirling dervishes" dance on a hill crest below the Great Comet.

THE BAB'S FAMILY RESIDENCE, SHIRAZ

Shiraz:
House of the Bab

Credit: Julio Savi

Illuminated by a lantern, a beautiful, very young baby lies still in a Persian style crib. Its eyes are open. It is absolutely motionless. After a few heart beats, the horror of this sight hits home. All is not well.

These are the moments after the death of the only child of a quiet young man, who will later assume the title of "the Bab," meaning "the gateway" to a new era of history, our modern age.

The Bab's Wife and Mother, tears gushing, sob and wail, hugging the lifeless child and clinging to each other.

It is a silent night, but for an ethereal and profoundly sad Persian chant. These intonations are prayers offered by her husband, the Bab, on this solemn occasion.

Later, the Bab's Wife, despondent, sits on a bench in the small courtyard. She looks up in the direction of the source of the chant, coming from the roof of a second story of the house. Her eyes are wet and red. The Bab's Mother appears and comforts her.

She tells the mother, "He said he was not destined to leave any children."

"Come to bed ... He will not stop until morning."

The Great Comet dominates the night sky. From the courtyard, it appears to connect with a place on the roof of the house. The prayerful chanting continues.

COURTYARD OF SIYYID KAZIM, KARBALA
December, 1843

According to custom, Siyyid Kazim has been prepared for burial. This is not a dream. He is dead. Light filters through moving tree leaves illuminating his figure. Prior to his death, however, there was a dream of a modest Shepherd of similar age to Siyyid Kazim. Consider his story, near the mosque of Baratha, not far from Baghdad.

BARATHA, COUNTRYSIDE NEAR BAGHDAD

In the same position as Siyyid Kazim now lies on his back, the sun-burned and wind-worn face of this Shepherd appears, also in the shade, illuminated by light filtering through moving foliage. The Shepherd opens his eyes and rises to a sitting position, as if rising from the dead. He smiles, seeing his livestock and dog nearby. But he just had a disturbing dream.

IN FRONT OF MOSQUE-I-BARATHA

Baratha aka "Bad Boy" mosque   creativemarket

Camels loaded with possessions mill about in front of the mosque. A group of some twenty men have gathered under a palm in the foreground. The Shepherd and his dog approach with hesitation. He is about the leave, when two men in the group, Sadiq and Javad smile and beckon him to join them.

Just as the Shepherd finds himself among the men, one of them turns for a close look at him. It is Siyyid Kazim. The Shepherd almost collapses. His dog whines when the one-eyed Mamaqani approaches.

Recomposed, the Shepherd quotes from his dream to Siyyid Kazim, "'When you shall have returned to Karbala, there, three days after your return, you will wing your flight to Me'."

Sadiq and Javad, but not Siyyid Kazim, become disturbed.

The Shepherd finishes his account, "That's what the voice said, 'Tell him, from Me'."

Suspicious that a conspiracy might be afoot with respect to their leader, Siyyid Kazim, some of the men can barely restrain themselves. No fool, the Shepherd realizes what methods might be used to extract further information. He sees that he cannot make a run for freedom. He is surrounded. Siyyid Kazim's men would not have harmed him, but the Shepherd is relieved when Siyyid Kazim intervenes smiling, "This was a dream?"

Looking around at the men, the Shepherd carefully

Siyyid Kazim Rashti

21

pronounces in his most credible tone of voice, "Yes, that's right. A dream." His dog wags its tail.

Then Siyyid Kazim states, "There is no doubt of the truth of this dream."

The emotions of the men shift from anger and suspicion toward confusion and grief as Siyyid Kazim continues,

"Would you not wish me to die, that the Promised One may be revealed?"

COURTYARD OF SIYYID KAZIM
1844

Tahirih's uncle had personally delivered Siyyid Kazim's reply to her letter. This kind uncle, Tahirih and her sister, Mardiyyih, then embarked on the long journey to Karbala to study under Siyyid Kazim. Upon their arrival, Mardiyyih awaits a reunion with her husband, Ali, who was already in Karbala as a student of Siyyid Kazim.

Alas, Siyyid Kazim had passed away before their arrival. Now Karbala was buzzing with the expectation that a new era was beginning and a new prophet might appear.

ALI, TAHIRIH's uncle and brother-in-law

The courtyard of Siyyid Kazim's residence is empty. Mardiyyih stands in the doorway to the women's area of the household.

Three men enter the courtyard from the street entrance, Shaykh, Tahirih's uncle and Ali, about 22.

"Ali!" cries Mardiyyih.

Shaykh and Tahirih's uncle stop at the entrance and politely look away as Ali runs to embrace Mardiyyih.

"To have traveled so far only to find that Siyyid Kazim had..." Ali says.
Mardiyyih whispers, "Umm ... you're here."

Husayn, 31, is another of Siyyid Kazim's students. As many of Siyyid Kazim's following, he is a scholar, devoted to religious studies, a Muslim cleric known as "Mulla Husayn." He is handsome and on this day, as he appears on the street in front of Siyyid Kazim's residence, his popularity is evident.

Husayn is not large, either by build or stature and may even be considered on the fragile side physically. He is serious, determined and possessed of an attractive personality that makes him a natural leader. A slight tremor is seen whenever he uses his right hand.

Mounted on horses, Husayn followed by his Brother and Nephew ride toward the residence of Siyyid Kazim. Husayn's Brother and Nephew, younger men, are almost constant companions devoted to Husayn.

Attracted by the sound of a crowd, Tahirih's uncle and Shaykh emerge from the front entrance of Siyyid Kazim's residence to see the three men near the stand of a bread vendor.

BREAD, Arab vender in Karbila

This vendor -- let us call him **"Bread"** -- is short, stout, flabby, unkempt, gruff, without class.

In the threshold of the dwelling next to Siyyid Kazim's, Husayn's mother, early 40's and his sister, Bibi, mid teens, wearing face veils, scarfs and dark dresses, watch the scene.

"Look at him!" Bibi says.

Husayn's mother, standing behind Bibi, wraps her arms around Bibi and replies stoically, "Take a good look at your brother."

A young boy, who will be called Street, then 10 years old, is thrilled to touch Husayn's saddle, as the crowd presses in.

From a window on the outer side of the parlor of Siyyid Kazim's residence, Tahirih lifts her shawl to cover her face and peers out at Husayn.

Near the rump of Husayn's horse, Street cups his hands to form a step to hoist his younger brother -- call him Kid, only five years old -- up on to the horse. High-strung and prancing in place, the horse shifts position. Street and Kid hit the ground.

Kid and **Street** are brothers visiting Karbala with their father, a widower; are "lower class" and often seem unaware of "manners"; they wear something distinctive to be easily recognized about three years later.

STREET, 12
Babi hero from Shiraz

Above the voices of well-wishers all speaking at once, the Bread vendor calls to Husayn, "Stay in Karbala! It is you they want. Thousands are coming! Big business!" as if a bread vendor could select or appoint the Promised One.

Husayn is expressionless. His Brother and Nephew are shocked by the crassness of this remark.

Street and Kid, grinning, are again positioned beside the rump of Husayn's horse.

We notice the tremor in his right hand when Husayn pulls out a coin. He tosses it to the Bread vender, who eyes it before enclosing it in his fist.

Plop! Kid lands on the horse's rump behind Husayn.

The Bread vender steps back from his stand, opening his arms. No one doubts the meaning. Quickly and orderly, the group cleans all the bread from the stand.

Joy in her eyes, Tahirih chuckles. Everyone is having fun.

Kid pulls himself up to sit behind Husayn. Though very young and with his hands on Husayn's shoulders, clearly Kid is daring and agile. The crowd cheers him.

Two glassy-eyed men seated smoking water pipes stare straight ahead, as if none of this activity was taking place.

Surveying and enjoying the near anarchy, the Bread vender notices that Husayn is staring at him and runs into his shop.

Kid manages to stand behind Husayn on the horse.

The Bread vendor reappears, carrying more bread from the shop for the people. More cheers.

Husayn's Brother and Nephew laugh, seeing that Kid behind Husayn and out of Husayn's view, has raised an arm in a victory expression and bows to the crowd, as if the cheers were only for him. Realizing what is

KID, 10
survives Tabarsi siege

happening, Husayn also laughs and snatches Kid down to his lap and hugs him.

At that instant, the eyes of Tahirih and Husayn meet and remain interlocked as Husayn's horse continues shifting position. No question of the profound mutual admiration.

HUSAYN, 35

Tahirih turns away from the window. The shawl raised to cover her face slips down. She is glowing. She repositions the shawl over her face when she notices that Mardiyyih and Ali are standing on the other side of the room in the doorway. Looking out the window again, she says, "Mulla Husayn will not rest until he has found the treasure hard to attain."

Turning to Mardiyyih and Ali, she touches a sealed letter to her cheek, crossing the room toward them.

"And when you, Ali, shall have also found him, would you offer this expression of my love and devotion?" she asks as she places this letter in Ali's hand.

Mardiyyih beams with pride at her husband.

Proclamation of the Mission of the Bab

THE BAB'S FAMILY RESIDENCE, SHIRAZ

Uncle, early 40s, raised the Bab almost as a father and is a successful merchant. His dress is elegant but not ostentatious. He is a gracious host to the new friends of his nephew, Siyyid 'Ali-Muhammad (later known as the Bab).

UNCLE of the Bab beheaded in Tehran

The house of the Bab is part of a complex near to the residence of the Bab's Uncle.

It is night. Looking up from a small courtyard, Husayn can be seen standing at the top of a stairway to the second floor. His posture is casual but it might seem that he is guarding the entrance. The Bab's Wife emerges carrying a tray with tea cups and descends the stairs.

Quddus: 22, confident, relaxed, but respectful; handsome, with a sensitive face of a poet; clean-shaven. His dress is colorful and unusual, even bizarre, compared to other young men of his class who were religion students.

Ali and Quddus sit in the courtyard. The Bab's Wife passes them. Uncle asks, "Would you men like some tea?"

Ali, "Oh ... no thank-you, sir, we're fine."

Uncle, "I hope my young 'Ali-Muhammad is not keeping you waiting."

Ali, "Ah ... no ... Actually, he..."

In the interior hallway behind Husayn, Mulla enters from a room and heads for Husayn and the stairs.

Quddus nudges Ali to signal that Husayn and Mulla are descending the stairs.

Quddus chimes in to Uncle, "Actually, sir, we were just on our way out. You have been more than kind."

QUDDUS, 22
Babi leader, martyr

Mulla: named Mulla 'Ali, a little older than Husayn and sports a full beard with strands of gray.

The four men exit the house of the Bab to the street from the front entrance, which is a double door in a wall enclosing the residence. As Husayn closes the doors, Mulla grabs both arms of Ali in a friendly, excited manner, "Listen to this."

Back against the wall, Ali looks to Quddus, "I was going to tell him..."

Quddus, "Tell him what? What would you say to the uncle of the Bab who has been like a father to him?"

Mulla, "Listen, 'Ali. I am to deliver a message to Qurratu'l-Ayn."

Across the narrow street on the second story, a woman opens a curtain to look.

Husayn, "Gentlemen, let's go."

SMALL GUEST ROOM, SHIRAZ
Summer, 1844

Night in a small room. Husayn, Mulla, Ali and Quddus have joined thirteen others, including Brother, Nephew, Eyes, Hadi, Ahmad, Yusuf, Jalil and Mahmud, in these cramped quarters.

Husayn remains standing as the others settle in to help in a bee-hive of activity. By candle and lantern light, groups are engaged in copying documents written in beautiful Persian script. If any discussion is heard, it would be comments such as "more paper", "out of ink here", "here's an error", "compare this with the original" and the like. It would seem that we are in a crude ad hoc 1840s copy shop.

Husayn, "The first nineteen with the Siyyid-i-Bab is now completed ... by a woman..."

Brother, "A woman."

Husayn replies to his Brother, "Don't look so amazed."

Nephew, "He is amazed, Husayn."

Husayn, "It is the poetess of Qazvin, Qurratu'l-Ayn."

Brother to the others, "Like he said, don't look so amazed."

Husayn to Quddus, "And the last of our number to have spontaneously recognized the Siyyid-i-Bab is Quddus."

Quddus to Husayn, "The last thanks the first."

Husayn, "'The last' may be 'the first'."

These 17 men, along with Tahirih and the Bab, are the initial Dawn-Breakers.

Husayn, "We shall soon leave Shiraz."

بسم الله الرحمن الرحيم

الحمد لله الذي ينزل الكتاب حقا معيّنا من عباده وما ادركم الا الله الأمر

لقد جاءكم ٥ وما نزل الكتاب لا ريب فيه قد فصّله حكم بالحق القرآن

تنزيلا من الله على حكيم ٥ وان ذلك الكتاب خير من بقية الله رب بات

لا بغير من عالمين بله ما في السموات وما في الارض وان المؤمنين

وحكم الكتاب لله حاشكم وت ٥ ان امنوا الله يا اصل الرق ثم اعلموا

ان حجر الله بالغير عليكم بعد ما سمعتم امن عالمك عبدنا ما حكم ٥ وقد

قد ارسلنا اليكم ان نزل كتابا مبراب بينات من الله القوم يوقنون

وانزل الكتاب بعد انزل نحكم بالحق القرآن من الله عاصرا طنوديم

ما يترها الله لا كثر كرلايا كلمه الشرك لا ترك ضوف حكم الله يوم القيمه بينكم

والعلا فيوسك ان يبدوا الاحسنكم من ولي علي الاظهر ؟ وكمكر الله

Text by the Bab in the handwriting of Mulla Husayn.

These 17 initial Babis travel from Shiraz in every direction to far-flung destinations.

CENTRAL SQUARE OF TEHRAN
Capital of Persia

Sunny day in the large open central square of Tehran. Around the square are government buildings, businesses and some offices of diplomatic legations. People are going about their business. Wright and Bishop walk by the Golestan palace of the Shah.

Tehran: Golestan Palace

Credit: Julio Savi

OFFICE OF PRIME MINISTER AQASI

Prime Minister Haji Mirza **Aqasi** is an old man who to all except the Shah is insolent, arrogant and sarcastic. As long as he can maneuver the Shah to approve his actions, Aqasi has complete power. Corrupt, cunning, vain. His dress appears almost shabby compared to what might be expected for a man in his position. Short, long nose, poorly dyed hair, shrill voice, rat-faced.

Aqasi sits at his desk holding a sealed written Epistle. Husayn stands by the closed office door and is not impressed by any display of pomp and circumstance. Aqasi eyes Husayn as he revolves the document in his hands. A Persian knife lies on the desk surface.

Aqasi, "The Shah is suffering these days. The gout. And this? From whom..."

Husayn, "Mister Prime Minister, it is from the Siyyid-i-Bab to the Shah. The epistle itself contains everything."

Husayn opens the door and moves to leave. Hearing a snap, Husayn sees that Aqasi has opened the document with his knife. Almost out, Husayn pauses saying firmly, "For the eyes of the Shah."

Husayn now gone, Aqasi is miffed and proceeds to read.

Aqasi repeats the line, "For the eyes of the Shah."

He abruptly folds the document and puts it in a lower desk drawer.

CENTRAL SQUARE OF TEHRAN

Now in September, outside in the central square of Tehran, the mysterious halos around the sun seen at the beginning of the year, reported in the press around the world, are seen again in yet another pattern.

Wright and Bishop walk out of the square down a street toward the British Mission. Other people are about.

BRITISH LEGATION

Inside the British legation, Major Justin Sheil, 40, now the envoy to the Shah, is seated. Lt.-Col. Francis Farrant, 36, soon to be Secretary of the Legation, stands nearby and hands to Sheil some paper work.

Farrant, "This report to London is ready for your signature, sir."

Sheil skims the pages as Farrant continues.

SHEIL, 42
British Envoy

"Captain Hennell in Bushihr reports that near anarchy reigns in Shiraz."

Sheil, "Rebellious tribes, kidnappings, common criminals. The Shah has appointed Husayn Khan as the new governor. He'll straighten it out."

Farrant is disgusted, "Through mutilations and executions."

Sheil motions his reply with arms and face, "What do you expect?"

Bishop and Wright arrive in the legation parlor. Bishop, "May I introduce our new envoy to Persia, Maj. Justin Sheil. This is an American friend, Reverend Austin Wright."

Wright, "An honor, sir."

Sheil and Wright shake hands. Sheil is self-satisfied; Farrant is jealous. Sheil wastes no time to hand to Wright a London "Times" newspaper from a stack,

"The pleasure is mine ... Beyond souls, you might be interested in ... what is it called ... the telegraph of Mr. Samuel Morse."

Wright examines the headline, "What Hath God Wrought", then looks up as Sheil continues,

"Quite a choice for the first message, don't you think?"

HOUSE OF BAHA'U'LLAH, TEHRAN

Meanwhile, outside the house of Baha'u'llah in Tehran, Husayn waits. Facing away from the house, he glances back, but not enough to see Musa looking out of a second story window at him.

PARLOR OF SIYYID KAZIM, KARBALA
Autumn, 1844

Mulla stands in the center of the room and is tensely waiting for the reply of Tahirih. Behind a curtain in an adjacent room, Tahirih looks at the letter that the Bab instructed Mulla to deliver to her. The form and appearance of these pages is similar to those seen previously being copied by the disciples of the Bab. Tahirih and Mulla cannot see each other.

Tahirih, "Mulla 'Ali, you there?"

Mulla, "Yes."

Tahirih now reads with pride. "'All praise be to God, Who hath, through the power of Truth, sent down this Book unto his servant, that it may serve as a shining light for all mankind'." Mulla's tenseness vanishes.

ROOF OF JAVAD'S KARBALA HOME

Haji Siyyid Javad, about 40, is a distinguished follower of Siyyid Kazim. He and Mulla share a few moments in the cool night air. Javad looks up from a manuscript, "This is a great event. Who is it? Who wrote this?"
Mulla, "It is forbidden. We cannot mention his name to anyone."

KARBALA STREET

Mardiyyih runs as best she can in the full body veil down the street through the people.
At his bread stand, Bread chuckles delighted with the news he imparts to Javad and Tahirih, "Mulla 'Ali went to Najaf. The Mullas there were incensed by the news that some one would dare to claim to be the expected prophet."
Mardiyyih finds and embraces Tahirih. In panic, out of breath, she whispers, "Mulla 'Ali has been arrested."
Tahirih, "Oh, no."
Mardiyyih, "Blasphemy is the charge."

BRITISH LEGATION, TEHRAN
Winter, 1845

Farrant reads a dispatch to Sheil, "Rawlinson writes from Baghdad, 'The Court of Inquisition convened for the trial of the Persian priest ... witnesses stated that he had in their presence declared his adoption of the spurious text, of which he was the bearer'."

The dispatch describes events in the Turkish Courtroom in Baghdad, where Mulla sits cross-legged, back straight gazing up. He looks defiant and unyielding. He bears cuffs on neck, wrists and ankles, connected with heavy chains.

Farrant continues reading, "The Sunni law-officers adjudged the culprit to be convicted of blasphemy and passed sentence of death on him accordingly, while the Shi'ihs returned a verdict, that he was only guilty of dissemination of blasphemy and liable in consequence to no heavier punishment than imprisonment or banishment."

UNCLE'S PARLOR, SHIRAZ
Spring, 1845

Uncle sits on a divan behind a table. He has received a guest, Quddus, who stands while Uncle briefly inspects him and his somewhat tattered appearance from a long journey.

Uncle, "My nephew's friend, greetings."

Quddus, "Now, more than a friend, sir."

Quddus steps forward. He spreads several pages of beautiful Persian writing on the table, "The Siyyid-i-Bab sends this to his beloved uncle."

Uncle, "My nephew? ... Gate? Bab? A 'gate' to what?"

Uncle looks up at Quddus.

Quddus, "These are the 'Seven Qualifications'."

Uncle picks up the first page and reads. Meanwhile, with a warm sympathetic chuckle, "Young man, my dear 'Ali-Muhammad is qualified as a merchant. But he had almost no schooling ... Qualifications? ... Could this be?"

The State Reacts - Shiraz

MOSQUE-I-NAW, SHIRAZ

Near sunset inside the Mosque-i-Naw staircase. Seen from above from a dark interior, Quddus is now freshened up in a new, clean outfit. He is with Ali-Askar, a conventionally dressed young man. They stand in a sun-drenched arched entrance looking up as Sadiq, an old man with ample beard and simple yet distinguished appearance, slowly climbs the stairs upward into near darkness.

Shiraz: The New Mosque (Mosque-i-Naw)

J A V Willians, Persia Past and Present, 1906

Outside, the courtyard is active with groups of people in conversation. Some are spreading prayer mats. Others are alone, kneeling and reading the Qur'an. A Shiraz Mulla, an elderly distinguished teacher and leader, instructs a group of young Islamic theology students, waving his arms.

At the top of the mosque in the late afternoon light, Sadiq emerges from almost total darkness, except for bright slits of light entering small openings in the side of the stairway.

SADIQ, mulla crusty, old reformer

With a panoramic view of Shiraz behind him, Sadiq begins to chant the Adhan, which is the Islamic call to afternoon prayer.

As Sadiq's chants, much background sound is hushed. The students of the Shiraz Mulla disperse to spread their prayer mats.

Suddenly, visibly upset, the Shiraz Mulla looks up at Sadiq at the top of the mosque. He then walks briskly off. Two similar mullas join him. They march off with determination.

RECEPTION ROOM OF KHAN

Later, in his reception room at dusk, Khan stands in front of a window. His powerful position is reflected by his ornate military dress, his demeanor of authority, deference shown to him by others and the rich interior of this reception room of the provincial governor. Past a table with expensive ornaments is beautiful wall mirror work and wood carvings in this impressive room.

The main entrance doors burst open. Quddus, Ali-Akbar and Sadiq, all three cuffed with chain from neck to wrists to feet, are pushed into the room. As they move forward, the Shiraz Constable enters.

Then the Shiraz Mulla and the two Mullas who joined him at the mosque enter, looking concerned, but satisfied. They tell Khan about Sadiq's call to prayer.

Khan, "Go on."
Shiraz Mulla, "The call for evening prayer is a tradition twelve centuries old ... Ah ... they changed it."

KHAN, 40
Fars Governor at Shiraz

Khan steps to a table and picks up the first page of a document. He angrily addresses Sadiq, with sarcasm, "Tell me if you are aware of this text wherein this 'Siyyid-i-Bab' addresses the rulers and kings of the earth in these terms." Khan reads from the document, "'Divest yourselves of the robe of sovereignty,...'"

While Khan reads, Quddus, on the floor next to Sadiq, smiles and glances at Sadiq who maintains his gaze on Khan. Khan continues, "'...for he who is the king of truth, hath been made manifest. The kingdom is God's' and etc and etc."

Khan sits looking away out the window and says, "If this is true, it must apply to my sovereign, Muhammad Shah, whom I represent in this province. Must he lay down the crown? Must I relinquish my power?"

Sadiq replies without hesitation, "If these are the Word of God, the abdication of Muhammad Shah and his like can matter but little. It can..."

The Shiraz Mullas are shocked. Their reaction ranks well into the upper half of the "miffed mulla" scale.

Khan, still looking out the window, interrupts, "Enough! Who are you people? Strip them ... One thousand lashes ... Ride to Bushihr. Arrest this 'Siyyid-i-Bab'."

MOSQUE-I-NAW, SHIRAZ

The next day, a crowd has formed in front of the Mosque-i-Naw. The three prisoners, Sadiq, Quddus and Ali-Akbar, no shoes, loin cloths only, bloodied from lashes, are led by the Constable and four soldiers. The crowd moves back as they proceed.

Some stones are thrown, as another soldier suddenly appears with a lit torch. Sadiq's beard is completely burned off producing serious skin burns.

CONSTABLE, under KHAN at Shiraz

The torch is maneuvered to burn off the beard of Ali-Akbar, too. The faces of the three are blackened with pigment.

In a dimly lit Shiraz dungeon, inch-deep sewage covers the stone floor. Sadiq, Quddus and Ali-Akbar lie, backs up with their wounds exposed, appearing to be dead. However, hands or arms prop their faces above the water level. A key in lock and heavy door opening signals somebody is coming. A rat runs across their backs towards Sadiq. He opens one eye, saying sweetly, "Good morning."

Back in front of the Mosque-i-Naw, today's situation is similar to yesterday's -- Quddus, Sadiq, Ali-Akbar, Constable, four soldiers, the crowd.

The noses of the prisoners are pierced and through this incision a leather cord is passed. At each step, the crowd screams of approval increase in volume. Coins are thrown to encourage the soldiers. Dogs bark.

The prisoners are led by these cords through the streets of Shiraz. People jeer, many positioned on building tops for a better view.

BUSHIHR TO SHIRAZ ROAD

A soothing sound of the wind contrasts the din of crowds during the punishment of the three Babis in Shiraz.

With beautiful mountain peaks in the distance, a rider makes his way on the Bushihr to Shiraz road. This is the Bab's Ethiopian servant. Large bundles of belongings attached to his horse, moving slowly down an incline at a walk pace. He stops, stands in the stirrups and calls ahead to the Bab, "Siyyid-i-Bab! Seven days to Shiraz!"

Twelve horsemen appear charging up the rocky trail, framed by a steep mountain slope on the right and a precipice on the left. Even without their soldiers' garb and gear, they would look fierce and menacing. The mere sight of these types causes villagers to flee to their homes and bolt doors.

The horsemen almost run right over the Bab when they suddenly pull up. Keyed up and dripping with perspiration, their horses snort and shift around. But the horsemen appear subdued when the Bab addresses them, "Where are you going?"

Shiraz Horseman, the leader, is uncomfortable, "Ah ... We're conducting an inquiry ... in Bushihr."

Ethiopian cautiously rides up to the horsemen. Meanwhile, the Bab says, "Here I am ... The governor has sent you to arrest me. I came out to meet you, to shorten your trip and make it easier to find me."

One of the horsemen grins and pulls out chains with leg and neck cuffs. Affected by the clanging sound, his horse spins around, prancing in place.

Ethiopian's concern is visible.

Startled by the candor of the Bab, Shiraz Horseman motions to his men to ignore the Bab. The horsemen prepare to leave, but the Bab continues, "I know that you are seeking me. I prefer to deliver myself into your hands, rather than subject you and your companions to unnecessary annoyance for my sake."

The Shiraz Horseman dismounts and approaches the Bab's horse, saying, "Please, escape from this place! The governor is a wolf. My men. Their word is their bond. We pledge not to betray your flight."

The Bab replies, "You do not yet know the mystery of my cause ... I will never flee the decree of God."

The Shiraz Horseman glances around to see if his horsemen are reacting to this unusual response of a supposed fugitive.

It is not evident that these rough types comprehend much of anything.

The Shiraz Horseman holds the reins near the bit of the Bab's horse. He is a practical man, knows what might be in store and shakes his head in disbelief, "But we wish you no harm."

"Do not be afraid ... no one will blame you," the Bab replies.

The Bab and the Ethiopian followed by twelve horsemen wind their way through the spectacular panorama of the mountainous terrain toward Shiraz.

SHIRAZ STREET

With the Bab and Ethiopian in front, the twelve horsemen arrive in Shiraz. As they pass by, people watch. Others scamper along roofs for a view. Others emerge from interior bazaars to enter the street. Some cheer and some jeer. Khan watches from an upper window of the governor's palace. He is incredulous, "He is leading my men!"

RECEPTION ROOM OF KHAN

Later, a lone chair has been placed in the center of Khan's large reception room. To the right, Khan stands behind his table. To the left stands an Attendant of the governor's palace, near a closed double door. Uncle and Abu-Turab stand by a divan.

Abu-Turab: By his advanced age, his bearing and distinctive clothing, it is clear that Shaykh Abu-Turab is a man of high standing. Indeed, he is the chief Mulla of Shiraz.

The doors open. The Bab enters and sits in the lone chair at the middle of the room.

Khan firmly addresses the Bab, "Do you realize what mischief you have caused? Disgrace of Islam. Of our sovereign. Are you not the man who claims to be the author of a new book which annuls the precepts of the Qur'an?"

As Khan speaks, he bears down over his table leering at the Bab, who replies, "If any bad man comes to you with news, clear up the matter at once, lest through ignorance you harm others and later be forced to regret what you have done."

Khan, "Are you calling us ignorant?"

Clearly, no one speaks to the governor as the Bab did. Khan motions to his Attendant, who steps forward and plants his feet directly in front of the Bab. The Attendant strikes the Bab on the head.

The Bab's green felt fez hits the floor and rolls. Uncle is distraught and sighs in anguish.

Abu-Turab is also displeased. He intervenes, "The youth has merely quoted a verse from the Qur'an."

Now Khan is embarrassed in addition to being vexed. After all, he had apparently not realized that his "heretic" prisoner had cited the holy book of Islam.

Abu-Turab crosses to pick up the fallen fez, saying, "The wise course, I feel, is to inquire into this matter with great care."

With Attendant standing nearby, Khan looks intently at Abu-Turab. Slowly collecting his thoughts, he suddenly turns his gaze toward the Bab, "All right!" Calming down and turning away, "All right."

Biela's Comet Split in Two

TEHRAN
1836

A cold night ten years ago. No electric lights. The glow from many light sources provides of warm sight of many colors as light filters through curtains. Darkness obscures a clear view, but the moon illuminates the south gate to the city in the foreground. Dim diffuse light from within the city reveals its expanse, framed above by the majestic snow covered peak of Mount Damavand in the distance.

Above the city on this cloudless night, a stunning "raining of comets" peppers the constellations of stars. Still higher in the night sky, a spectacular view of Biela's comet dominates even the historic rare comet shower. The gigantic tail of Biela's comet occupies much of the sky. With a telescope one could have seen the breaking off of the material forming the comet's tail. The comet literally splits into two comets.

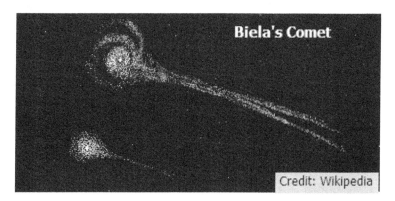
Biela's Comet
Credit: Wikipedia

HOUSE OF BAHA'U'LLAH, TEHRAN
Winter, 1846

Outside the house of Baha'u'llah, Quddus looks up recalling the spectacle of the split Biela's comet ten years ago. He knocks on a door. A Servant opens the door, cautious in view of the late hour and the stranger. They speak in hushed tones.

Servant, "Yes."

Quddus, "Siyyid-i-Bab, servant of Jinab-i-Baha."

As if this were the correct password, the Servant opens the door more, enough for Quddus to slip in.

Inside the house of Baha'u'llah, Quddus meets Majid and Musa.

MUSA, 30
Persian nobleman

Majid: early 30s, secretary to the Russian Legation and brother-in-law of Baha'u'llah, later called "Jinab-i-Baha".

Musa: also about 30, a brother of Baha'u'llah.

Both Majid and Musa appear distinctly older than Quddus, now 24, if only because of their more formal dress. Baha'u'llah's family was of noble lineage, had extensive acquaintances with high government officials and therefore walked a tight rope due to their allegiance to the Bab.

Tea is served by the Servant. Musa and Majid are seated on the divan.

Quddus, an affable and good-humored conversationalist, must stand and pace to punctuate his story with gestures and "body English".

Quddus, "I remained with the Bab after everyone had been sent on missions throughout Persia and beyond.

Each received their instructions. Mulla Husayn was to find someone in this city."

Musa, "Husayn was here."

Quddus, "He was?"

Majid, "At this house ... Go on."

Quddus, "The Bab and I left Shiraz to go on pilgrimage. We made our way to Mecca and Medina where he proclaimed the new message."

Majid to Musa, "As foretold by tradition."

Quddus, "Back in Shiraz, Sadiq altered the call to prayer and we were shown the way out of town!"

Quddus chuckles, shaking his head.

Turning serious, Majid interjects, "We heard considerably more than that! Now the Bab is under house arrest. His uncle posted bond. Tehran has been swept by rumors."

Musa smiles, "They say the Bab is a magician. Few know what is really happening."

Majid, "Which reminds me. A new envoy has just arrived from St. Petersburg. As secretary to the Russian Legation, I must be present at the palace. The Shah is hosting a reception."

Musa, "But you, young man, are envoy of the real king."

PALACE OF THE SHAH, TEHRAN

Cut to a night view of a large room in the palace of the shah.

Major Justin **Sheil**: now 42, British Envoy, blond, a bit on the stern side reflected in his manner and military dress.

Prince Dimitri **Dolgorukov**: 49, Russian Envoy, just arrived at his post in Tehran; handsome, suave, largish mustache, subtle sense of humor, more the relaxed type, dress that of a Russian nobleman. A generation before, his family almost assumed control of the monarchy in Russia.

Sheil and Dolgorukov chat as they stroll down the opulently furnished room. They are in a good mood. Each exudes confidence and is everything a great power could want in an ambassador to an important country.

Dolgorukov, "Astronomers in St. Petersburg say this exceeds the shooting star display over ten years ago which itself had no historic comparison."

**DOLGORUKOV, 50
Russian Envoy**

Sheil, "Umm. Soon after the first one, Fath-'Ali Shah fell. Let's hope we don't have to stabilize Persia again this time."

They reach the door of the office of War. Aqasi is heard shouting within. Sheil moves to enter. There is no visible movement of the posted guard to intercede. Dolgorukov gestures for a pause.

Dolgorukov, "Can we just walk right in?"

Sheil smiles, "My men are inside."

OFFICE OF MINISTER OF WAR

Aqasi: Prime Minister, resents his dependency on Britain and Russia, who had assisted Muhammad Shah to the Crown of Persia and hence his own ascent to Prime Minister. Britain has long provided military training and equipment in return for trading concessions throughout Persia and has a network for intelligence on activities in the country that is often more efficient than that of the Prime Minister.

About 20 years earlier Russia had defeated Persia, gaining vast lands north of the Aras river near Mt. Ararat. As he often did, Aqasi is dressed almost as a beggar in a dark woolen cape, to emphasize, as he would say, his spiritualism and humility, both of which he totally lacked. This outfit contrasts the formal dress of the elite in an almost comic manner.

War: Mirza Aqa Khan, about 40, Persian Minister of War, ambitious, a bit conceited, unreliable; chubby but not fat; overshadowed by Aqasi.

Lt.-Col. Francis **Farrant**: had trained Persian cavalry forces and is now in the British diplomatic legation.

Officer: currently a British military advisor.

WAR, 40
Persian Minister of War

Speaking loudly, Aqasi taps his cane as a pointer to the NE section of a large wall map of Persia. The map shows a "distorted view" because it's an authentic version circa 1845. War seems insignificant sitting on a divan. Farrant and Officer stand listening.

Aqasi, "In the northeast..."

Sheil and Dolgorukov enter, interrupting Aqasi. No need for introductions. They have all met previously.

Dolgorukov sees Aqasi switch his cane to the NW of the map, previous Persian territory now marked "Russia". Tapping his cane on this spot, gazing at Dolgorukov, "And in the northwest, we are concerned by ... nothing! Russia took those lands from Persia ... and their problems, too."

Aqasi bursts out in laughter. One might think he is a madman if his sarcastic character were not known, as was the case, to some extent, by the new Russian envoy, Dolgorukov.

A man of considerable experience, Dolgorukov is unfazed and is about to issue a no-doubt-diplomatic reply when Aqasi chimes in, "Just a joke ... for Nicholas, if you had been Tsar Dolgorukov and Nicholas, your envoy here."

Sheil, "Such was almost the case ... by a hair."

Dolgorukov smiles, "By a hair."

An attendant to Aqasi opens the door enough to pop his head in, nods to Farrant, then retires.

Farrant, "Your highness, dinner."

Aqasi, "Ah. To think about. We had over 20,000 Persians in Karbala waiting for ... God knows what."

Sheil to Dolgorukov, "A Persian Babi was arrested, but the Turks refused to deport him."

Aqasi, "He might have provided useful information." Tapping map sites with his cane, Aqasi continues, "Now we have reports of Babis in Tabriz, Ardibil, Qazvin, Takur,

Mashhad, Bushruyih, Yazd, Kirman, Kashan, Isfahan and Shiraz."

Dolgorukov is adjusting to the situation. Although he is very proper, he is not beyond subtlety goading Aqasi.

Dolgorukov, "Almost all of Persia."

Aqasi, "By a hair."

Sheil, "There is an unusual influx of people into Shiraz."

Aqasi, "We don't know who is really behind this, but a young lunatic in Shiraz has written this:" Then reading, "'O concourse of kings ... Lay aside, one and all, your dominion which belongeth unto God'. This is seditious!"

Dolgorukov to Sheil, "And to think that Christians were climbing mountains to gain a better view."

Aqasi, "Excuse me?"

Dolgorukov, "Nothing important, sir. Umm. Some say the comet and the Bab are one and the same."

Aqasi, "Hysteria of a few Persians. Is not the same comet seen by the Queen of England?"

As if ready for the right moment, Sheil pulls out a copy of the "London Times", Nov 19, 1845, handing it to Aqasi, "Well, a serious incident with some Babis in Shiraz was reported in the 'London Times'."

Examining this article, headlined "Muhammadan Schism", the sarcastic attitude of Aqasi yields to one of concern, which he would rather not show.

Aqasi, "The Shah awaits us."

PALACE OF THE SHAH

A room full of women of the highest class exhibits the ladies of the palace entertaining the female guests of the reception for Dolgorukov. The chatter is interrupted when Prince Nasiri'd-Din, an insecure, aimless 15 year old boy, partially opens a curtain blocking a corner entrance and peers in. He sounds unhappy.

Nasiri'd-Din, "Mother."

He nervously surveys the room trying to spot his mother, when a hand appears on his shoulder. The

Prince reluctantly brings down his arm holding the curtain open, allowing it to fall back into position. Behind the curtain is a larger room full of men.

It was the hand of the Prince's Tutor, an old scholarly type, on the shoulder of Prince Nasiri'd-Din. A sitar player with the traditional Persian instrument plays music. Aqasi stands behind Muhammad Shah and carefully studies the situation. Muhammad Shah sits on a rug-covered royal platform looking at his son, Nasiri'd-Din. Among many guests, Majid talks with Vahid. Sheil talks with Dolgorukov, the guest of honor. Refreshments are available, as are water pipes and other accessories for tobacco, hashish or opium.

Tehran: Golestan Palace interior

Muhammad Shah: 38, with absolute power of life or death over anyone at any time, nevertheless appears feeble in his royal garb as he chews on chunks of meat. No wonder he suffered from the gout.

Vahid (the "Unique One"): 35, known here as "Siyyid Yahya", probably the most erudite man in Persia; trusted by the Shah because of his integrity and therefore posed a threat in the eyes of Aqasi. If any of the figures seen so far are truly urbane and suave, they are Dolgorukov and Vahid.

Sheil leans slightly to narrate the scene to Dolgorukov in a low voice.

Across the room the Prince's Tutor apparently reasons with Prince Nasiri'd-Din.

Sheil, "Prince Nasiri'd-Din is in line for the throne. His tutor, there, says the prince is imperfectly acquainted with reading and writing in his own language."

MUHAMMAD SHAH, 38 sickly monarch

As Sheil speaks, Nasiri'd-Din, sulking, steps over to and up on the platform and sits on the rug by Muhammad Shah, who reinforces the bored young Nasiri'd-Din, "That's better. You are a part of all this."

Dolgorukov sees that Aqasi is staring at him, but quickly looks away.

Dolgorukov, "Does not Prime Minister Aqasi have a single friend?"

Sheil, "His type have stripped peasants in his province of all possessions. The army is fat. The people eat grass."

Dolgorukov, "I have seen much starvation."

Sheil, "And Aqasi knows that the last Shah ordered the killing of his own Prime Minister."

Sheil snaps his fingers to highlight this last point.

Majid and Vahid approach the two diplomats, "Prince Dolgorukov, may I present perhaps the most distinguished citizen of Persia, Siyyid Yahya."

53

Dolgorukov, "Mirza Majid said you are most well informed and have committed to memory over 30,000 Islamic traditions and know the Qur'an by heart."

Majid appropriately steps back out of the picture, as Vahid and Dolgorukov exchange bows.

Vahid, "Such might be true, sir, but you might find it hardly noticeable."

Dolgorukov, "Oh, not at all."

Vahid, "It is said that your honored colleague, Major Sheil, has on his desk the most intimate communications within this government, even before they are received by their intended recipients."

VAHID, 40
suave, urbane scholar

Sheil, "You will allow that that could be a slight exaggeration?"

Dolgorukov, "What a pleasure to be with two humble men."

Sheil, "Prince Dolgorukov has learned that people compare the great comet to the Bab in Shiraz."

Dolgorukov, "Actually, Ambassador, I made that up."

Vahid, "Well, you were close to the mark. The Bab has gathered around him a group of devoted adherents. He is noted for extreme simplicity of manner, engaging gentleness and charm of appearance. They say the writings of this youth are elegant in style and have produced an immense sensation in Persia. As soon as he enters a mosque in Shiraz, it becomes surrounded."

Dolgorukov checks Sheil's reaction, one of cool interest.

Dolgorukov, "Fascinating."

54

Vahid, "I myself am intrigued. Indeed, his Imperial Majesty the Shah has assigned me to investigate this episode of the Bab."

Muhammad Shah calls Aqasi to his side and whispers something to Aqasi who then beckons to the envoys to approach the platform of Muhammad Shah. A more refined man would have crossed the room to summon them in a more polite manner. Dolgorukov further probes the situation.

Dolgorukov, "My, my. The Prime Minister seems unhappy."

Vahid, "It might be me. I shall excuse myself."

Sheil to Dolgorukov, "It annoys him to see us together for so long. He would like to think he can put Britain and Russia at odds to his advantage in Persia."

COUNTRYSIDE OUTSIDE ISFAHAN
Central Persia
Spring, 1846

Husayn stops his horse on the crest of a slope overlooking the ancient provincial capital of Isfahan, located midway between Shiraz and Tehran, more than 400 miles north of Shiraz on the road to Tehran.

He and his Brother and Nephew, have been joined by about 35 Babis, from teenagers to old men. Many are on foot. The others are mounted on horses, mules and camels. Many of the animals are loaded with possessions. The scene is typical for migrating groups in these regions, in the 1840s and even today in some remote regions.

Husayn, "So large a group might excite curiosity and suspicion. We shall disperse and enter the gates of Isfahan in small and inconspicuous numbers."

ISFAHAN BAZAAR

In an Isfahan bazaar, shops line a narrow passageway covered with an arched roof. Bustling with activity, this "indoor street" is part of a network, which explains why exterior views of portions of the city often appear as one interconnected roof. In such a site famous for all nature of intrigues, Husayn, with Brother and Nephew not far off, is conferring with a wool merchant.

WOOL, merchant
Babi, unpredictable

Wool, "Shiraz is in a state of violent agitation. With the crowds attracted by any public appearance of the Siyyid-i-Bab, the governor Husayn Khan cannot know who is or is not a Babi. Now all manner of contact with the Siyyid-i-Bab is forbidden."

Husayn, "And he will decline assistance."

Wool, "A visit to Shiraz could be dangerous. You are too well known. Agents of the governor are trying to penetrate Babi circles. The mullas and the governor have joined to distort our aims."

Wool: short, stubble beard; looks manic; is sort of crazy.

Vahid Investigates the Babis

RECEPTION ROOM OF KHAN, SHIRAZ

In his reception room, the provincial governor, Khan, is entertaining Vahid, on special assignment from Muhammad Shah to report on the situation in Shiraz. Although Khan is a formidable figure, he is by any measure a clear step below the caliber of Vahid, a man who had achieved universal renown in Persia. They have finished dinner. Although Khan tries to seem relaxed, his nervousness is evident as he fidgets with a tea cup. A great deal is at stake for him.

Khan relates to Vahid a false version of the story of the three Babis he had severely punished previously. He points away from the Persian-style meal setting on the floor, saying, "They stood right there. Three 'Babis'. They said that this 'Siyyid-i-Bab' is an impostor."

Vahid, "And you released them?"

Khan, "Of course. The writings of this Youth are pretentious."

Vahid is lost in thought.

Khan continues, "Some mullas offer to sign a death warrant, if I would cosign it. What do you think?"

The next events might be seen as a flashback. However, the present meeting between Vahid and Khan may also be seen as a flashback with respect to the next scenes. This ambiguity among the following locations and events continues as Vahid's thoughts and suspicions among the characters are explored.

UNCLE'S PARLOR

Uncle sits on the divan in his parlor. Shaykh, Eyes, Javad and Karim (young, fragile, intense) stand around Uncle, directing their attention to Vahid.

Shaykh, Eyes and Karim have been serving as assistants in recording and transcribing the writings of the Bab. They are serious and determined, but are gracious and respectful to the high position of Vahid when they speak. A certain irony might be noticeable, namely that Khan had dominated Babis by force previously, while Vahid had easily overshadowed Khan, but Vahid seems hesitant in the presence of the Babis. They discuss the writings of the Bab. Manuscripts are stacked on the table.

Vahid says, "These writings ... umm ... their many references to ancient Islamic traditions are all correct."

Eyes, "If you had found an error, could you explain it by a gap in your own research?"

Uncle to Eyes, "The esteemed Siyyid will ask the questions."

Vahid massages his tired eyes.

RESIDENCE OF KHAN

Vahid and Javad talk in front of Khan's residence. In the doorway, out of earshot, Khan looks on.

Vahid, "If only the Bab would produce a miracle."

Javad, "So that people will laugh that you have lost your senses?"

Vahid, "hmm."

Javad, "The proof is his book. None can produce its like."

BACK TO UNCLE'S PARLOR

Vahid with Uncle, Shaykh, Eyes, Javad and Karim as before.

Vahid, "Does the Bab alone produce these writings?"
Eyes, "I myself have seen him pick up a pen and reveal over 3,000 verses without any pause or hesitation."

BACK TO RECEPTION ROOM OF KHAN

Vahid's response to Khan's question is pending. Having collected his thoughts, Vahid turns to Khan. His response is a cool, blank look.
Vahid, "A death warrant?"
Khan, "Well, that might be premature. With a man of your prestige and knowledge investigating..."
Vahid, "I can easily overcome the Bab in any argument."
Khan, "...this unbalanced young man will no doubt retract his claims."
Vahid, "I would not be too sure. Some prominent people throughout Persia have adopted his cause. This spread of his message so widely in so short a time is unprecedented, not the work, as you say, of an 'unbalanced' man." Vahid pauses to think.

BACK TO UNCLE'S PARLOR

The situation remains as before.
Vahid, "During my journey from Tehran, I made a list of questions for the Bab."
Shaykh, "We are happy to comment on all of your questions."
Vahid, "There are certain questions that no one has ever been able to answer for me. I shall state these questions only to the Siyyid-i-Bab himself."
Eyes steps into the hallway as if the moment was expected.
Uncle, "He will meet with you."
Eyes, "Come this way, please."
Eyes motions to Vahid. Vahid follows.

BACK TO RECEPTION ROOM OF KHAN

Khan and Vahid are seated in the after dinner conversation as before.

Khan, "But his youth. He could not understand. I mean, he should respond to your position and experience."

HALLWAY IN UNCLE'S RESIDENCE

Vahid follows Eyes leading him down a hallway off Uncle's Parlor. Eyes glances back at Vahid as they approach an open door from which light flows.

BACK TO RECEPTION ROOM OF KHAN

Vahid, "His uncle states that his knowledge is innate. I have not yet seen him."

Khan, "Why, he is our prisoner! You have every right..."

Vahid, "I think his Imperial Majesty the Shah would approve of my methods."

Ferrier opens the door and walks right into the room as if he owned the place. He sees Khan is not alone and pauses, "Oh, excuse me, Your Excellency. I did not know you were busy. They said I should come up."

Khan, "That's all right. Do join us."

Khan continues as Ferrier nods and makes himself at home sitting directly across from Vahid. Khan is

FERRIER, French advisor and agent

between the men at the head of the dinner setting.

Khan, "May I present Gen. Ferrier. This is the renowned Siyyid Yahya. Did you know that our sovereign has commissioned him to report on the Siyyid-i-Bab?"

Ferrier, "No I didn't. How interesting."

Both Khan and Ferrier are lying in the pretense of Ferrier's ignorance. Vahid studies Ferrier who chews on a piece of fruit.

Gen. Joseph Philippe **Ferrier**: a late-30s Frenchman; had long worked for the Persian Army with the rank of Adjunct General. He is now paid by Khan as a key military advisor, but he also later functioned as a French Agent and would file frequent reports to France on affairs in Persia.

FRONT OF THE BAB'S FAMILY RESIDENCE

Ferrier recalls watching Constable confer with Two Guards at the closed front doors on the narrow street. Constable steps toward Ferrier, saying to him, "They're surprised to see us here after dark."

Ferrier, "Good that they know we are watching."

Constable, "No one has entered or left except Siyyid Yahya who is still inside."

Ferrier, "When did our visitor from Tehran arrive today?"

Constable, "Early afternoon."

Ferrier, "Umm. Each day he stays longer."

BACK TO RECEPTION ROOM OF KHAN

Continuing the meeting in the reception room of Khan, Ferrier tries to look casual as Vahid watches him.

Ferrier, "How is your report coming?"

Vahid, "Too early to comment."

Ferrier, "Of course." Ferrier glances to Khan.

Khan, "The British presence in Persia is great enough, so I have employed some French experts."

Ferrier, "Thank-you. The Shah must see your point. He just employed a Frenchman as his personal physician."

HALLWAY IN UNCLE'S RESIDENCE

Vahid sees Eyes becoming illuminated as he reaches the open door in the hallway off Uncle's Parlor.

BACK TO RECEPTION ROOM OF KHAN

Ferrier continues, "Can't be too careful."
Vahid looks at Khan, who says, "Gen. Ferrier has our troops ready for any situation."
Ferrier, "We tightened up a little and the crowds of Babis that we had, well, they just left Shiraz."
Vahid stands to excuse himself, "Your efforts may have simply helped the Siyyid-i-Bab."
Khan, "Really?"
Vahid, "No doubt Persia will now receive a new wave of admirers of this movement."

BACK TO UNCLE'S PARLOR

Now with night lighting, the situation has changed. Javad and Karim are not present. Looking faint, Vahid returns to the room. Uncle and Shaykh guide Vahid to sit on the divan.
Uncle, "You look weak. Shall I call a physician?"
Vahid, "No, thank you, I'm fine."
Uncle, "It has been a long day for you. We can continue tomorrow."
Vahid, "I'm fine, thank-you."

RECEPTION ROOM OF KHAN

After the foregoing exploration of thoughts and motives of the players, our narrative returns to real-time.

In Khan's reception room, the arrangement is as before except that Khan sits alone. His plate and the plate at the spot where Vahid had sat, are full of food. In the previous scenes, these plates were empty but sullied by the remnants of a consumed meal. The implication is that Vahid did not show up for his private meal with the governor. Khan fidgets contemplating the situation.

BACK TO UNCLE'S PARLOR

In Uncle's parlor, Vahid explains to Uncle, Shaykh and Eyes, "When I entered the room, I could not even remember my own questions. Known for my memory, such a thing has never happened even when I appear before the Shah. 'Seek from me,' the Bab said, 'whatever is your heart's desire.' I was speechless. He then revealed a text that set forth the answers to all of the questions I had prepared but could not ask. Verses streamed from his pen with a rapidity that was truly astounding."

BACK TO RECEPTION ROOM OF KHAN

Sitting alone with dinner served for two, Khan boils over. He turns his plate of food over in anger and stands up looking to the window.

Khan, "He has become a Babi."

CENTRAL SQUARE OF TEHRAN
Summer, 1846

Muhammad Shah rides his horse across the central square toward the palace steps, attracting a group of well-wishers.

Aqasi and several attendants emerge from the palace. Aqasi observes the scene as attendants run down to assist.

Javad passes as Muhammad Shah reaches the palace steps and addresses Muhammad Shah from some distance.

Javad, "I pray that Your Highness had a pleasant excursion on this fine day." The attendants steady the Shah's horse so he may dismount. Several of the well-wishers, Tehranis, appear displeased by Javad's remark.

Muhammad Shah, "Why, thank you. Indeed I did."

Javad continues on his way.

A Tehrani close to the Shah confides to him, "Does not your Imperial Majesty realize ... that man has proclaimed himself a Babi."

The Shah has dismounted and looks the Tehrani in the eyes, "How strange! Whoever is distinguished by his conduct and courtesy, my people denounce him as a Babi."

One can read Aqasi's expression as "not good".

Aqasi and Muhammad Shah climb the steps to the palace.

Muhammad Shah

Credit: Jules Laurens

Muhammad Shah, "We have been lately informed that Siyyid Yahya has become a Babi. If this is true, we should cease belittling the cause of the Bab. Remind me to announce this at a state function."

Aqasi, "You can have no doubt."

Shiraz Governor Ordered to Kill the Bab

RECEPTION ROOM OF KHAN, SHIRAZ
Autumn, 1846

Foliage outside the window of Khan's reception room featured previously has turned brown marking the change of season. Khan sits with his head buried in his arms on the table. Khan's long-nosed servant, Nose, pours tea beside him. Typically such a servant is unable to read. But Nose scans documents on the table and focuses on the Persian script of a particular letter. Nose mixes the tea and leaves.

Khan's Agent, a wiry young psychopath seated across from Khan, speaks, "An eager crowd visits the Bab each night, more people than come to this palace by day. Peasants and celebrated men."

Khan lifts his head. He looks tired, at the end of his rope.

Outside, Nose sprints down a Shiraz street. He pauses, panting and sweating. His eyes are moist with tears. After a moment, he dashes off.

NOSE, Babi father of STREET and KID

Meanwhile, Agent continues his report to Khan, "Your subordinates pretend that the house is guarded. This is a joke. I myself have seen the Bab visiting sites in Shiraz by night. The Babis use drugs to put whoever they want in a trance."

When Khan speaks, he is more energetic than he looks, "Do you believe that?"

Agent, "Why, yes."

Khan, "Have you seen any Babi put any drug in a drink?"

Agent, "Ah ... no."

Khan, "You ... are a fool. I can tell better than you what the interests of the State require ... Watch me."

THE BAB'S FAMILY RESIDENCE

Nose, disguised as a beggar, approaches the two Guards in front of the Bab's family residence.

Window Woman across the street peeks out of her window.

BROWS, 22
early Babi

Nose passes a note to Guard #1, who unfolds and reads it, as Nose departs.

In Uncle's parlor at night, Uncle and a Babi, Brows (real name Siyyid Kazim-i-Zanjani), are present. Vahid is not. They are engaged in reading and quiet discussion. Bang, bang, bang. They look up.

Brows swiftly descends stairs. Bang, bang.

At the inside of the front entrance, in a short passage from an interior patio, Brows removes the bolt securing the double doors. Brows opens one of the doors enough to see Guard #1.

Brows, "What is it?"

Guard #1 passes to Brows the folded message from Nose, "This."

Shiraz: narrow street

In front the residence at night, Guard #1 and Guard #2 are back at attention. Footsteps to their right. The Guards look. Nothing. The street is empty.

At the end of the block, Nose and Street, now 13 years old, father and son, hide around the corner with a freshly saddled horse.

Uncle looks up after reading the unfolded message passed from Guard #1 to Brows, "Prime Minister Aqasi has ordered Governor Husayn Khan to kill the Bab and his companions. This will be done tonight in secret."

Back outside, from the other end of the street, opposite to the end where Nose and Street are hiding around the corner, the Constable with ten fully armed Soldiers carrying a ladder appear marching up the street.

Guard #1, "Stall them."

Guard #2 steps in their direction to meet them.

Street peeks around the corner to observe,

"We're too late."

Nose, "Shhh."

69

Inside, Uncle to Brows, "Out the back. There's time."

Brows pulls back his cape to reveal a weapon, "I'm staying."

The Bab's Wife emerges from the hallway and confers with Uncle.

Shiraz: old residential quarter, narrow paths, tall fences

A Soldier creeps along the roof of the residence. Another Soldier moves from ladder to roof behind him. They are two stories up on the roof where the Bab had prayed at the death of his only child.

At street level, the Constable stands at the base of the ladder about 30 feet down the street from the entrance with Guard #2. Blade, a young soldier, about 17, begins to mount the ladder behind the Constable, who orders Guard #2, "Get back to your post."

From the direction where Nose and Street are, an incredible sound is heard in the distance: wailing and shrieking voices. The two Guards, Constable and Blade look down the street. Not a soul is seen all the way down to the intersection where Nose and Street are hiding.

Starting to climb the ladder, Blade would not normally speak, due to his low rank. But he blurts out, "What in the hell is that?"

Constable snaps, "A diversion. Get in there and open that door!"

The wailing hysterical voices increase in volume.

Uncle directs Brows out of the room, "Open the front door. There will be no bloodshed here. We will meet them outside to protect the women."

Soldiers descend from the roof into the interior courtyard.

Brows has descended from Uncle's parlor. He opens the front doors to the street. Now screams of the Bab's Wife and the Bab's Mother add to the wailing voices outside.

Soldiers burst into an empty room. They stuff books, papers and manuscripts into sacks. They pocket valuables for themselves.

The Bab's Wife runs into the room of the Bab's Mother, who jumps out of bed. Terrorized, they hug and slip down into a dark corner of the small room.

Blade moves from ladder to roof on the second story. He peers down at the street. The Constable and the remaining Soldiers have moved down to the now open doors to the street. Brows comes out.

Filled with fear, Blade crouches on the edge of the roof. He tries to block out the sound of the wailing and screaming voices in the distance. He covers his ears and closes his eyes, but the sound rings louder in his head.

In the courtyard of the residence, another Soldier runs out of a doorway with filled sack, knocking the dazed Ethiopian off his feet.

Blade looks again from his vantage point on the roof.

The residences are being sacked and a group of soldiers and prisoners is forming in the narrow street.

Shiraz: House of the Bab courtyard

Credit: Baha'i World Center; photo taken at a later time.

Nose and Street bravely move into full view in the intersection. The Constable sees them. Standing on the edge of the roof, Blade sees Nose and Street, unarmed and appearing helpless at the intersection at the far end of the street. The source of the sounds of moaning people in grief remains unknown.

Blade, "God help us."

Blade runs off across the rooftops in panic. He makes his way toward the intersection where Nose and Street stand alone, no longer hiding, holding the reins of the now agitated horse.

Second story windows covered with curtains light up as people along the street are awakened by the ever-louder sound of wailing.

Window Woman prays in her chamber.

Nose and Street hold their ground at the intersection. Constable marches up the street toward them, followed by 3 or 4 rows of people: the soldiers and the prisoners. Uncle has been left in the house. The Bab is one of the prisoners. The Constable, followed by a row of three of his soldiers, fill the narrow street, approaching fast. One soldier draws his sword.

Constable shouts to Nose and Street, "You. Go home."

Blade jumps from the roof of a single story residence and rolls in the street connected with the intersection where Nose and Street stand.

Nose and Street look at him briefly. Now the sound of hysterical voices is very loud.

The Constable and group close in on the position of Nose and Street. A soldier cocks his rifle aimed at Nose.

Around the corner, Blade picks himself up from the dirt of the connected street. Street motions for him to stay back.

The Constable and group are nearly descending on Nose and Street. The horse is spooked and rearing. Its reins slip out of Nose's hand as Nose and Street try to stare down the Constable and soldiers.

Constable shouts to them, "Get out of the way."

Nose and Street hold their ground as their horse runs off. The moment of truth is upon him. Street can only glance at Blade. Street shouts to him, "Save yourself." Blade seems paralyzed.

The Constable and group step forward briskly.

Around the corner, Blade draws his sword. His hand shakes. The blade quivers in the air. Behind it, a mob of people appear running toward the intersection.

Now everyone is gripped with fear. At the intersection, the Constable witnesses the press of people flowing toward him. The sound of hysterical voices in grief fits the picture. The crowd is in panic carrying belongings, caskets and cadavers wrapped in cloth.

Nose and Street do not know what is happening, but they seem a bit relieved.

The Constable knew that things were not going according to plan, but this is a total surprise.

All of these people have mixed into one mass of disorder.

Constable, "What is going on?"

Passerby, moving on, "Outbreak of cholera."
Constable, "Wait."
Another passerby, "The Plague. Hundreds are dead since midnight. Run for your lives."

RESIDENCE OF KHAN

At the residence of Khan later that night, the sound of hysterical people continues, volume reduced. The street is filled with people moving in one direction, carrying their dead for burial. Moving against the flow the Constable, alone, runs up to the front of the house of Governor Khan. Doorman, seemingly unaffected by the anarchy in the street, sits on the steps.

Doorman: old man, in his day has seen it all. Who knows? Maybe he is drugged or simply does not care. Maybe he even appreciates the excitement. His relaxed presence provides a contrast.

The Constable has been running, something he is not in shape for and naturally, is excited, "The Governor. Husayn Khan. I must see him."
Doorman flicks his cane in the air and uses it to gesture, "Too late. He fled the city."
The Constable steps closer moving up the steps.
Constable, "He has got to be here."
Doorman slaps his cane in the Constable's path.
Doorman, "I wouldn't go in there."
The Constable can now see a body lying on the floor inside the open entrance.
Doorman, "The Governor is outside the city. He didn't even stop to bury the dead of his own house."

SHIRAZ STREET NEAR GATE EXIT OF CITY

On the Shiraz street near the gate in the walls around the city, an orange glow above the hills at dawn increases the level of illumination.

Voices of despair have subdued but some people still suffer from attacks of hysteria as they exit the city to the open country, with gardens and orchards outside, hills in the distance. They move down the street through a large arched gate carrying the dead, some on mules. The bodies, adult and child, are wrapped in cloth or in caskets. Footsteps, some crying, hysteria attacks are heard. The people are in a state of shock. No one speaks.

Street, dazed, walks along a wall toward the exit. He spots the Constable and he tries to hide in a small doorway indentation. Before he knows it, the Constable has spotted and grabbed him. A boy about his age, 12-13, the Constable's Son, dress reflecting the wealth of his family, sticks behind the Constable.

Street struggles to break loose, "Bastard!"

Constable, "Listen ... please."

Kicking, pounding, spitting, anything, Street is a tough little cuss.

Street, "Let go!"

Constable, "I want to help."

The Constable's Son is now by the Constable's side, sort of cornering Street.

Street shouts, "Liar."

Constable's son, "Please."

Street, pointing, "Who did that?"

Street can see over the Constable's shoulder the top of the arched city gate. Hanging from the top is a dead body. The body has been mutilated. This sight is shocking, silhouetted against the dawn morning light. Oh, yes, the top half of the dead man is hung from the right, the bottom half hung from the left side of the arch.

People continue passing below out the gate to the countryside. No one looks up. This is a common sight.

Constable, "That was a criminal."

Street, "Was not!"

Constable's son, "Please."

Constable, "The Bab is safe. I wanted to embrace you, son."

Street pushes between them, stepping into the street. The Constable and his Son turn.

Street, "Liar."

As people carrying their dead pass behind Street, the Constable crouches to Street's eye level, one arm around his son.

Constable, "Listen, son. My boy almost died last night. I took the Bab to my house. He prayed. The Bab washed his face and gave me the water for my son to drink. Now he is cured."

Street, "You O.K.?"

Street touches the cheek of the Constable's Son just as tears start to run down the Son's cheek. The Son grins, "O.K."

The Constable and Son step toward the city. The Constable points over Street toward the outside of the city.

Constable, "Look, son. The governor is out there. He has released the Bab and his friends. They are at my house. Come on. I have resigned my post so this will be our last chance to see my beautiful house."

The Constable and Son start down the street, against the flow of the crowd. Street is hesitant, still in shock.

Constable's son, "Come on. Help us find your father."

With hardly a moment of reflection, Street runs after them.

The State Reacts - Isfahan

POST HOUSE OF ISFAHAN
October, 1846

Brows and Wool walk from the walled city to the post house.

Brows, "Husayn Khan released the Bab on condition that he leave Shiraz. He and I, alone, rode north. After 14 days, we made camp outside Isfahan. I took a message in his own hand to the Governor Manuchihr Khan."

PALACE OF MANUCHIHR KHAN

Isfahan: Palace of Governor

J A V Willians, Persia Past and Present, 1906

In the Governor's palace, Brows sits Persian-style on knees on a rug before Manuchihr.

His movements somewhere between "masculine" and "effeminate", Manuchihr sits on a divan. He picks up the message which Brows had delivered. With the other hand, he maneuvers a tea cup from a nearby table to his lips. He sips some tea, peering over the cup to examine the message. Manuchihr lowers the cup.

As if to an imagined audience, he expresses that he is amazed, amused and curious, "Hundreds of

MANUCHIHR, eunuch Isfahan Governor

siyyids pass through Isfahan. They seek lodging where it can be found. The youth from Shiraz, however, addresses himself in an exquisite manner directly to the governor."

Manuchihr Khan: about 40, a Georgian eunuch, worked his way up from service in the royal harem to be perhaps the most powerful governor in Persia. He helped Muhammad Shah to secure his crown with his funds and troops and was therefore highly esteemed and trusted by the Shah. Manuchihr is stout, round, but not overweight; light complexion, no beard; high-pitched voice; jewel-handled dagger at his waist.

BACK TO POST HOUSE SOUTH OF ISFAHAN

Later, Brows and Wool approach the post house south of Isfahan. Brows is proud of the results of his appearance before the governor. He points to the ground ahead of him, "Manuchihr Khan ordered that the chief mulla provide lodging."

Isfahan: Post House

C J Wills, In the Land of the Lion and Sun, or Modern Persia, 1891

A post rider arrives at the post house. He dismounts the sweat-covered horse and hauls saddle bags filled with mail into the dark post house interior.

Wool, "You see. Isfahan is unique!"

Brows, "A step closer to Tehran."

Wool, "A step away from Shiraz."

ABU'L-QASIM'S RESIDENCE, SHIRAZ

Steam rises from vigorously boiling water at Abu'l-Qasim's residence in Shiraz at dusk where sounds of footsteps, some weeping, voices, street noises, shovel digging dirt and boiling water mix.

. A huge copper colander over a raging wood fire on the ground contains the boiling water, tinted with red and black ink. Sheets with lovely Persian script are thrown into the water. The heat and turbulence churns the pages around in the colander.

This is the front patio with a number of similar large colanders over fires. Uncle, Abu'l-Qasim, the brother-in-law of the Bab, and other family members are busy.

By a wall on his knees, Uncle gathers pages of writing, strewn on the ground like litter. As he stuffs sheets of paper in one hand, more pages float to the ground around him.

Limping, Abu'l-Qasim steps to a boiling colander. The rising steam covers him with sweat. He feeds more pages into the boiling bath. Another man digs a hole, one of many.

People in the street outside quickly approach, throw manuscripts over the high mud brick wall and move on.

A page sinks into the boiling water. The writing on it fades as the ink dissolves.

Uncle is also covered with sweat from the steam and heat. He uses a twig to fish pages from the boiling water. He slings the now clean, soggy paper on to trays on the ground.

Others dump the soggy paper from the trays into the holes dug in the ground. A shovel quickly moves earth on top to fill each hole.

Having received news in the post from Shiraz, Wool narrates this activity, "The family of the Bab has suffered beatings, threats, fines. Now they are ostracized. Governor Husayn Khan has vowed to punish anyone found to possess even a single page of the writings of the Bab."

A WOMAN'S QUARTERS, KARBALA

A figure appears in the doorway covered completely by a black full-body veil. It is Shams. In one motion Shams removes the veil to reveal a gorgeous brightly colored dress worn by an extra fine example of young womanhood. She appears intense, innocent.

Shams, "Is this what you meant?"

An "Ohhh" exclamation of admiration is the reply from Plump, Bibi, several other woman, some old, some plain and Tahirih, dressed in similar bright, happy outfits.

Tahirih takes Shams' hands in hers, "Oh ... breathtaking."

The young Shams bubbles, "I'm so happy."

OFFICE OF MINISTER OF WAR, TEHRAN

War is napping at his desk.

Aqasi, preoccupied, bursts into the room. He sees War napping and purposefully slams the door, arousing War. Aqasi moves behind War and in front of the wall map of Persia and neighboring regions. Aqasi grabs War's ear to shake him, "You are a disgrace. Could you rise from the dead?"

War, "I, ah,..."

Aqasi, "Never mind. What do we have today?"

Still groggy, War shuffles papers on his desk to find the right dispatch. Aqasi stands behind. War finally replies, "In the post from Baghdad ... there was ... I'll find it ... Our foreign minister reports that the Turkish authorities are holding a woman ... you know ... the Babi poetess from Qazvin ... here it is ... she was arrested in Karbala and transferred to Baghdad."

BACK TO WOMAN'S QUARTERS, KARBALA

Sunlight from a window illuminates the women, seated in a circle on a Persian rug. Tahirih speaks to Shams and the others. Sounds from the nearby street can be heard.

Persian girl. S G W Benjamin, Persia and the Persians, 1887

Tahirih, "For some of you, I owe an explanation. Today is the birthday of the beloved Bab, born 27 years ago. Two years ago he began a new era, one that shall witness the total emancipation of women."

Karbala Woman appears in the doorway. She pulls up her full body veil to show her dress, all black, and her face. She is middle-aged, graying hair, shocked and angry.

Karbala Woman, "What is going on here?"

Shams, "Oh, it's beautiful."

Tahirih, "Come in."

Karbala Woman, "This is ... this is ugly! This cannot be permitted."

She had been holding her veil up. She lets it drop back in place and hurries off. Plump shakes her head and to Shams, "Why don't you talk to her."

BACK TO OFFICE OF MINISTER OF WAR

War continues summarizing to Aqasi the dispatch from Baghdad, "Some Babi women in Karbala committed a blasphemy on the day of mourning for the Imam Husayn."

BACK TO WOMAN'S QUARTERS

Now in the doorway, Shams "disappears" as her full body veil covers her.

Tahirih, "Go slow. Don't push her."

Shams, "Oh, sure."

Shams paces through a dark passageway. Street sounds become louder. Ahead of her is the open entrance to the bright street.

BACK TO OFFICE OF MINISTER OF WAR

War, "The Baghdad governor is waiting for word from Constantinople on what to do with the Babi poetess."

Aqasi, "He doesn't know?"

KARBALA STREET

Shams emerges to the Karbala street. She looks both ways. Her movement belies uncertainty.

Sham's vision is limited by her veil grid, "Where did she go?" With Shams' limited field of vision, she does not realize it, but a group of fully veiled women is forming, moving in around her. It is a scary sight, as if the black figures were a pack of dogs surrounding their prey.

BACK TO OFFICE OF MINISTER OF WAR

War, "Meanwhile there's the question if we want to request that she be deported to Persia."

Aqasi, "Absurd! We requested that the Turks hand over that Babi Mulla 'Ali and they refused. That was their mistake. Because wherever you put a Babi..." He claps his hands, "...more Babis! They multiply like rats."

BACK TO WOMAN'S QUARTERS

Shouting and screams of Shams outside are heard.

The women with Tahirih look up, startled.
Plump, "Ahhh!"
Tahirih cries out, "That's Shams!"

BACK TO KARBALA STREET

Karbala Women are stoning Shams, curled up on the ground. Some men observe keeping their distance.
No time to put on full veils, just face veils, Tahirih, Plump and Bibi run out to the street.
Karbala Women, "Unclean! ... You all stink!" The shouting women provoke several dogs to start barking.

BACK TO OFFICE OF MINISTER OF WAR

War turns to another page of the dispatch, "It's reported that even some of the Babis have protested to the Turks over the teachings of this so-called poetess."
Aqasi, "Her own family in Qazvin is outraged."

WOMAN'S QUARTERS

Shouting women in the street still heard, Tahirih holds the limp, possibly lifeless body of Shams in her arms. Plump peals up the full body veil and removes it along with Shams' scarf, revealing her face and head. Shams is cut and bruised, covered with sweat, blood all over her face, hair, hands and dress.
Tahirih hugs her tightly at the sight of her wounds, "Acchh. I'm so sorry."
Shams opens her eyes, "Let them stone me."
Tahirih rocks Shams in her arms, "Let them stone me."

BACK TO OFFICE OF MINISTER OF WAR

War, "So...?"
Aqasi, "Oh, no, never. No extradition request from us. Let the Turks keep her ... and her madness."

War, "What about the British? They were too interested in the Mulla 'Ali case."

Aqasi, "We must keep this one quiet."

BRITISH LEGATION, TEHRAN

William **Cormick**: 26, had worked for Muhammad Shah's father, appointed physician to the British Mission in 1844.

DR. CORMICK, 27 British physician

Walking briskly, Dr. Cormick enters the Legation yard from the street and paces up the lane to the building. Sheil and Farrant exit the legation office to meet him. The three march back out toward the street. Sheil to Dr. Cormick, "Let's go, Doctor."

Dr. Cormick, "What is it?"

Farrant, "Capt. Hennell reports that the cholera epidemic has spread from Shiraz as far as Basra and Baghdad in Turkish domains, with deaths up to 200 a day."

Dr. Cormick, "What about medical assistance?"

BACK TO OFFICE OF MINISTER OF WAR

Aqasi, "What else do you have?"

War tries to look organized as he shuffles through the dispatches, "More protests from the mullas in Isfahan."

Aqasi, "I told them to resist the author of that obscure and contemptible movement!"

War, "Well, this Siyyid-i-Bab seems to hold the provincial capital in his hands."

Aqasi reflects, "Who could have dreamed that an unknown frail ignorant shopkeeper could take Persia ... without an army. I tell you, he's very smart. He escaped us in Shiraz. We'll just have to be smarter this time. That's all."

He looks out the window. In the central Tehran square, Sheil, Farrant and Dr. Cormick approach the palace.

PALACE OF THE SHAH, TEHRAN
November, 1846

Muhammad Shah sits at his writing table. Nasiri'd-Din stands behind, a hand on each of his father's shoulders. Nasiri'd-Din is motionless and stares directly ahead. His expression is confident, unblinking. His look is chilling, capturing attention.

Meanwhile, Muhammad Shah speaks as he signs and seals an order, glancing up to a listener, "The Siyyid-i-Bab shall be brought at once from Isfahan to appear before me in person."

MANUCHIHR'S GARDEN OUTSIDE ISFAHAN

Snow falls in Manuchihr's garden outside the Isfahan city walls. Light snow collects on the ground.

Manuchihr with twelve armed horsemen arrive outside the garden mud wall. He dismounts and enters the garden.

His gardener rushes up. He had swept the path Manuchihr will walk free of snow. Manuchihr gives him a coin. The gardener scurries ahead to further sweep the path as the snow continues to fall. Trees in the garden are leafless.

Manuchihr steps off the path into the snow and takes a leafless branch of an orchard tree in his hand. He studies the branch as he turns toward the garden gate. Aziz has also dismounted and stands at the garden entrance some ten yards away.

Manuchihr, "Aziz."

Aziz immediately falls to his knees awaiting his command. Manuchihr motions that Aziz should approach him and Aziz jumps up to comply. Manuchihr quietly says to Aziz, "Make ready 500 horsemen at the barracks."

Aziz: well-paid, faithful body-guard; recruited from the fierce nomadic tribes of central Persia; could have been a championship wrestler.

MOSQUE-I-JUM'IH, ISFAHAN

Through falling snow, this magnificent Mosque-i-Jum'ih of Isfahan sparkles, even on this overcast day.

The pulpit inside is a simple seven-step stairway. Standing by the pulpit, an Isfahan Mulla speaks to another mulla, "Manuchihr Khan has invited us to a meeting with the Siyyid- i-Bab. I will excuse myself. You should also."

Isfahan Mulla spreads this message to the other

Isfahan: mosque pulpit.

congregated mullas, "It is most unwise for you to meet the Siyyid-i-Bab face to face. He will no doubt reassert his claim and adduce whatever proof you may desire him to give and without the least hesitation, write verses equal to half the Qur'an. If we cannot answer him, our impotence will be exposed. If we submit to his claim, we forfeit our prerogatives and rights."

ISFAHAN BAZAAR

Wool sits next to Street and Kid, now about 7 years old, at the front of his shop. Nose appears, grabs Wool by the upper arm and leads him forcibly toward the rear of the shop.

Nose, "Let's talk." And to Street, "Run the shop."

Wool, "He doesn't know the prices!"

Nose to Street, "If they're smiling, the price is right."

Kid, "I'll help!"

As Nose and Wool disappear into a rear stock room, Wool calls to Street, "Please, little smiles."

Bazaar scene | S G W Benjamin, Persia and the Persians, 1887

In Wool's stock room, Nose says, "I've been here one day and I don't like the picture. I saw hundreds of people clamor for the water the Bab used in his ablutions."

Wool, "That's good."

Nose, "'That' leads down the same road we saw in Shiraz."

Wool, "Take it easy."

Nose, "The mullas are condemning us. We have a few people looking for miracles to face mobs of religious fanatics."

Wool does not see any problem. To the contrary, "Easy. The Bab is now a special guest of the governor."

Nose, "Manuchihr Khan? The man who leads armies to secure the Shah's throne? ... who crushed the Bakhtiari tribes? This man built a tower with mortar and the living bodies of eighty prisoners. These are facts."

Wool glances out to his shop. The shop is brimming with smiling clients. Street and Kid are doing a brisk business. Now Wool sees the problem, namely, Nose himself, "The fact is, Manuchihr Khan is the richest man and most powerful governor in Persia ... and close to the Shah. You understand? Right now, your kids out there are making me broke ... And that tower crumbled over the years."

NORTH GATE OF ISFAHAN

From the north gate of Isfahan, five hundred armed tribesmen ride north along a trail that disappears in the hills. They ride in rows of two or three horsemen, surrounded by the on-looking public.

Outside the gate, a "royal tent" has been erected. In front, Manuchihr and Brows observe the departure. Nearby, Aziz is mounted and ready, awaiting Manuchihr's signal.

Nose, Street and Kid are among the onlookers.

Manuchihr announces loudly, "These are 500 of the best from my own personal bodyguard, to escort the

Siyyid-i-Bab to Tehran." Then to Aziz, "Go!" Aziz instantly jumps his horse into a gallop toward the distant lead of the procession of troops.

In Manuchihr's tent, Shaykh, Eyes, Hasan (the brother of Eyes) and Karim are packing manuscripts and belongings for their departure. Manuchihr and Brows enter. Manuchihr produces a document from an inner pocket of his cloak and hands it to Shaykh, "You would not want your Siyyid in Isfahan."

Shaykh reads and says, "This condemns the Bab to death."

Manuchihr, "Signed and sealed by 70 notables and ecclesiastics. You see. The Bab is safer with my men."

The Babis in the tent cannot suppress their relief. Smiles of admiration are spontaneous. Eyes and Hasan laugh out loud and slap each other playfully. Shaykh passes the document to Brows. In mock seriousness, "Listen to this," Brows says while reading, "'The extravagance of his claims and his disdainful contempt for the things of the world, incline me to believe that he is devoid of reason and judgment'."

Now the Babis are all laughing, continuing to pack.

Manuchihr looks on with a "Mona Lisa" smile, "My men will move slowly. You will be able to remain in Isfahan for a while."

WRIGHT'S STUDY, URUMIYYIH
Winter, 1847

Wright ignites a match and starts an oil lamp, revealing scraps of paper and clippings arranged as pieces of an unfinished puzzle across his desk. Some scraps are as mixed as Wright's thoughts, pieces of envelopes, fragments of stationery, etc. The scraps contain notes in Wright's handwriting.

A cluster of four "puzzle pieces" at the left read: "Book Of Revelation", "Great Earthquake", "The Dark Day" and "Stars Falling to Earth".

To the right, a note reads, "When??", bordered by a scramble of more puzzle pieces. Below the "When??", Wright adds these pieces: "1844 = 2300 year period of Daniel", newspaper clipping of "What Hath God Wrought, The Telegraph of Samuel Morse.", "Abomination of Desolation" and "Jews Back To Palestine". Wright says, "The Edict of Toleration gave Jews the right to return to Palestine, for the first time in 1200 years."

Wright adds another puzzle piece, "1844 AD". He puffs his pipe and stands over the table in the dimly lit interior, "If 1844 was 'when', then who and where?"

From the scramble of items on the table, Wright picks up another piece of paper with the notes, "Thief in the Night, ii Peter 3:10", "He will come as a thief in the night."

TURKISH COURTROOM, BAGHDAD

Something -- a handrail, the tile floor -- helps us immediately recognize this courtroom, where Mulla had sat bound in chains for committing blasphemy.

Before the Judge, Tahirih looks up coolly. Shams, Plump and Bibi stand behind. The four women are dressed for a formal public appearance, wearing face veils.

Judge, "I hereby order that you be deported to Persia. We shall provide an escort from Baghdad to the Persian border."

Relieved, Tahirih turns to Shams and Plump. Though the veils cover their noses and mouths, their eyes sparkle. They are all smiles.

Baghdad panorama

The Bab Disappears

Street playfully chases Kid, both giggling, through the people to the front of Wool's shop. Startled, Street and Kid stop. Smiles vanish from their faces.

Kid, "Hey?" The front doors to Wool's shop are open, but the shop is empty. Counters and shelves are bare. Catching up with his kids, Nose steps ahead into the shop, with that "Something is wrong" look. Kid steps forward. Nose barks to Street, "Take him outside."

Street, "What...?"

Nose, "Right now, go on."

RUSSIAN LEGATION, TEHRAN

An oil lamp illuminates Majid, busily translating a document into Russian at his desk. Dolgorukov enters. Each are surprised to see the other at this late hour.

Dolgorukov, "You work hard enough by day."

Majid, "You had asked for the Russian translations."

To examine Majid's work, Dolgorukov moves beside Majid, "Then for me, more to read, more to worry."

Majid, "I try."

Dolgorukov, "Please, you have proved yourself ... And the Siyyid-i-Bab?"

This last phrase alerts Majid, who raises a brow slightly. Majid is seated, facing in the same direction as Dolgorukov, standing behind. Majid looks up at Dolgorukov.

Majid, "Excuse me, sir?"

Dolgorukov, "The Siyyid-i-Bab."

Choosing his words carefully, pushing back from the desk, "Yes, the Siyyid-i-Bab ... what may I tell you."

Dolgorukov, "Well, he has disappeared, hasn't he?"

A large army encampment spreads across the hilly terrain. Smoke rising from fires, tethered horses, artillery, tents, etc, dot the hills. Cannon and musket fire, commanders shouting orders.

A low ranked British soldier supervises Persian recruits learning to load a cannon on this cool day.

Credit: Jules Laurens

Though a quite wealthy man, Prime Minister Aqasi is dressed in the tattered garb of a poor priest and rides a mule, another symbol in his pretense of humility. Frankly, Aqasi looks ridiculous, his short figure, perched on the small mule, riding next to his well-dressed Lackey, high on a well-appointed sleek horse. Behind, another British advisor shows Persian recruits how to handle a rifle.

Looking proud, Sheil and Officer stand by two Persian soldiers who are modeling British Military uniforms. The two Models look awkward and nervous.

Aqasi dismounts with Lackey who takes the reins of the mule. Similar to all of the other Persian Soldiers, except the Models, Lackey is dressed in the traditional Persian military garb.

Sheil, "Your Excellency."

By his expression, something between a grimace and a smile, Aqasi notices the Models wearing British uniforms.

Aqasi pushes Lackey aside, "Get out of the way."

Aqasi steps over to the Models, both much taller than he. He looks straight up into the painful expression on Model #1's sweaty face.

Sheil is upbeat, "What do you think?"

Aqasi pats Model #1's cheek, "Poor boy."

Officer, "They ... they'll get used to it."

Sheil, "These uniforms are very functional, sir."

Now Aqasi focuses on the Model's trousers.

Aqasi, "Pants."

Officer, "Yes, sir."

Aqasi, "Here is what will happen."

Aqasi directs a bit of theater.

He steps back, "I am a villager." To Model #1, "A soldier of the royal army walks by." Aqasi points the way, "Go ahead, walk by me."

Model #1 is stiff and uncomfortable. He walks by Aqasi who faces Sheil. Just as Model #1 has passed and cannot see what is happening behind him, "Stop there!" Aqasi doubles in a shocking, ugly outburst of laughter. Model #1 is petrified. Model #2 faints to the ground. Smiling, Aqasi steps between the Models toward Sheil and Officer. In apparent complete sincerity, he explains, "Our people think soldiers with pants are funny. Imagine a soldier in pants. No respect."

Muscles, a higher ranked Persian soldier, gallops up to a nearby tent and jumps off his horse.

Aqasi, "Excuse me."

Before anyone can say anything, Aqasi scurries over toward Muscles, away from Sheil, Officer and the Models. He loudly calls back to Sheil, "No respect!"

Aqasi to Muscles, "What took you so long?"

Muscles, "We rode day and night. There are dead horses back there."

As Aqasi and Muscles disappear into the tent, "Don't snap at me."

Inside War's tent, War sits smoking hashish. At the sight, in a sudden swift move, Aqasi whips out Muscles' sword slapping War's pipe from his mouth to the ground.

War, "My hashish!"

Aqasi, "Next you'll say, 'My head'!" Then to Muscles, "Please, speak."

Muscles sits on his knees on a rug below Aqasi who stands over him,

"We searched 1000 kilometers between Isfahan and Tehran. If the Bab's escort had 500 men, we would have seen them."

Aqasi's mental wheels are spinning.

Aqasi whispers, "The mountains or the desert." To Muscles, "What about Isfahan?"

Muscles, "No one wanted to talk. The troops there knew we were not attached to Manuchihr Khan. A larger force would be required."

Aqasi, "And on the way back?"

Muscles, "Then, of course, we asked at each stopping place about the Bab's escort. Nothing."

Aqasi returns the sword to Muscles, "Nothing."

BACK TO ISFAHAN BAZAAR

Alone in Wool's bare shop, Nose hears voices coming from the rear stock room. He cautiously opens the door.

In lantern and diffused light, the room is like a stone prison cell. The stacks of merchandize are gone. Shaykh, Eyes, Hasan, Karim and Brows sit on the floor around the walls. Wool jumps up smiling ear to ear, "A friend!"

Nose, "What is..."

Wool, "Going to Tehran, aren't we?" Showing purse of coins, "I sold out. It's all here."

Nose sardonically, "For what?"

Wool sits a worried Nose down near a tea set on the floor.

Wool to the others, "He's excitable."

Nose, "Most of the men in that escort are back in Isfahan. So where is the Bab?"

Brows, "The rumor is ... they killed him in the desert."

Shaykh, "To avoid riots in the city."

Nose, "I'm afraid that..."

Nose is interrupted by a knock on the door behind him.

Nose to Wool, "Are you expecting...?"

The door opens. Everyone inside is sitting. So they look up at the large figure of Aziz.

To Aziz, it looks like a room containing seven men who expect they might be executed within minutes.

Brows stands up, "Welcome, sir." Trying to smile to the others, "He represents the governor."

Aziz, "Excuse me. I seek one Mulla 'Abdu'l-Karim."

Wool and the others rise to their feet.

Wool, "Come in." Karim steps forward to the center of the small room, "That's me."

Aziz, "This is for you, sir." Karim receives a written page from Aziz.

The beauty of this Persian calligraphy is amazing.

Karim inspects the document, "In the Bab's hand ... today's date ... cannot be a forgery!"

MANUCHIHR'S GARDEN

The Persian calligraphy just seen dissolves to the silhouette of an intricate pattern of ice-covered twigs on a leafless tree branch against the overcast sky. Manuchihr holds the branch, studying it.

Like in a dream, Manuchihr recalls and narrates events, "Though I had received the order of my sovereign, the Bab would not be safe in Tehran."

Nearby, Karim is kneeling on the frosted ground and further behind, Aziz stands alone at the garden entrance.

Manuchihr continues, "Along the route, Aziz sent contingents of 20 horsemen off to collect taxes, until only a few remained with the Bab."

MANUCHIHR'S PRIVATE RESIDENCE

Manuchihr selects from his stock what he considers to be the best of Persian paintings and personally arranges their display on a wall.

Isfahan: House of Manuchihr Khan

Credit: Julio Savi

Manuchihr narrates, "Before dawn, Aziz and my most trusted security guard returned the Bab to my private residence, unseen by anyone."

Manuchihr arranges pen, ink and clean writing paper on a table. Then he positions a satin covered chair at the table, "For secrecy, all of the servants were reassigned to other residences."

PALACE OF THE SHAH, TEHRAN
February, 1847

Muhammad Shah is impatient, "The Bab left Isfahan almost four months ago with a well armed escort."

Without any real answer, Aqasi must stall for time.

Aqasi, "Yes, you are ... absolutely right."

Muhammad Shah, "And?"

BACK TO MANUCHIHR'S NARRATION

Manuchihr continues to prepare the room, almost as an expectant mother, just before "the new arrival". In a corner, he sets several layers of rugs, some pillows on top, for a sleeping area.

Manuchihr silently recalls, "As a youth, I was castrated to serve as a slave in the royal harem. They converted me to Islam, but I never believed until the Bab convinced me."

By the sleeping area, Manuchihr pours water from a pitcher into a silver bowl for ablutions (washing).

Manuchihr's thoughts continue, "From the heights of power and wealth, I then became a servant again ... of the Bab."

ISFAHAN TO TEHRAN TRAIL

This location is a flat, near desert plain, strewn with small rocks, mountains in the distance. The only indication of a "road" is a relatively rock-free lane, cleared by caravans on this route over centuries.

A caravan, people, camels, mules, horses, etc, approaches, plodding along. Behind, a Post Rider nears rapidly at full gallop.

Unable to afford the rental for a beast of burden, Nose, Street and Kid, parched, walk carrying sacks.

The Post Rider pauses in front of them and shouts the news to the travelers, "Manuchihr Khan is dead!"

BACK TO MANUCHIHR'S NARRATION

Manuchihr sits on knees at the head of a rug in the middle of the room. He gathers dishes and cups from settings before and near him, placing the articles on trays next to him, clearing the area. This "after dinner" scene is illuminated by a candelabrum centered on a nearby mat.

Manuchihr recalls, "Before I died, I offered to win Muhammad Shah to this cause. I prepared a will leaving my entire estate with 5,000 horsemen to the Bab."

Eyes sits at the table, illuminating this will with a detailed border design in colored inks.

Manuchihr, "The French valued my riches at 40 million francs."

Eyes is now gone in Manuchihr's dream-like recollection. The table is now as Manuchihr had prepared it before.

Manuchihr stands and bends to pick up the full tray, preparing to leave, "The Bab declined this offer. He may have known that my will would be destroyed as soon as it was found."

Manuchihr blows out the candles leaving complete darkness, "It was destroyed."

The State Reacts - Tehran

POST STABLE, KIRAND
Turkish-Persian Border
Spring, 1847

Bread, the Arab baker turned Babi, saddles a horse. Tahirih, in black full-body veil, slips into the stable unseen by anyone outside. Bread chuckles reassuringly, "I'm off."

Tahirih produces some coins and speaks softly, "I thought ... your expenses."

Bread ignores the coins, mounts a stout strong horse and slaps the horse's neck.

"I'm fine. He's paid for. Ten days." Referring to himself, "This tub of lard will fly to Tehran. Maybe less."

Tahirih, "Yes ... you will ... I know."

Sensing that Tahirih is apprehensive, Bread leans to touch Tahirih's veil near her cheek, "I will make contact and send news in the post." Tahirih's eyes are watery, "The Siyyid-i-Bab ... I am..."

To further reassure Tahirih, Bread switches from the "happy-go-lucky" approach and tenderly whispers, "Shh, shh ... I'll fly."

HILL NEAR KIRAND

The spring weather, a gentle slope blanketed with wild flowers -- what a place, what a day! At the top of the hill, dozens of carpets have been spread under giant shade trees. The Kirand Prince seeks the attention of hundreds of people, a cross-section, a major part of the small population of this border village. It's a picnic. Children eat sherbet. People socialize waiting to bid farewell to Tahirih.

Down the slope coming from the village, Tahirih's party walks up the hill. First the men, Ali and Brother, several other Persians and about 30 Arab Babis. Then the women. There is Shams, Plump, Bibi and finally Tahirih, all dressed for a public appearance wearing scarfs and face veils.

They all look forward at the activity higher up the slope, except Tahirih. She slows slightly to watch Bread in the distance ride away on the trail to Tehran.

Tahirih recalls telling him, "You must stop to rest only at remote places. Do not risk speaking with anyone until you cross the threshold of Husayn-'Ali of Nur in Tehran."

At this moment, as Bread disappears among the hills leading to the Zagros mountains beyond, Tahirih is struck by the silliness Bread had used moments ago to calm her. She chuckles recalling Bread's whisper, "I will fly."

The Kirand Prince will speak above voices still heard from the scattered crowd. Ordinarily, his mere snap of the fingers would produce instant silence, but this is not an ordinary occasion. People position themselves to observe Tahirih's party approach. Loudly, "Qurratu'l-Ayn! In Baghdad, the ablest leaders of the Shi'ih, Sunni, Christian and Jewish communities sought to convince her of the folly of her actions."

Bibi drops back down the slope toward Tahirih.

Kirand Prince continues, "The force of her argument silenced their protests."

Behind Bibi, Ali also approaches Tahirih.

Bibi, "If my brother could see this!"

Embracing the shorter Bibi, Tahirih closes her eyes. She recalls Husayn mounted on a horse and seeing her in the window of Siyyid Kazim's parlor in Karbala.

Between Tahirih and Ali, the shorter Bibi follows the conversation as if she were by the net of a ping-pong game, her teen mind concentrated on each word.

Ali, "Are you all right?"

Tahirih, softly, "Yes ... a little embarrassed."

Ali, "They think you will march to the capital and address the royal court. They regard you as..."

Tahirih with feigned annoyance, "Oh, no more praise." Self-depreciating, "It is far more likely that I shall die as a martyr in the capital."

Ali's expression droops. He had not thought of that possibility, nor had Bibi.

Bibi to Tahirih, "Huh?!"

Ali to Bibi, "Shhh."

Tahirih smiles with mock scold to Ali, "Don't 'Shhh' this girl!" To Bibi, "Later, we'll talk, O.K.?"

Bibi acknowledges Tahirih's affection with a small smile.

Ali, "Well, the prince and local chiefs offer to place twelve thousand men under your command, to follow you ... wherever you go."

Tahirih, "Now I am going to faint."

Ali, apologetic, "They insisted I tell you."

Tahirih, "I know."

Ali, "I shall gratefully decline on your behalf."

Tahirih, "Yes ... with my blessings. Can I have a minute?"

Ali, "Of course."

Bibi and Ali march off signaling the others to proceed. Brother and Plump had paused a way up the slope to observe.

Bibi to Plump, "She's O.K.!"

Tahirih's party reaches the villagers and notables. It settles in with the crowd around Kirand Prince. Most are already sitting. The men in Tahirih's party seem like "secret service agents", alert, watchful for the safety of Tahirih as they position themselves.

When Tahirih crosses the perimeter of the circle, all conversation ceases. Only the breeze rustling the leaves of the shade trees and a few bird calls remain.

Ali, Brother and Kirand Prince are the last to sit down in the first row of people around Tahirih.

Standing, almost no gestures with her arms or hands, Tahirih projects her voice speaking in the round, "Since I returned to Persian soil, we have spoken of how in each age, a great message inspires a new civilization. Who can we praise more? We spoke of Moses, Jesus and Muhammad. Each manifested the same sun. We believe that His Holiness Muhammad is 'the Seal of the Prophets'. From the time of Abraham until today was 'the age of prophesy'. The world now enters a new era: the age for fulfillment of those prophesies."

DOLGORUKOV'S RESIDENCE, TEHRAN

Dolgorukov and Ferrier enjoy a quiet dinner European-style. That is, they sit at a dining table and use utensils to eat.

Dolgorukov, "You have traveled a great distance from Shiraz."

Ferrier, "I hope to support recognition by the Shah of a French embassy in Tehran."

Dolgorukov, "I wish you success."

Ferrier, "Thank you."

Dolgorukov, "Of course, our Persian friends tend to suspect the motive of every European who travels in their land. It is never just 'to visit compatriots' or 'to admire the ruins of ancient civilizations'."

Ferrier laughs pouring more wine for himself and Dolgorukov.

Dolgorukov, "It is 'to seek wealth' or 'to spy for information and power'. How often they are right. How were conditions along your route?"

Ferrier, "Isfahan was in turmoil. With Manuchihr Khan dead, incredible disorder."

Dolgorukov may abruptly redirect a conversation to probe the reactions of others, "That mysterious young Siyyid was actually hidden there by the governor himself."

Ferrier is surprised, "The Siyyid-i-Bab?"

Dolgorukov, "Yes, but this is not generally known in the capital. The Shah issued an imperial order summoning the Bab in disguise to Tehran as a prisoner, I believe."

Ferrier is thinking fast to digest this intelligence, "Well, that is appropriate. These Babis are like the socialists and anarchists who plague France."

Dolgorukov smells that he might have hit pay-dirt, "Oh? You have something on their doctrines?"

Ferrier pauses, "No."

Dolgorukov, "I see."

OFFICE OF MINISTER OF WAR

Big, of the Nusayri tribe, reports to Aqasi who taps his cane on the tiled floor impatiently, standing in front of the wall map.

Big, "We camped in your gardens south of Tehran."

Aqasi, "Good."

Big, "The Siyyid-i-Bab wishes a meeting with His Imperial Majesty the Shah."

Aqasi mocks Big, "So you are a spokesman of the Siyyid?"

Big is tense, "No, sir."

Aqasi, "Now, you will proceed as you have to Tabriz. On your way, you will not enter Qazvin or Zanjan or any other city. After the Siyyid arrives in Tabriz, your men will deliver him to 'Ali Khan at the Mah-Ku fortress."

Aqasi uses his cane to trace the path on the wall map from Tehran to Tabriz and then Tabriz to Mah-Ku.

With a little smile, Aqasi turns and peers past Muscles. He tilts his head, putting on his "look for approval" expression. But from whom? There is an additional person in the room -- the solemn Shiraz Governor Khan, who signals his delight with a subdued toss of his head.

Haji Mirza Aqasi: Visier to Muhammad Shah

Aqasi's reaches down and pulls open the drawer that still contains the Bab's Epistle to Muhammad Shah that Husayn had delivered to him.

"Oh, I forgot to give that to the Shah," he says.

HUJJAT, 35
Babi leader in Zanjan

Hujjat cranes his head to see, but the contents of the desk drawer remain out of his view.

Hujjat, "Give what?"

Looking surprised at himself, Aqasi lightly strikes his temple with the palm of his hand, pushing his hat off center, "Oh, nothing. I can be so forgetful! It's pitiful."

Aqasi's sarcasm again. He never had any intention of delivering that Epistle to Muhammad Shah.

Hujjat (the "Proof"): 34, large, husky, beard clipped to quarter inch length, was leading Mulla in Zanjan, northwest of Tehran, early convert to the Bab's Cause, self-confident, outspoken and brash; highly educated, long famous as a controversialist, quick-witted, highly intelligent.

Aqasi pulls a pouch of tobacco from the drawer, places it on the desk and shuts the drawer, "To what good fortune do I owe this visit by the important mulla from the important city of Zanjan?"

Aqasi calmly prepares and lights the water pipe on his desk.

Hujjat is angry, "Visit? Your men abducted me from Zanjan and keep me like a prisoner confined in Tehran."

Aqasi, "The Shah complained that two-thirds of the people in Zanjan identify with the Siyyid-i-Bab ... because of you."

Aqasi puffs the water pipe. Hujjat boldly circles the desk to stand over Aqasi. This action would not be done by anyone who feared for his life. Aqasi, however, takes it in stride.

Hujjat, "What's that? Opium?"

Aqasi, "Definitely not ... I thought you had exhausted the supply of opium and prostitutes to lure the innocents of Zanjan to your immoral Babi fanatics. That's why you're here, you know, I have to protect them ... from you."

Hujjat, "We teach purity of conduct and character. You know that."

Aqasi, "I know, one, that you are not the only 'leading citizen' of Zanjan. Two, that the mullas of Zanjan have come here to me to condemn your behavior and..."

As Aqasi speaks, Hujjat folds his arms, moving to the front of the desk, just across from Aqasi. Then he leans over the desk, speaking loudly directly into Aqasi's face, "You mean the mullas who 'rent' a 'wife' to any man, for an hour, day, or week, as one might wish! They make me look like a saint."

Aqasi glances toward the closed door, "Not so loud. They'll think you're killing me in here."

Hujjat, "That's not such a bad idea. But the Bab prohibits violence."

Aqasi, "Oh, good ... While you scheme to 'free' the Bab, perhaps by an attack on my escort?"

Hujjat, "That is not true!"

Aqasi rises and shouts, "Arise and deliver me from the hand of the oppressor!"

Aqasi punctuates that remark with a slam of his cane on the desk. Suddenly, Aqasi acts out a sham confusion, blinking and banging his forehead again with his palm, saying softly, "Oh ... what is this? Those were words of your prophet." Then scorn, "Or do you deny that, too?"

Hujjat, "I do not. There was no 'attack'. Your men were asleep. Our friends spoke with the Bab, but he refused to escape. Any comments?"

Aqasi bites his lip.

Hujjat moves away to leave and with mock admiration, "But you did prevent a meeting between the Bab and the Shah. Congratulations." He laughs, "No need to worry for now ... that your impressionable king would befriend the Bab or that the Bab might cure his illness and win his tender heart."

Aqasi replies calmly, "You know, I ought to have you killed right now."

Hujjat tosses a dagger from a wall display to Aqasi's desk, "Go right ahead." Aqasi picks up the dagger and uses it clean his nails, "Get out of here."

Hujjat exiting, "OK, I'll die on another day.

Tehran: Golestan Palace inner courtyard

The Bab Imprisoned at the Mak-Ku Fortress

MAH-KU, NORTHWEST PERSIA
Summer, 1847

Mah-Ku: Town populated mostly by Kurds following the Sunni division of Islam; at the NW corner of Persian territory overlooking territory of both the Russian and Ottoman empires; the birthplace of Prime Minister Aqasi. Above the town, on the side of a hollow mountain, is the castle in which the Bab, Eyes and Hasan are imprisoned.

Mah-Ku mountain fortress

Médiathèque Baha'ie Francophone

The first morning light makes the massive mountain with its prison fortress visible. In the foreground is the little mud-brick village of Mah-Ku surrounded by a wall.

A group of some 20 people press in closer to the closed town gate. They repeat a rhythmic chant of "Dhikru'llah-al-Azam" (meaning "Mention of God, the Most Great").

Campsites dot the trail to the gate. The campsites are a scattered and disorganized mix of all classes, rich to poor, fancy tents to those with only a few tattered bags. People mill about. Many are still covered by the dust of the road from traveling. Some appear to be arriving just now.

One family is just waking from sleep on mats over the dirt. A woman places a metal tea pot on a small fire.

Another family erects a tent.

Dervish sits smoking a hand-held pipe. His tattered clothes, unwashed long stringy hair, eyeglasses and face are so dusty that they look powdered. Kid eyes him.

Dervish extends the pipe offering a puff to Kid, "Want to try some, boy?" Kid looks up to Nose, standing behind Dervish and says, "Oh-oh." Nose kicks Dervish in the kidney with the side of his foot, knocking Dervish's glasses and pipe to the ground, more from surprise than the force of the blow.

The Mah-Ku gate opens. Warden rides out. Hasan follows on foot and slips to the side along the wall. A group again chanting "Dhikru'llah-al-Azam" presses in to Warden's horse. Warden stops and this suffices to silence the group. Warden surveys the group and campsites disparagingly.

WARDEN, rough Kurdish chief at Ma-Ku

Warden: named 'Ali Khan, Chief of the Kurdish town of Mah-Ku; warden of the prison castle; a Kurd, clumsy, unrefined, rough.

Hasan moves along the wall toward a spot where Shaykh awaits.

Shaykh, "Not a word for two weeks!"

Hasan, "My brother and I were allowed to accompany the Bab."

112

Warden gruffly shouts to the group, "Go back to your homes! My orders do not permit you to see your 'Dhikru'llah'."

Nose and Kid look up at Warden, who emphatically concludes, "And you will not."

Warden rides off down the trail through the campsites passing Dervish.

Dervish sneers, laughs and throws a stone after Warden, now well out of range.

Hasan says to Shaykh, "You will be able to enter Mah-Ku and visit the Bab."

Shaykh, "Now?"

Hasan, "No, the Bab will speak with the warden today."

Hasan sees that the gate to Mah-Ku begins to close.

Shaykh, "But he just said, 'Go home'!"

Hasan departing to reenter Mah-Ku before the gate closes, "Got to go."

Warden sits on his horse on the crest of a hill. His panoramic view includes the mountain fortress of Mah-Ku to the east. The early morning light is now brighter. The sun has risen just above the mountain. Enjoying his morning ride, Warden breathes deeply and rides back toward Mah-Ku.

Kurdish horseman

On his knees at the edge of a wide stream, Street prepares to toss a fish net into the water. It is very quiet, no wind, except Warden's horse slowing to a stop and the chant of Street, praying as he works with the net. Street notices Warden dismounting at the top of a slope behind him, as he stands to position himself to toss the net.

Looking down the slope, Warden ties his horse to a bush. He mumbles angrily, "Damn it to hell!"

Squinting, Warden watches Street continue his chant, standing facing away toward the stream, starting to swing the net. The light of the rising sun reflects in the water, so that Street's image is silhouetted in almost blinding brightness. Warden is mystified, "What's he doing out here?"

Warden makes a fist and punches the palm of his left hand with a loud slap sound. He struts down the slope, reproving the guards at the fortress under his command, "This man was to be strictly confined."

Warden marches further down the slope toward Street. Seen from the rear against the reflected sunlight in the water, Street swings the net with arms raised in the air. Warden stops abruptly, still upset, simpering, "Oh God, he's praying!"

Warden squints, molested by the bright reflection.

Chanting loudly, Street slings the net into the air. It spreads out, falls downward and splashes into the water, which had been flat and unperturbed.

Warden raises a hand to block the bright light, but has to look away closing his eyes.

Strange images reverberate in his head from his last glimpse of the net spreading out and flying upward leaving Street's hands. Sparks fly everywhere like a swarm of bees originating from Street's hands, while the components of the image become painted with a rainbow of pastel colors, his "white" garments, his shoes, skin and hair, the river bank, the water, everything. Through the swarm, the images blink. With each moment, the color of a particular thing changes in hue or intensity. Now the swarm of sparks is gone and the images step rapidly through views of the same action, from different angles, as if Warden's imagination had left his body. Not only do we see views impossible for Warden to behold from his position, but the order of events is also mixed up.

114

Though the net had fallen in an instant, its intricate pattern of lines glowing as multi-colored laser-like threads float gracefully downward. In one image, the "net of light" surrounds the almost black silhouette image of Street with outstretched arms releasing yet other nets. The net's impact with the water releases steam and giant cartoon-like splashes and droplets.

As little waves ripple out in the water, Street bends to pull in his net, chanting and unconcerned, looking up at Warden some half way up the slope behind him.

Warden looks confused and fearful but is still angry and snaps, "Let him pray!"

He abruptly turns and marches with determination toward his horse.

Later in the morning, against the background of the town gate and campsites, Nose and Kid walk down the trail away from the village.

Like a bat out of hell, Warden gallops past them.

At the closed gate, Warden jumps off his horse. Irked and confused to see the gate closed, "What in the hell is this?"

Warden bangs on the gate with both fists, shouting, "Open up, damn it!"

Dervish, washed up, eating with Shaykh at one of the campsites, cranes his head to see what the shouting at the gate is about. The gate opens. Warden swings back on to his horse and maneuvers it inside to see Blinky Kurd, handling the inner side of the gate.

Warden, "You negligent slob! You left this gate open!"

Blinky Kurd is confused, "Open? Ah. No, sir."

Warden, angry smirk, "I'll bet!" Warden gallops into the town.

Eyes hurries down the incline from the fortress to greet his brother Hasan and take from him some packages to divide the load of purchases Hasan had made in the Mah-

Ku village. Warden struggles up the incline and jumps off his mount, "Your 'leader' thinks he can escape!"

Eyes is incredulous, "What?"

Warden, "But we'll go get him!" Pointing angrily, "I saw him out there."

Hasan, "Go where?"

Eyes frowning to Hasan, "Nowhere." To Warden, "The Bab is in his cell." To Hasan, "Let's go."

Unperturbed by the strange behavior of Warden, Eyes and Hasan walk up the incline away from the shocked Warden.

Hasan turns to address Warden, "Aren't you coming to see your prisoner?"

The chant of morning prayers by the Bab originates from the prison fortress on the mountain above.

Dervish sleeps like a baby on the ground.

Sadiq, sullied by the dust of travel on foot, steps over Dervish. Shaykh, Nose, Street and Kid sit beside him. As Sadiq sits, he passes a sack to Shaykh, who removes and passes bread and cheese to Kid, Street and Nose. He whispers, "We can't enter Mah-Ku, so I brought food from a distance."

Sadiq bends over Dervish and looks right into his face. Dervish snores. Sadiq rustles Dervish, "Wake up. It's time for the morning prayer."

Dervish opens his eyes to a close look at Sadiq's weathered face, scarred from beatings, stonings and the torching of his beard that he had suffered in Shiraz. He feigns fearful shock at the sight of Sadiq, "Haa-aaa! ... I thought," impish grin, "I thought you were a nightmare."

Nose, "Just a Babi heretic." Sadiq grins at Nose.

The gate of Mah-Ku opens. Warden appears on horseback. His attitude is still harsh but noticeably less so, as he announces loudly, "Is there a Shaykh Hasan?"

Shaykh jumps up and runs to Warden, who dismounts.

116

Warden leads Shaykh, startled, into Mah-Ku. Blinky Kurd begins to close the gate. Warden tells him, "Leave the gate open."

Blinky Kurd is confused, "Open?"

In the campsites around the gate, people stand incredulous looking at the open gate.

The last to stand up, Dervish positions his eye-glasses, "Well? Let's go in."

Sadiq extends an arm in front of Dervish, blocking his path toward the gate. No one else makes a move. To Dervish, "Wait a while."

The Babis Act

PLAIN OUTSIDE MASHHAD
Autumn, 1847

Kneeling on the plane outside Mashhad, Husayn bends to touch his forehead to the ground, chanting the afternoon prayer. He faces the setting sun, about to disappear below the southwest horizon of this vast flat plain. Husayn appears miniscule in this dry, barren, open place.

Later, after sunset, Husayn sits up, positions himself W-NW, wiping his hands together to remove the dust.

Now in almost complete darkness, Husayn still meditates in the same position. Far off in the direction he faces, the Bab remains imprisoned in the Mah-Ku fortress. An hour passes.
In the total night silence, Husayn sits, erect posture, eyes closed. Now his forearms are extended before him, palms up. The moon is higher in the clear star-filled sky.
He hears voices and horses from behind and turns eastward to look.
Banner, Cannon, Baqir and Qambar ride horses westward at walk pace. Behind, some faint lights from oil lamps in the city of Mashhad are detectable on the horizon.

Banner: early twenties, stubble beard growth, son of a mulla.
Cannon: named 'Abdu'l-'Ali Khan, admirer of Husayn; resident of Mashhad; captain of artillery in the forces of Prince Hamzih Mirza, who was governor.
Baqir: 40s, large man, successful merchant.
Qambar: 30s, graying short beard, a poor man, uneducated, simple manners, personal attendant of Husayn in Mashhad.

"I say we ride north to the Salar's camp of the rebels against the central government," Banner suggests to Cannon.
"The Salar learned of Husayn's large following and wished to win the support of Husayn for his revolt," Baqir adds. "Husayn might be there now."

"But to what end?" Cannon replies. "How could the Salar understand that our movement does not further its aims by armed struggle."

Looking ahead, Qambar exclaims, "There he is!"

The four men stop near the solemn figure of Husayn, now standing, facing south. Husayn tosses his head in the W-SW direction, "The sun has set on Shiraz."

Husayn turns toward the men, raising his right arm behind indicating the W-NW direction, "I shall now go to Mah-Ku."

The four men are concerned, "Let us provide you with horses and men."

Acknowledging this offer, Husayn nods respectfully, "Thank you, but I shall go alone." He looks westward away from the men, "I have vowed to walk the whole distance that separates me from my beloved." Before anyone can respond, Husayn turns toward Mah-Ku and walks off into the darkness.

Baqir to Cannon, "Why, that's 2,000 kilometers. Winter approaches."

Suddenly, Qambar dismounts, passing the reins of his horse to Banner, who reacts to Qambar with a touch of condescension, "What are you doing?"

"If I go with nothing, he might let me go with him," replies Qambar, who runs off into the darkness after Husayn.

COUNTRYSIDE NEAR MAH-KU

In the early morning fog, Dervish sits against the trunk of a shade tree. Some distance behind him are large boulders and more trees. Otherwise, Dervish's tree is alone in this expansive, remote, lonely place, featuring clumps of dried wild grasses on rolling hills.

Dervish lights a water pipe taken from his pouch. As he puffs away, he takes from his pouch five simple clay figures, which look like crude "ginger-bread men". No doubt it is hashish. Dervish begins to giggle a bit, the pipe smoke tube still in his mouth, pipe smoke mingling with the fog. He sticks the five clay figures into the soil, so they form a 90 degree arc before him, "standing" in the earth facing him. He removes his glasses, while he mumbles, "A new day." He giggles, then in a serious tone, "This tortured soul shall now persevere in its search for enlightenment."

When Dervish giggles, it is of the uncontrolled pant type and not hard-toned or childish.

Dervish places his curved hatchet on the ground to his right. His left hand wields a heavy club, another implement commonly carried by wandering dervishes. He addresses the leftmost figure, "O Moses! You freed people and gave mighty laws. But when Jesus appeared, people were ill-prepared. Explain this mystery!"

Among large boulders behind Dervish's tree, Wright awakens from a night's sleep on a simple bed roll, concerned by the voice he hears, but does not recognize.

C J Wills, In the Land of the Lion and Sun, or Modern Persia, 1891

Dervish continues loudly, addressing the little clay figure before him, "Speak now, or forever hold your peace! You can, you must!"

Wright fears that bandits are about. He jumps for cover between two boulders, to hide his position, scanning his surroundings.

Scared, Wright peeks over the rock to locate the source of the voice he hears. He can see this much.

From behind the tree trunk, the left arm of Dervish waves the club violently in the air. To the right of the trunk, a ray of light from the rising sun penetrates the mist, reflecting off the blade of the hatchet, as Dervish shouts, "Your silence will seal your fate!"

Wright sees the club descend with great force to the ground, shattering the clay figure to pieces, with a rending thump.

Quite frightened, Wright slumps down, pondering his options, as he hears a threatening loud laugh from Dervish, drugged and near psychotic.

From the pathetic pieces of the first figure, Dervish moves the end of the heavy club to the second clay figure, which becomes "spot-lighted" by another ray of sunlight shining through foliage.

Wright decides to try to reach out to retrieve his bedroll to better conceal his position, when the mysterious voice booms loudly, "O Jesus! You have uplifted the souls of men! I beg you."

At these words, Wright realizes he may have misgauged the situation. He rises to take another look.

Dervish now holds the club with both hands in its position on the ground before the second figure, saying sadly, "The people scorned Muhammad." Then inquisitively, "Surely your divine wisdom could have prevented this."

With Dervish behind the tree trunk and facing away from Wright, only the sides of Dervish's arms are visible. But Wright notices the water pipe at the left near the tree trunk. Puffs of smoke emerge from behind the trunk. Dervish giggles some more.

Wright is still cautious, but now curious.

Dervish raises his club in the air, "This lowly servant beseeches your exalted self!" There is no reply and Dervish is angry, "What? You remain silent?"

Dervish delivers a mighty blow pulverizing the second clay figure.

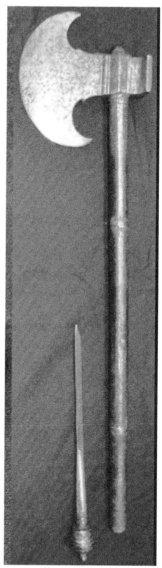

Careful to avoid making any sound, Wright moves toward the tree as Dervish leans forward to address the third figure, saying loudly, "O Muhammad! Perhaps you can free me from this torment!"

Dervish's face is distorted by his rising frenzy, looming ominously over the third clay figure. Dervish trembles with rage, "Now the Siyyid-i-Bab has been banished and imprisoned!"

Awed by the grotesque scene, Wright cautiously peers around the tree as Dervish again slowly raises his club.

Dervish, "O great one! Show forth your infinite powers to purify this worthless atom!"

The third figure falls forward, flat on the dirt. Dervish's left hand sticks it back in the soil, "I shall be patient. Pronounce to me your secret knowledge!"

Behind Dervish and the tree, Wright cannot be seen by Dervish. Unaware that he is being observed, Dervish waits for a reply, "Not a single word?!"

Dervish smashes the third figure. Wright flinches and turns away. He is disgusted and wary of this raving maniac.

Dervish puts the pipe tube back in his mouth.

Wright carefully stoops, molested by a fresh cloud of pipe smoke. Another Dervish giggle. Wright extends his right arm toward the hatchet handle, as Dervish intones, with gravity, loudly, "O Siyyid-i-Bab! You have been witness to the penalty which your brethren have suffered!"

Tree trunk to his left, Wright's extends his fingers toward the end of the axe handle. But Dervish's right hand snatches up the hatchet. Wright withdraws his hand.

Wright springs to his feet pressing body and cheek to the trunk, wondering if his presence had been detected.

With club and hatchet in hand, Dervish raises both arms menacingly over the fourth clay figure. He continues, "Perhaps your sublime words shall calm this humble servant." Trying to show fairness and patience, Dervish tilts his head slightly, to better hear any sound that might emerge from the fourth clay figure. Bloodshot eyes, eyelids quivering, raised arms beside his distorted face, Dervish shouts, "Nothing? ... You choose to stand mute?"

Another swift blow of the club destroys the little figure, driving fragments into the soil.

Behind the tree trunk, Wright decides that the most prudent course is to withdraw from the scene of this mad-man, whose identity still remains unknown to him. His total disgust is evident as he takes a parting look to see the club move before the fifth and last clay figure, the hatchet blade hovering above it.

Wright begins to depart. Barely one step completed, Dervish cries out, "O thou Lord God of heaven and earth!" whereupon Wright stops, unable to continence this additional blasphemy. No longer wary, without any further trace of sympathy for the obviously deranged Dervish, Wright returns decisively to his spot behind the tree.

Addressing the fifth figure before him, Dervish slowly flexes his arms in, lifting his gaze upward, "Shall thou also ignore my plea?" Dervish listens for a reply, with club and hatchet in clenched fists framing his face. Wright booms, "Wretch! Thou hast slain my prophets in your perverse ignorance! How dare thee threaten the Creator!"

Dervish's eyeballs rotate upward. He emits one loud brief howl, fainting. Club and hatchet fall near the shattered clay.

Dervish's limp body slumps to the right of the tree trunk, sprawling at Wright's feet, revealing Dervish's face to Wright for the first time in this episode.

Recognizing Dervish, Wright exclaims, "My gosh! It's you!"

WRIGHT'S STUDY

On this bright and hot day with the window shudders open, Wright can see the distant mountains. He sits in undershirt and short pants at his work table preparing to write on a clean page.

His "puzzle pieces" are still laid out to his left. To the right of that, just next to his ink well and writing paper, there is a new cluster of three pieces with the notes: "Where??", "Look to Elam, Daniel 8:2" and "Elam = Fars = Shiraz". Wright begins to write, "Three years ago, a man in Shiraz claimed to be inspired by God and adopted the name 'Bab', the Arabic word for 'Gateway'."

Wright stops writing and groans, as if frustrated or recalling something unpleasant. He recalls his incident with Dervish as he continues writing.

BACK TO COUNTRYSIDE NEAR MAH-KU

Wright lifts Dervish's head, resting at the same spot but now on Wright's bed roll. Wright offers a cup of water, but Dervish is still out cold.

Fog and mist gone, mid-day sun, some wind and rustling leaves, Wright stands over Dervish. The text Wright wrote continues, "He was taken toward Tehran, but his guard was diverted to Tabriz, where the population greeted the arrival of the prisoner chanting, 'God is the Most Great'!"

Dervish opens his eyes and recognizes Wright with a sheepish wide grin. The impressive sound of masses of people crying "Allah-u-Akbar!" mixes with that of the wind and leaves. Wright stoops again to offer water.

The text continues, "The populace of that city was warned that those seeking to approach the Bab would be stripped of possessions and imprisoned themselves."

As Wright recalls it, leading his horse loaded with packages of supplies purchased in Tabriz, he converses with Dervish. They walk up a slope from the tree behind them.

Wright's text, "He was then banished to a remote prison castle on the border of Russia and Turkey."

Speaking to Wright as they approach the top of the slope, Dervish points ahead of them over the crest.

Wright adds, "Anyone who wanted to see him was soon admitted."

From this distant slope, Wright and Dervish witness the forbidding sight of the prison fortress of Mah-Ku, perched on the side of a craggy rock mountain, abruptly protruding above the surrounding hills.

Wright continues his story, "His friends had become fairly numerous throughout Persia."

Wright bids farewell to Dervish who walks down the slope toward Mah-Ku. Wright mounts his horse. Dervish and Wright exchange final waves. Wright adds to his notes, "He was visited by persons near our mission, who then became his followers."

BACK TO WRIGHT'S STUDY

Wright concludes his text, "He dictated to scribes and the sentences flowed so fast from his mouth that many believed him to be inspired."

Appearing irked and unsatisfied, the perfectionist Wright suddenly crumples up the pages of his text.

Like two spots in a sea of white snow as seen from a distance, Husayn and Qambar, about twenty yards behind Husayn, march through two inches of freshly fallen snow.

Mt. Damavand

S G W Benjamin, Persia and the Persians, 1887

The whitened mountains of Mazindaran, including the towering peak of Mt. Damavand to the north rise above them. They walk west. There are no other footprints to indicate the trail. Few travel in this weather. There are no signs of civilization.

Husayn's mustache and stubble beard are covered with ice. He and Qambar have wrapped themselves in blankets. Qambar falls into the snow. At a cry from Qambar, Husayn turns and scurries back to him.

In the best of spirits, Dolgorukov pours two drinks of Vodka, picks them up and offers one to Russian. Both smiling broadly, "Welcome to Tehran!"

Russian, "Thank you, sir, for everything ... the dinner..."

Dolgorukov, "It is a joy to host a traveler from mother Russia. But you have said nothing of your trip."

Russian: early 20s, handsome lad, stern face, Russian dress, from well-to-do family, appears to be a student.

RUSSIAN, 20
"student" traveler

Russian stands in front of a large portrait of Nicholas I, Tsar of Russia, "South of Astrakhan, when I entered the newly acquired Russian territory, I became quite disturbed."

Seating himself on a divan, Dolgorukov is sympathetic, "Well, the Georgians and Armenians there are difficult to rule, even when they belonged to Persia."

Russian sits, "What bothered me was the Babis. I estimate over 30,000 of them."

Dolgorukov usually directs a conversation toward his ends. In this instance, this intelligence catches him off guard. He leans forward, "Babis?"

Russian, "Yes, an old Persian walked many hundreds of kilometers spreading this belief."

At a new dawn, Sadiq again brings food to Shaykh, Nose, Street and Kid. This time, Sadiq is seen arriving from a different angle showing Russian was there, not far off, studying Sadiq.

Russian narrates, "Reaching Persia, I saw him. He looked decrepit, yet he crossed that rugged country."

Flashback of people standing staring at the open gate to the Mah-Ku village, including Russian at the perimeter, "Later, I saw their prophet teaching a multitude on the side of a mountain at Mah-Ku."

Mulla Husayn Walks from Mashhad to Mah-Ku

CARAVANSERAI ROOM, TEHRAN

Tehran: Caravanserai
Weighing merchandise

S G W Benjamin, Persia and the Persians, 1887

Qambar is asleep.

Husayn looks terrible. He peers into a small mirror, perhaps a few inches long, held in his left hand. His right hand brings a razor to his cheek, covered with stubble, a little longer than before, no shaving cream. His right hand trembles a bit. Mad at himself, he drops the razor hand, exhaling audibly in frustration, "Cheee!"

The mud-wall room has no furniture, just a tattered rug on which Qambar sleeps. Husayn sits on his knees, trying to shave. He switches the razor to his left hand, mirror to right hand.

Raising razor to his neck, at the "moment of truth", he peers into the mirror for guidance. The mirror held in his right hand shakes, but Husayn can proceed shaving.

PALACE OF THE SHAH

Muhammad Shah lies on rugs and pillows, feet propped on pillows above his head. Prime Minister Aqasi stands behind, leaning on his cane. Muhammad Shah looks sick, the gout. Aqasi is in total control.

Muhammad Shah chuckles, "Tell me that story again, the one about the traveler terrorized by the Sufi dervish in the wilderness." He notices that Aqasi looks away at Dolgorukov, standing in the entrance and gazing gravely at them.

Muhammad Shah looks Dolgorukov over, signaling with an arm to Aqasi, "Could you take care of it, Haji?"

Aqasi, "Certainly."

All too happy to handle the affairs of state out of the presence of the Shah, Aqasi quickly circles the Shah to cross toward Dolgorukov.

HOUSE OF BAHA'U'LLAH, TEHRAN

Accompanied by the elegantly dressed Musa, Husayn and Qambar, all cleaned up in fresh clothes, approach the front door. Though of noble lineage, Musa follows the two men into the frost-covered patio leading to the door, showing obvious deference even to the lowly servant, Qambar.

Bread, laughing, emerges from the house to greet them in the front patio. He is exuberant, "Remember me!"

With a strained smile, Husayn thinks but to no avail, "Ahhh."

Bread bends a knee, leans slightly to the side, extends his arm and replays how he had caught the coin that Husayn had tossed to him when he was a bread vender in Karbala. Throughout, Bread grins and at the moment he palms the imaginary coin in his fist, he winks at Husayn. Eureka!

Husayn, "The Karbalai!"

Husayn and Bread embrace with a burst of sustained laughter. Meanwhile, Wool runs from the house throwing himself at Husayn's feet, "Husayn!" Releasing Bread, helping the overwhelmed Wool to his feet, "Come on. This is the New Day! We do not worship people."

They move toward the house. At the front door threshold, Brows and Karim beam at Husayn and wait their turn to greet him.

OFFICE OF PRIME MINISTER AQASI

For the first time, Dolgorukov is seen in a truly humorless mood. He addresses Aqasi, who looks petite seated at his big European-style desk. Formal and serious, "We ask that your government send the Siyyid-i-Bab, on whom be peace, to some other part of Persia. Mah-Ku is on the frontier of Russia and we feel the Babis there will be the cause of disturbances."

Aqasi tries to act statesman-like, but it is too much for him to ask of himself. Relieved that the matter raised by Dolgorukov is less weighty, in his mind, than what he had imagined it might be, Aqasi exhales loudly, as if bored or minimizing Dolgorukov's statement, "Is that it?"

Acquainted with Aqasi's crudeness, but nevertheless irked, Dolgorukov retorts, "My government views this as a quite serious matter."

Aqasi perfunctorily, "Then consider it done."

Dolgorukov, "The Bab will be moved?"

Aqasi, "Yes, right away."

Dolgorukov glares at Aqasi, whose attitude seems to him to be somehow inappropriate. Then, the "diplomat" in him, "Thank you, your excellency. I shall inform St. Petersburg of your act of friendship toward Russia."

BACK TO HOUSE OF BAHA'U'LLAH, TEHRAN

Husayn, Qambar, Musa, Bread, Wool, Brows and Karim sit around a rug sharing tea and sherbet.

Musa addresses Husayn, "When the Bab passed Qazvin, he directed a strongly worded epistle to the mullas there."

Bread, "Get this. Two of the leading mullas are brothers. One is the father of Qurratu'l-Ayn. The other is the father of her husband. Figure that out."

Brows, "Well, her ex-husband. They divorced."

Bread, proudly and dramatically, "The party of Qurratu'l-Ayn was approaching the capital!"

Musa, "But she was taken back to her 'family' in Qazvin."

Brows, "They sent horsemen to get her."

Musa, "Reluctantly, she bid her Babi companions to return to their homes."

Husayn, "I don't like what I'm hearing."

Bread, "Definitely. It's a mess. Then, the father of her ex-husband, that's her uncle ... right? ... was murdered."

Husayn, "But is she all right now?"

Musa, "That's the question, we don't know."

Nasiri'd-Din, now about 17, sports a little mustache and has more self-confidence. He and Taqi enter the front patio of the British Legation in Tehran, walking briskly toward the front entrance. It is below-freezing weather, the ground is frosted and the street outside is frozen mud.

TAQI, 41
new Prime Minister

Taqi: Mirza Taqi Khan, 40, large, stout, round man; round beard, heavy eyebrows, long pointed nose; regal dresser. Son of a lowly cook; a wrestler in his youth; married to Nasiri'd-Din's sister; a man with few other friends. Able and clever; subject to extreme avarice; often harsh and cruel; suspicious of Europeans and Western ways. Taqi was opposed by Nasiri'd-Din's mother, but he seems to know even now that he shall soon be Prime Minister for Nasiri'd-Din, in line for the crown of Persia.

From a tray with all the ingredients on a side table, Dr. Cormick pours himself a cup of tea.

Farrant, "Prince Nasiri'd-Din asked to meet you here, doctor."

Dr. Cormick, "More than a bit strange. Why didn't we go to the palace?"

Farrant, "I don't know. He wanted to come to the Mission."

Nasiri'd-Din and Taqi appear in the vestibule off the reception room of the mission. With deference, Farrant meets them at the entrance of the room, "Welcome, gentlemen. Please, make yourselves comfortable."

Taqi remains by the entrance near Farrant just inside the room, while Nasiri'd-Din marches right to the center of the room, where he remains standing, "Is not Major Sheil here?"

Farrant, "He is on leave in London, excellency."

Nasiri'd-Din, "Yes ... I knew that."

Farrant, "I am now Charge d'Affaires."

Ignoring Farrant, Nasiri'd-Din addresses himself to Dr. Cormick, who stands at attention across from Farrant, "Dr. Cormick, I thought it best to address this particular request to you at this site, since you are now physician of the British Legation."

Dr. Cormick, "I am at your service."

Nasiri'd-Din, "My desire is that you come with me, as my personal physician, to Tabriz, where I shall assume the post of Governor of Adharbayjan."

Nasiri'd-Din and Taqi are not positioned to see that Farrant winks approvingly at Dr. Cormick, while Nasiri'd-Din continues, "Your salary would be ample."

Acting properly overwhelmed and thankful for such an honor, Dr. Cormick, "Well ... I gratefully accept!"

Nasiri'd-Din to Farrant, "Lieutenant-Colonel Farrant?"

Farrant realizes this is a coup both in foreign relations and in intelligence-gathering potential, "With my profound blessings."

As if he does not know what to do next, Nasiri'd-Din appears awkward. He abruptly marches out of the

Legation, saying nothing, followed by Taqi. Struck by this abrupt behavior (no "thank you" or "good day" from Nasiri'd-Din), Farrant and Dr. Cormick, suddenly alone, snicker audibly eyeing each other as if they are about to burst out in laughter.

TEHRAN TO QAZVIN TRAIL

With Qambar close behind, Husayn walks west on this cold, cloudy day. Remnants of snow scattered on the landscape, the snow-covered peaks of the mountains of Mazindaran behind. Husayn recalls saying, "Is she all right?"

And Musa saying, "We don't know." Followed by Bread saying, "Husayn! Look at this!"

Husayn walks while deep in thought, stoic expression. He remembers Bread's words, "It's a poem by Qurratu'l-Ayn." After a pause, Bread had called out louder, "Husayn?"

Husayn had said, "Please ... read it to us."

Qambar folds his arms to protect from the cold. Other traffic, some on foot and riders on mules and horses, passes. Husayn replays Bread's words, "Aaww! You should have heard her recite it in Baghdad ... It is addressed to the Bab."

Husayn continues his march, closing his eyes, while he repeats in his mind recitation of Tahirih's work, "The thralls of yearning love constrain, within bonds of pain and calamity, these broken-hearted lovers of Thine to yield their lives in their zeal for Thee."

Husayn replays the moment in Karbala when the gazes of he and Tahirih were briefly interlocked. But this time, it is Husayn image of Tahirih looking out the window.

HADI'S HOUSE, QAZVIN

Tahirih, eyes closed, recites her poem, continuing from where Bread left off in Husayn's recollection. Her graceful gestures complement each word perfectly in her inspired delivery, "As in sleep I lay, at the break of day, that tempting Charmer came to me," As she recites, Tahirih stands in the center of the parlor.

"And in the grace of His form and face, the dawn of the morn I seemed to see."

Tahirih opens her eyes. Gazing admiringly, Husayn stands by a window.

In addition to Husayn, seated on rugs are Qambar, Qanitih, the older woman attendant of Tahirih, and two couples, all much younger than Husayn and Tahirih. First, Hadi and his wife Khatun-Jan. Then, Ali and Mardiyyih.

Mardiyyih to Tahirih, "That's translated from Arabic to Persian. Please, go on."

Tahirih is filled with emotion. Her expression mixes elements of a frown above and a smile below, "I'm sorry ... I feel..."

Rising to his feet, Hadi clears his throat and says, "You might want to talk with Husayn alone."

Tahirih, "No, that is not it. Stay." With an ironic laugh, "Our detractors have already used the murder of my uncle as an excuse to throw our friends into chains and put them to death. My ex-husband himself calls me a conspirator in his father's death! What would be the wild rumors if you left me with Husayn?"

No one moves. Tahirih emits a brief, but emotional sigh of frustration and looks into the eyes of Husayn. About six feet away at the perimeter of the room, he is still gazing at her.

Hadi: 18, nephew of Tahirih, original disciple of the Bab.

RESIDENCE OF DOLGORUKOV, TEHRAN

By lantern light, Dolgorukov sits alone at a writing table in his parlor drafting a dispatch, "For some time now, Tehran has been subject to the influence of sinister predictions. A Siyyid, known in this country as 'the Bab', was exiled from Isfahan after a rebellion and last year, on my demand, he was removed from the vicinity of our frontiers, where he had been exiled."

MAH-KU
Spring, 1948

Husayn and Qambar reach a crest along the trail where they see the imposing sight of the distant mountain fortress of Mah-Ku.

Note: Husayn and Qambar are in an obvious change of dress. Believing that the Bab was strictly confined by Warden, known to be harsh and severe, Husayn and Qambar had disguised themselves and are now dressed as the Kurdish people of this remote place.

The sun rising at dawn above the hilly horizon behind them, Husayn and Qambar walk briskly. Qambar nervously scurries up to Husayn, slowing him, gesturing ahead of them, "We won't pass as Kurds!" On a bridge over a river crossing the trail Warden sits alertly on his horse, holding the reins of two saddled horses. His position blocks the way. He stares at Husayn and Qambar as they approach.

Husayn says, "Keep walking."

Qambar, "What's going on?"

Husayn, "I don't know."

Warden shouts out loudly with force and pride. His statement brings Husayn and Qambar to a halt, "I am 'Ali Khan, warden and chief of Mah-Ku!"

Husayn and Qambar fear the worst and attempt to appear as ordinary travelers. Warden dismounts and leads the three horses toward Husayn and Qambar, "Last night, I dreamed of your arrival."

Warden kneels at the feet of Husayn as if Husayn was his king. Amazed, Qambar looks on.

Warden, "I beg you to complete your journey on these horses."

Pulling Warden to his feet, Husayn is firm, but respectful, "I have vowed to complete my route on foot. I will walk to the summit of this mountain to visit your prisoner."

Islamic Clerics Agree to Execute Tahirih

HOUSE OF BAHA'U'LLAH, TEHRAN

The Servant arouses Musa from deep sleep to notify him that an unexpected guest has arrived. In his bed clothes, Musa meets Hadi in the parlor. Profoundly distraught, Hadi reports to Musa, "Qurratu'l-Ayn is now confined and the mullas have already agreed to her execution."

The unflappable Musa is concerned but remains cool, "At least we have time before this mock trial ends."

Hadi, "No we don't! Qurratu'l-Ayn has, ah, issued an ultimatum."

Musa, "What do you mean?"

Hadi, "She told them, that if she spoke the truth, the Lord would deliver her from their tyranny ... within nine days. If not, then the mullas were free to pass sentence, without any further delay."

Musa, "Oh God. Where is she being held?"

Hadi, "In her father's house."

OFFICE OF MINISTER OF WAR

Teeth grinding, clenching his cane, Aqasi stands fuming in front of the wall map.

Whistling, War enters looking happy, carrying a bundle of documents. He closes the door and is surprised to see Aqasi, who shouts, "Where have you been? Damn it!"

War, innocently, "Getting the dispatches..."

Aqasi still shouting, "I mean, for the last year!"

Speechless, War slumps dumbfounded on the divan by the door. Aqasi approaches, softly, "I just had a nice little visit with a family relation..." Then with raised voice, "...from Mah-Ku! Instead of being 'strictly isolated', I learn, our prisoner there has been free to meet with visitors coming from all over Persia!"

Now Aqasi stands over War and continues scolding him loudly, "How did I not learn of this through official channels?" With a sarcastic laugh, "Why, it would seem that the Russian Envoy knows more than I of our internal affairs!"

At this moment, Dolgorukov opens the door and enters the room, unexpected and unannounced, anxious to show his anger at every opportunity, "Conferring with an aide?"

Straightening up, Aqasi puts his free hand to his forehead, as if he suddenly has a migraine headache. He feigns a limp pacing with his cane back behind War's desk before the wall map, laughing nervously and saying authoritatively, "So ... we are again honored..."

Dolgorukov, bluntly, "You lied to me."

Aqasi, "Lied? Perhaps the Persian can be vague. But, lie?"

War seems to enjoy seeing Aqasi getting some chastisement.

Dolgorukov, "I took your word to the point of informing the Russian government that this Bab was removed from Mah-Ku. Now, three months later, I find, to my embarrassment, that nothing has been done!"

Aqasi looks like he is about to burst out in laughter. But he contains himself, remaining defensive, "... Well, of course..."

Dolgorukov, "I shall petition the Shah on this matter."

Dolgorukov moves to leave. He pauses to listen when Aqasi offers a compromise, "One moment. I will approach the Shah today to issue such an order, if you wish to observe."

QAZVIN

There are no lights on this night in the front door vestibule of house of Tahirih's father. In diffused moonlight, Tahirih and Qanitih wait apprehensively, dressed all in black with gowns down to the floor, scarfs and face veils.

They hear a faint tap, tap on the door.

They were waiting for this signal because the door had been already unbolted and Tahirih opens it immediately. She and Qanitih slip out.

Qazvin: House of Tahirih

Tahirih and Qanitih emerge into the moonlight and are met by Khatun-Jan, similarly dressed, wide-eyed, hands trembling. They are careful not to make a single sound.

As they leave the front door area, the posted guard sleeps on the ground nearby. Wary of the danger of being seen, the three women hurry off down the street.

Moonlight illuminates a tree outside the Qazvin city wall. Hadi sits on the ground against the wall next to a pile of rope ladder with short wooden steps.

A rock hits the ground in front of Hadi.

Recognizing this signal instantly, Hadi jumps up and throws the rope ladder over the wall. As soon as he secures his end to the nearby tree trunk, tension appears in the rope ladder, as one of the women climbs up it on the other side of the wall.

Now poised on the top of the wall, Khatun-Jan jumps. Hadi catches her to break the fall. They fall to the ground.

Four saddled horses are tied to the nearby tree. They shift position nervously in reaction to the sudden activity. Their footsteps and a few horse grunts break the silence.

Khatun-Jan unties the horses, mounting one, holding the reins of the other three.

Meanwhile, the older Qanitih reaches the top of the wall and jumps to Hadi's outstretched arms, knocking him to the ground again as he breaks her fall. In Hadi's arms on the ground, Qanitih is frightened by the sight of the horses looming above them. She whispers, "I cannot ride!" Now Tahirih waits to jump.

Holding all the reins, Khatun-Jan dismounts and helps Qanitih up on a horse.

Agitated voices emerge at a distance within the city, perhaps "Search everywhere!", "Check the gates!", etc.

Tahirih jumps. Hadi stumbles. Tahirih hits the ground unassisted, rolling to avoid injury.

Now Qanitih is mounted. Khatun-Jan remounts. Tahirih rushes to a free horse. Hadi whips the rope ladder off the wall, doubling it over his shoulders, so he can mount as rapidly as possible. The voices in the city become louder, "Get that woman!", etc, banging on doors and "Shut up!", "Be quiet!" from angry people.

All four mounted, Khatun-Jan hands Hadi the reins of Qanitih's horse, so that Hadi can lead it.

Trembling, Qanitih grips the horse's mane in anticipation of a rough ride.

Hadi nods. Khatun-Jan and Tahirih gallop off.

As he finishes consolidating the rope ladder lashing it behind him on the horse, Hadi smiles confidently looking at Qanitih, saying softly, "Ready?"

Qanitih is almost too tense to move, but manages to nod "yes".

Hadi and Qanitih charge off after the others, Hadi leading Qanitih's horse. Clearly Qanitih has never even been on a horse before. She barely hangs on.

Persian Woman in Varamin

Christian Missionary Watches the Babis

CHRISTIAN MISSION, URUMIYYIH
South Of Chihriq

Carrying his bible, Wright descends a gentle slope from the stone Christian Mission building. He approaches a large shade tree where about six young Kurdish men sit on mats. Meanwhile, he recalls the text he had written about the Bab, "It was also said that he did miracles and whole masses of people believed this rumor, since he ignored material comforts and spent the greatest part of his time in prayer. The Bab was brought south from Mah-Ku to the Chihriq prison fortress not far from here."

Standing before the Kurdish young men, Wright opens his Bible and addresses them, "Today, I will speak of the meteoric ministry of Jesus!"

Wright continues his speech. While he speaks, he notices someone approaching and seems bothered.

He replays in his mind more of the text he wrote, "In the town of Chihriq, a crowd saw him. They were all mysteriously moved and burst into tears."

Looking a little less unkempt, Dervish nears the group and sits on the periphery. He grins widely and directs a childish, eager expression of attentiveness to Wright, exaggerating the attitude of Wright's young Kurdish students.

Wright continues his sermon, "Youthful, his ministry was brief. He challenged laws, creeds and corruption, both religious and secular. The purity of his life shamed the authorities who heaped indignities upon him, including a public interrogation." As Wright speaks of Jesus, his emotional fervor becomes evident.

Dervish is not aware that Wright speaks of Jesus and develops an expression of incredulous astonishment. Finally, he blurts out loudly in rapt amazement and joy, "The missionary has become a Babi!"

147

A few of the young Kurds giggle at the absurdity of Dervish's assertion.

To Wright, this is not only a rude interruption, but also a thoughtless personal affront, if he heard correctly, "What's that?"

Since he missed the beginning of Wright's class, Dervish thinks he was not heard or understood, "You're talking about the Bab, aren't you?"

Wright, "God forbid! Definitely not!"

Acquainted with the story of the Bab, the young Kurds recognize that Dervish had mistakenly thought Wright spoke of the Bab and they burst into laughter.

Later after sunset, Wright and Dervish visit in the Mission building. Though there are comfortable chairs in the front parlor, Dervish sits on a rug. He looks and feels out of place, as he converses with Wright who sits in a cushioned reading chair.

In general, the boorish behavior of Dervish is partly a personal characteristic, partly a reflection of a life spent mostly alone in the wilderness sleeping in caves or under the stars. Although the behavior of Dervish has been outrageous for Wright, he nevertheless has a curious empathy with Dervish and Dervish has been a source of information on a topic that has fascinated Wright, namely, the Babis.

Dervish utters the first statement we have from him in a serious, concerned tone of voice without his burlesque personality so evident, "They will take him to Tabriz for a public trial."

Wright has seen enough to immediately recognize that Dervish is, for once, sad and serious. Wright knows enough to realize the implications, "They?"

Dervish, "I don't know. The Prime Minister. The Crown Prince."

Wright, "And what of you?"

Dervish, proudly, "To Khurasan! The Bab has directed those who can to go to Khurasan."

Wright pulls out his money pouch from his coat's inner chest pocket, "That's over 600 miles! I shall help defray your cost."

Dervish emits a surly laugh and indicates "no" to the money, saying foxily, "A few months ago, we would have talked. I would have left you, unaware ... and broke!"

Recalling his previous encounter with Dervish, Wright feels the empty chest coat pocket from which he had just removed his money wallet. He now realizes that it was Dervish, on a previous occasion, as we now learn, who had robbed him, "It was you! Scoundrel! You robbed me."

Wright cannot help but laugh in admiration of Dervish's successful con. Dervish grins knowingly rolling his eyes acknowledging guilt. Then, smiling, looking around this well-appointed parlor, waving his finger "no" to the money, "No. I will walk and sleep under the stars."

Replacing his wallet securely in his coat, Wright is impressed, "Then, you are a Babi now."

This provokes Dervish to rise to his feet, "A Babi?"

Dervish frowns and grimaces at the thought. He snickers and raises his arms, his tone and gestures a mixture of pomposity and self-depreciation, "I am a free spirit, a poor wandering seeker of truth!"

Wright firmly takes note of Dervish's inconsistency, "What is a Babi, if not simply follower of the Bab? Who said, 'Go to Khurasan'?"

HOUSE OF BAHA'U'LLAH, TEHRAN

In a women-only room adjacent to the parlor seen previously and separated from it by a doorway completely covered by a curtain, Tahirih and Qanitih pack newly acquired clothes into bags, assisted by Khatun-Jan and Musa's Wife, who displays a dress to Tahirih saying, "My best gown ... for you!"

While Musa's Wife folds the dress to pack it, a male voice is heard from the "men-only" parlor behind the curtain separating the rooms, "This house is no longer safe for Babis."

In the parlor, Vahid sits on the divan, reading. Now the women's voices are heard vaguely from the other room, such as "You can't", "It's beautiful" and "I insist".

Near Vahid, Musa speaks to Fata and Hadi, these three all standing, "You will soon depart toward Khurasan to make preparations for the meeting." Vahid glances up from his book, "It should be historic."

Qanitih concludes a description of their escape from Qazvin to Musa's Wife, "I must be dreaming." Regarding Tahirih, "She would have been dead by now."

Vahid can be heard, "Think of the implications! ... Here's something else."

For the first time, we see a wide, foxy grin, not a smile, from Tahirih. She tosses her head to refer to the men in the adjacent parlor, saying, "Soon ... they may regret that I escaped execution in Qazvin."

Musa, "I shall take the women to a safe place outside Tehran." And to Fata, "You shall meet them there and escort them to Khurasan."

Vahid finds something of interest in the old, tattered book he is perusing, "Unbelievable! Here's another verse confirming the advent of the Bab's mission."

Tahirih hears the authoritative and intellectual tone of Vahid's remark. She looks up and calls through the curtain, loudly enough to be clearly heard by the men in the parlor, "Yahya!"

Vahid is surprised to be challenged. Tahirih shouts out, "Cease repeating traditions of the past!"

Tahirih continues loudly and firmly to Vahid, "Let deeds, not words, be your adorning!"

Qanitih, Khatun-Jan and Musa's Wife are wide-eyed, impressed and exchange glances. Tahirih smiles meekly and nods to them to confirm her "regret" remark, saying softly, "You see?"

Musa's Wife and Khatun-Jan snicker approvingly. Qanitih looks on, not sure how to react.

Mulla Husayn Back in Mashhad

BUILDING HOUSING A BABI CENTER, MASHHAD

Mashhad: Babi center ("Babiyyih") interior

Around a rug on the floor set for the purpose of serving refreshments, Baqir and Ali sit on their knees enjoying tea. They are suddenly disturbed by loud shouting, screams of women and other vocalizations from a violent scuffle outside. The mayhem is dominated by the fervent chant of "Ya Sahibu'z-Zaman!". Husayn runs out from a rear room. Ali and Baqir rise.

Ali, alarmed, to Husayn and Baqir, "That's our people!" Husayn, Ali and Baqir dash outside.

Expecting trouble, Husayn, Baqir and Ali emerge from the building to the street to meet Thin, a small thin personal attendant of Husayn, and Banner, with some twenty Babis. A crowd of onlookers discuss this episode, at street level and from the tops of the buildings. Thin is covered with dirt, bruised and bloodied from a beating and a cord still dangles from an incision made in his nose. He had been punished similar to the treatment that Quddus and friends had received previously in Shiraz.

Angry, Husayn takes Thin into his arms. Banner explains, "This! Because he is a Babi."

Now Husayn is furious. He stares at Banner, who continues, "We had to free him!"

A few of the Babis bear swords with fresh blood.

Thin, in pain, one of Husayn's arms still around him, looks up almost apologetically to Husayn, "I tried ... My tormentors..."

Banner, "One of them perished."

Husayn exhales a sigh to release his rage, so that his tone will be firm but not scornful to Banner and the Babis. Referring to Thin, "You have refused to tolerate his persecution." Then referring to himself, "then how can you reconcile yourselves to the martyrdom of Husayn?"

Mashhad: Babi center

By lantern light in the Babi Center, Quddus stands before Husayn, Ali and Baqir, all seated on their knees on a rug.

Quddus: now 26, still looks physically younger than his age. His dramatic change in demeanor and dress are evident. The "wild" clothes of a young rebel he had worn previously have been replaced with white, as Husayn had dressed. Although still warm and affable, we see by his behavior and manner that he has become a "young general" among the Babis.

Husayn: now 35, looks more than his almost ten years older than Quddus. He is regarded as a "commander" among the Babis. However, by his deference to Quddus, he clearly recognizes the leadership of Quddus.

Husayn to Quddus, "Many of the friends do not understand our mission."

Quddus, "They will understand ... Some may flee from our faces." Then to Ali, he says, "Ali and I will meet the friends approaching Khurasan." To Husayn, "We shall meet at whatever place the Almighty decrees." Indicating Husayn, Quddus says to Baqir, "Please follow him. Protect him."

ZAGROS MOUNTAIN WILDERNESS

Dervish walks eastward through this rugged mountain wilderness. There is no visible trail. The route is in Dervish's head.

Dervish replays his indignant reaction to Wright, "A Babi? Ridiculous."

He replays Wright's words, adding his own whining tone, "But you said the Babis are this and that."

Dervish interrupts himself and formulates an explanation for Wright. "Well", he says in a playfully indignant tone, "You are always asking about them."

MASHHAD-TEHRAN ROAD SOUTH OF MT. DAMAVAND

Riders on horses guide them in a graceful lope gait toward the right, eastward, if viewed from the south. Summer upon us, we see the mountains of Mazindaran again, but now only the highest peaks, such as Mt. Damavand, have snow. In this season, they are lush and green beyond the plain crossed by the riders: Tahirih, Qanitih, Fata, Wool, Brows, Ali-Akbar, Yusuf and Jalil.

They rapidly approach three travelers carrying small sacks walking toward the east: Nose, Street and Kid.

Hearing the approaching riders, Nose, Street and Kid turn and with instant recognition, cry out, "Babis!"

The riders surround them, amid laughter and the exchange of cheerful greetings. In this swarm of movement, male riders pull them up behind them on to their horses: Wool takes Nose; Brows takes Street; and Fata takes Kid, who cheers as they ride off without delay, "Yeaaa!"

PLAIN OUTSIDE MASHHAD

Quddus and Ali, their horses in a flowing lope gait, ride toward the left, westward. They look determined, but at this moment, they are engaged in a conversation and also seem carefree. Their conversation is not heard, but a comment by Quddus is apparently funny, because Ali laughs.

Badasht Conference and the Trial of the Bab

Badasht: small hamlet near the village of Shahrud. The area is in the country, green, grassy terrain with wooded areas nearby.

Riders approach. Babis chatter near Tahirih's tent.

Bread holds a stake which Blade drives into the ground with a mallet.

Bread straightens up. The tent patterned with broad green and white stripes lies on the ground nearby. Behind, some 40 yards away beyond a little ridge, another group of men raise into the air another similar tent for Quddus. Bread surveys the tent and to Blade, "Let's put her up."

Tahirih's group of riders arrive at Quddus' tent, exchanging excited greetings.

Blade, "More friends!"

Tahirih, Qanitih, Fata with Kid, Brows with Street and Wool with Nose continue on to Tahirih's tent, greeting Bread.

Bread helps Tahirih down. Blade helps Qanitih.

Street and Nose, jumping down from the horses, recognize Blade. Kid jumps down too and scampers right up to Blade.

Bread looks to Tahirih, now standing facing him, for approval. Tahirih whispers near Bread's ear, melting him, "You did fly to Tehran."

Street grins shaking Blade's arm, exclaiming to Nose, "Heeyy!"

Kid to Street, "Who is he?"

Nose greets Blade. Nose and Street recognize him from the night of the Bab's escape from Shiraz.

ZUNUZI'S HOUSE, TABRIZ
Northwest Persia

A very loud, no doubt massive crowd cheer the arrival of the Bab to Tabriz with the repeated chant of "Allah-u-Akbar" (meaning "God is the Most Great"). This chant is so loud that people inside the house have to speak a bit louder to be heard.

Youth: A handsome lad, presently about 17, energetic, strong-willed, intelligent, real name "Muhammad-'Ali-i-Zunuzi."

Zunuzi: 40, stepfather of Youth, large, stern, over-weight, not a Babi, notable citizen of Zunuz, related by family to Shaykh, real name "Siyyid 'Ali-i-Zunuzi."

YOUTH, 18
executed with the Bab

Grabbing Zunuzi's arm, Youth sulks and pleads, "Everybody is out there!"

Zunuzi is angry, "They're crazy!"

Youth, "He's arriving now. I just want ... I want to see his face."

Zunuzi shoves Youth back. While Youth slumps down to the floor, Zunuzi snaps loudly, "This so-called prophet..."

Youth, forcefully, "You can't keep me prisoner!"

Knock, knock on the door.

Zunuzi opens the front door, which admits a louder chant sound. Shaykh walks in and Zunuzi angrily wags a finger at Youth, "Prisoner? You got it, boy."

Shaykh, "I've come at a bad time."

Zunuzi, "No, no. Come in. I'm worried about this boy. He's dumb enough to declare himself a Babi! He has no idea of the danger." Exiting, he says to Shaykh, "Talk to him. I'll ask that tea be brought."

Zunuzi exits to a rear room, while Youth gazes into Shaykh's eyes. Shaykh looks up and away. At the instant that Zunuzi is out of sight, Youth pulls Shaykh to sit by him on the rug and whispers with conviction and anticipation, "You are a Babi."

Shaykh glances back to the doorway where Zunuzi exited, then softly, uneasy, "Ah-huh."

Shaykh and Youth speak in hushed voices, close to each other while the chanting crowd continues, "I knew it! Tell me!"

Shaykh does not know what to say, "Well ... Before the trouble in Shiraz, the Bab left all his property to his wife and mother."

Youth, "As if he knew."

Shaykh, foreboding, "Now, ah ... he has instructed me to deliver all of his writings to a safe place here in Tabriz..."

The enthusiastic expression of Youth droops as he considers the implications of this news.

Zunuzi returns to entertain his guest Shaykh, happy to see Shaykh talking to Youth, "Good! Talk sense to the boy!"

BACK TO TAHIRIH'S TENT, BADASHT ENCAMPMENT

Bread sits on the grass by Blade and watches the reaction of Tahirih and Qanitih, as Fata shows them the tent which Tahirih shall occupy, now fully erected. Rented by Jinab-i-Baha (later widely known as Baha'u'llah), the tent looks regal. It has four trapezoidal sides, with a five foot square top, high enough to stand up inside. Tahirih to Bread, "So often, ... I thank you again."

Bread inhales deeply with pride, glancing at Blade.

Tahirih and Qanitih, with their small travel bags, enter the tent. Fata appears to "stand guard" outside.

BACK TO ZUNUZI'S HOUSE, TABRIZ

The population outside continues chanting.

Shaykh rises to his feet, looking awkward and grim, and says to Zunuzi, "They are holding the Bab outside of the city wall, fearing disorder if the troops bring him into Tabriz."

Zunuzi to his son, Youth, "See what I mean?"

Shaykh, "Excuse me. I want to see..."

Youth jumps up to follow. Zunuzi snaps at Youth, "You're a prisoner, remember?"

As Zunuzi closes the door, he does not see that Shaykh, now beyond the threshold, directs a sympathetic, supportive nod to Youth inside.

GOVERNMENT HOUSE, TABRIZ

Random crowd voices, no chant.

The Government House interior has a meeting hall extending some forty feet deep from the twenty foot width of the room facing the entrance to the street. Shaykh positions himself in the crowd outside pressing toward the entrance. Shaykh's position provides him a good view of the interior.

Molested by the crowd, sweating from the heat of the day, Dr. Cormick passes by Shaykh. The Hall Guard at the entrance permits him passage such that Dr. Cormick enters the meeting hall without even breaking his stride. Dr. Cormick walks briskly straight down the middle of the sparsely furnished hall. A few tables along the long wall look small.

Rapidly arriving at the inner end of the hall, Dr. Cormick stops and bows before Nasiri'd-Din, who sits one leg under him on the only piece of furniture at this end of the room, a handsome throne befitting the Crown Prince. Two Persian Doctors and Tutor look on to the right of Nasiri'd-Din. Taqi on the left and Nasiri'd-Din converse briefly. Nasiri'd-Din seems to look to Taqi for guidance, but when Nasiri'd-Din pronounces a phrase, it is with an air of authority. Then, Taqi and Dr. Cormick address each other briefly. Dr. Cormick glances at Nasiri'd-Din.

During the above action, Dr. Cormick narrates the story of a letter he wrote to Wright, "Could you take a letter to the Reverend at the Christian Mission?" Pause. "You ask me for some particulars of my interview with the Founder of the Babis. Nothing of any importance transpired in this interview, as the Bab was aware of my having been sent with two Persian doctors to see whether he was of sane mind or merely a madman, to decide the question whether to put him to death or not."

NW GATE OF TABRIZ

Looking grim, Shaykh walks out of Tabriz to the open countryside, the sun descending lower in the W-SW sky. Five riders emerge from the city gate, passing Shaykh, directing their horses in a trot gait along the trail NW. They emerge in order: Taqi, Mamaqani, Dr. Cormick and the two Persian Doctors.

The one-eyed Mamaqani sees Shaykh. They both recognize each other. Mamaqani stops his horse in front of Shaykh, glaring at him as the other riders pass. Looking nervous and wary, Shaykh takes a stab at directing a smile at Mamaqani, who immediately spits in Shaykh's face and rides off.

Only the horses and the wind are heard.

Meanwhile, Dr. Cormick's narration continues uninterrupted, "With this knowledge, the Bab was loath to answer any questions put to him. To all inquiries, he merely regarded us with a mild look, chanting in a low melodious voice."

Mamaqani: old, white beard, one eye covered with a patch; vain, cruel; previously follower of Siyyid Kazim in Karbala, now "distinguished doctor of divinity" in Tabriz.

ROOM IN HOUSE OUTSIDE TABRIZ

Amid a low melodious chant of the Bab, Dr. Cormick stands in front of a window in the west wall of the room through which the low afternoon sun shines a directed beam across the room. His back to the window, he stares pensively slightly downward, in the direction of the rays of the sunlight. He is looking at the Bab seated on the floor against the east wall of the room.

Dr. Cormick looks to his right. Partially in the sunlight near the south wall of the room, Eyes and Hasan return Dr. Cormick's gaze, looking intently and stoically without blinking. Both Eyes and Hasan look older -- Eyes about 23 years old now, Hasan less than that. Having just completed a journey through over 100 miles of rugged country, brought as prisoners to Tabriz, Eyes and Hasan look haggard. Dr. Cormick's narration continues, "Two other siyyids, his intimate friends, were also present."

Taqi and Mamaqani stand on Dr. Cormick's right and the two Persian Doctors stand on his left. All stare solemnly at the Bab, who stops his chant.

Dr. Cormick speaks to the Bab, stepping forward in a concerned and sympathetic manner. His letter to Wright reports on this meeting, "He only once answered me, when I explained I was not a Muslim and was willing to know something about his religion, as I might perhaps be inclined to adopt it. He regarded me very intently on my saying this and replied that he had no doubt that all Europeans would eventually adopt his cause."

Eyes and Hasan watch defiantly.

Dr. Cormick straightens up as he listens to the Bab. The Persian Doctors and Taqi with Mamaqani, on either side behind him, look scornfully.

NEAR HOUSE OUTSIDE TABRIZ

Partially concealed in some bushes, Shaykh observes Dr. Cormick and the Persian Doctors ride their horses at a walk pace back toward the city limit of Tabriz. Dr. Cormick sees Shaykh and watches him sympathetically as he passes as if he recognized Shaykh or believed him to be a Babi. Shaykh returns this friendly look and makes no effort to conceal himself. Dr. Cormick concludes his letter to Wright, "Our report to the Shah at that time was of a nature to spare his life."

BADASHT ENCAMPMENT, KHURASAN

Badasht: The lovely pastoral landscape of this Babi encampment consists of three areas, about an acre each, in a row from east to west, in a larger open grassy area, surrounded by woods. South of the encampment horses and mules are tethered and graze. Each of the three areas contains a tent, assigned from west to east to Tahirih, Quddus and Jinab-i-Baha respectively. The campsites of some 80 Babis surround the tents. However, there is only one campsite in the area of Tahirih, that of Bread, Blade, Ali, Fata and a few others from Qazvin. Babis circulate and gather in groups throughout the encampment.

Near the middle tent for Quddus at dawn, Dervish sits, strikes a match to light his hand-held pipe and says cheerfully, "So I told him that we have no laws. It's a new era now, you know."

Nose, Street and Kid sit facing Dervish.

Nose is displeased, "You told who?"

Dervish, "Sadiq!" Snickering, "That old goat is very strict."

Dervish sees that he is being ignored. Nose, Street and Kid look beyond him, in admiration, as Kid, now 8, stands. Kid is in love and says, "There she is!"

Tahirih, wearing dull brown, and Qanitih, wearing bright colors, both otherwise dressed as usual with face veils, head scarfs and full gowns, walk from their tent.

Adjusting his spectacles, Dervish turns to view them and says, "Women! What in the hell is this?"

Dervish does not see that Sadiq, behind him, emerges from Quddus' tent and approaches to stand over him.

Nose to Dervish, "Idiot! That's Qurratu'l-Ayn."

Nose looks up at Sadiq, prompting Dervish to swing around, "Sadiq! Hey, friend!"

Sadiq, "Get rid of the opium and hashish now,... or leave."

Dervish, "Come on. Says who?"

Nose rises to his feet, "The old goat."

Tahirih strolls NE away from the encampment. Qanitih lingers behind and watches Tahirih continuously.

Tahirih meets Quddus near a tree. He says, "We each have spoken with Jinab-i-Baha about our purpose here."

Tahirih's face lights up with a confident smile.

They hear a galloping horse and loud exclamations from its rider and other Babis.

Quddus and Tahirih look toward the encampment.

A frantic rider gallops into the middle of the encampment. From the position near Quddus and Tahirih, the sun rises directly above the farthermost tent of Jinab-i-Baha. The rider jumps off his horse near Sadiq and loudly exclaims, "They took the Bab to Tabriz!"

GOVERNMENT HOUSE, TABRIZ

Shaykh stands with one hand on the side of the open entrance. Nobody else is present. Shaykh recounts the events that he witnessed there, "I watched with others outside the hall."

Cautiously Shaykh enters the hall, pacing down the middle toward the throne, recalling, "One hundred ecclesiastical dignitaries gathered to interrogate the Bab."

Halfway to the throne, Shaykh is chilled by sudden fear and gasps inhaling deeply.

In a flashback view from the throne, as Shaykh remembers it, Shaykh is frozen in fear as before, halfway to the throne. But now the walls are lined with mullas and notables of Tabriz sitting on the floor, all glaring at Shaykh. Shaykh exhales and turns toward the entrance behind him.

Shaykh sees the Hall Guard at the entrance. The Guard holds back a curious crowd and Shaykh sees himself clearly in the crowd, craning for a view. In other words, the Shaykh in the crowd outside is looking at himself.

Back to reality, so to speak, with the view from the hall entrance. The hall is empty as before, except the lone figure of Shaykh, who turns back toward the throne and approaches it.

Shaykh narrates what he saw, "When the Bab arrived, the only seat available was that of the Crown Prince. Without the slightest hesitation," Shaykh extends his arm slowly and reverently touches the arm of the throne, "the Bab proceeded to occupy that vacant seat." With a faint smile, Shaykh scans the empty hall, "Not one soul dared breathe a single word."

BACK TO BADASHT ENCAMPMENT

With a stern expression, Quddus emerges through the flaps of his tent.

Babis begin rising to their feet, directing their attention to Quddus. Sadiq stands next to Dervish with Nose, Street, Kid and Wool.

Inside Tahirih's tent, seated on a mat by Qanitih, Tahirih looks up at Fata who stands at the entrance holding the tent flap open.

Tahirih says, "Right now, please." Fata tensely nods "yes" to her.

Tahirih turns her gaze downward, "Thank you."

Just outside his tent, Quddus announces loudly, "Illness has confined Husayn-'Ali of Nur to his tent."

Quddus marches east toward the tent of Baha'u'llah, previously referred to as Jinab-i-Baha. Many Babis follow Quddus, joining those already near the tent of Baha'u'llah.

Fata closes the entrance flap of Tahirih's tent and dashes after the Babis following Quddus.

As Quddus approaches Baha'u'llah's tent, several Babis at its entrance lash it open so that Quddus can walk right in without breaking his stride.

Panting, Fata runs up through the group, "Quddus! Tahirih wishes that you visit."

Quddus reappears at the entrance to the tent of Baha'u'llah to meet Fata. Quddus scans the assembled Babis and says to Fata, forcefully but not loud, "I have severed myself entirely from her. I refuse to meet her."

Confused and disappointed, Fata backs off while Wool and Dervish nod their approval of Quddus to each other.

Fata runs off back toward Tahirih's tent.

BACK TO GOVERNMENT HOUSE, TABRIZ

Shaykh sits on his knees, bent over with forehead touching floor and facing the entrance. He is in front and to the side of the throne. He rises to a sitting position and looks at the entrance.

Back to Shaykh's recollection and imagination, the crowd with Shaykh in it peers into the hall. In the entrance in front of Hall Guard, Prince Nasiri'd-Din, hands on his hips, perturbed, stares into the hall. Smirking and glancing about, Nasiri'd-Din steps inside.

Shaykh continues his account of what he had witnessed there, "When the Crown Prince arrived, with the Bab seated in his chair, he reluctantly sat himself to the side."

One of the Ulama Islamic authorities interrogating the Bab in the hall booms in a scornful tone, "Whom do you claim to be?"

BACK TO BADASHT ENCAMPMENT

Inside her tent, Tahirih is dressed in bright colors wearing the elegant gown and accessories given to her by Musa's Wife in a previous scene. Qanitih busily prepares her outfit like a worried mother would.

Respiring heavily, Fata appears at the entrance. At the sight of Tahirih, Fata gasps in surprise and admiration, "Aaaaa!" Incredulous, "Quddus ... he refused to come!"

BACK TO GOVERNMENT HOUSE, TABRIZ

In reply to the Ulama question, the Bab proclaims, "I am ... I am, I am the promised one!"

The instant Ulama reaction is fuming rage, "You wretched immature lad!"

The Bab continues, "Your Honor. I have not come here of my own accord. I have been summoned to this place."

Mamaqani shouts at the Bab, "Hold your peace, you perverse follower of Satan!"

Shaykh is suddenly shocked by another loud voice, "Hey, you! Damn it!" No longer alone in the meeting hall, Shaykh looks around toward the entrance. Hall Guard stands over him and is quite mad, "Hey, get the hell out of here!"

BACK TO BADASHT ENCAMPMENT

Fata returns to the front of the tent occupied by Jinab-i-Baha and sits on his knees. Quddus stands over him surrounded by the assembled Babis. In what might be a bit of pre-arranged theatrics, Fata says firmly, "Tahirih insists that you visit."

Fata unsheathes his sword and places it before Quddus' feet, saying defiantly, "Go with me to Tahirih ... or cut off my head."

Expressionless, Quddus seems to decide to call Fata's bluff. He slowly stoops extending his hand down to pick up the sword. Amid the rising chatter of spontaneous conversation and excitement spreading among the Babis, Quddus says coolly, "I said I will not visit her. That leaves your alternative."

Unfazed, Fata slowly bends forward exposing his neck. With a dead serious expression, glaring at Fata, Quddus picks up the sword. With a sudden, swift motion, he raises the sword in the air and rises to an erect posture. The Babis gasp.

Beyond Quddus with sword over Fata with the Babi group literally horrified, all heads turn toward Tahirih, who now stands unveiled in the gorgeous gown of Musa's Wife.

At the periphery of the Babis, Tahirih without veil glows with a serene, confident smile. Qanitih is awe-struck, a bit behind Tahirih. Many of the Babis rise aghast. Without hesitation, Tahirih walks forward among them. This is the first time Tahirih has appeared publicly without face veil.

Tahirih moves among the Babi group toward Quddus, still frozen with sword held in the air above Fata. Quddus grips the sword with both hands.

Complete consternation seizes the Babis. Amid their cries of admiration or disgust and protest, they rise, all eyes riveted on Tahirih.

At the periphery, Qanitih watches Tahirih among the Babis approach Quddus. Some of the Babis disperse shaking their heads in disdain. In particular, two of them run past Qanitih frightening her with a sneer and a loud exclamation of disgust, "Let's get out of here!"

Chaotic movement and discussion erupts.

Near Quddus, Wool jumps to his feet, cursing, and pulls out his dagger in his fist before his face. Almost at the center of the Babis, Tahirih appears to glide past Kid, who watches entranced with eyes glued on her radiant face. Street and Nose look on wide-eyed.

Known to be emotionally unstable to begin with, Wool is hysterical. He shrieks loudly. Some others stand speechless. The Babis become more agitated.

Oblivious to the possible danger of the sword held aloft by Quddus, Tahirih sits below it by Fata, still bent over before Quddus. He now directs his gaze at Tahirih.

Without warning, Wool slits his throat with his dagger and runs off, shrieking at the top of his lungs with blood streaming down his neck and chest.

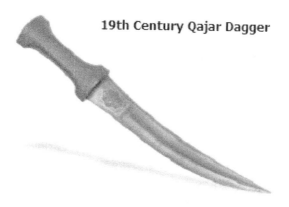

19th Century Qajar Dagger

ROOM IN HOUSE OF CHIEF LICTOR, TABRIZ

Dr. Cormick kneels on one knee over a large bowl of hot water next to his doctor's bag. While he rinses blood out of a white cloth and wrings the excess water from it, he looks ahead as if studying the wounds of a patient. That patient is the Bab. Directly behind, the legs and waists of the two Persian Doctors are seen standing against a wall. His lips pursed, his movements tense and jerky, Dr. Cormick appears mad and disgusted. Indeed, he abruptly throws two bottles of medication back into his bag.

Narrating this action, "On being asked whether a Persian surgeon should be brought to treat him, he expressed a desire that I should be sent for."

Rising to his feet by the Persian Doctors, wiping his fingers with the cloth, Dr. Cormick is angry, "I thought the bastinado was across the feet. Did your one-eyed priest have to let him be struck across the face!" The door opens.

Turning toward the door, Dr. Cormick exclaims loudly, "Look at that wound and swelling!"

Mamaqani, an ugly sight in the doorway, opines, "Ah, but the English doctor fails to consider that this self-appointed prophet got up and walked out of his trial before the Crown Prince and elite clerics of Tabriz."

BACK TO BADASHT ENCAMPMENT

It is now quiet after dark, except one can never stop the chatter of crickets.

Amid strategically placed lanterns, Wool is delirious. He lies on his back by the tent for Tahirih, dried blood on his clothes and wet cloths covering his neck.

As Wool mutters something incomprehensible, Nose and Street kneel beside him. Nose tells Wool, "Shut up!" Then grinning to Street, "Sad to say, he'll live."

On the other side of the encampment, Babis sit around Tahirih at their center in front of the tent of Baha'u'llah. Kid scampers through them toward Tahirih.

Tahirih rises to her feet. All eyes are on her. Kid plops himself down right in front of her, clasping his hands in his lap, smiling up at her.

Tahirih proclaims, "I am the 'word' which shall put to flight the chiefs and notables of the earth!" At the periphery of the Babis, Quddus and Qanitih look on with solemn expressions.

Tahirih, "This day the fetters of the past have been burst asunder."

Dream of a Tabriz Youth

TABRIZ

Tabriz: Public garden

Youth watches Zunuzi smile as he demonstrates, almost like a refrigerator salesman, how a door in the parlor has been installed with a latch on the outside. Zunuzi manipulates the latch on the parlor side of the new door, whereupon he shoves Youth to the floor in the storage room behind. This room appears like a prison cell with unplastered mud-brick walls. Zunuzi then slams the door shut, latching it locking Youth inside.

Inside this cell, Youth bangs his fist once on the locked door. An exaggerated, mystical version of Youth's escape from his house follows.

Against the wall opposite the door, Youth swings a large heavy sledge-hammer implement.

At the other side of this wall, a gaping hole blows open as if a cannon ball had hit the other side where Youth is.

Before the dust has settled and even before the pieces of brick have completely fallen, Youth emerges crawling over the lower part of the gaping hole, debris falling, seemingly in slow motion, around and on him.

Alone, Youth opens one of the pair of high, heavy, wooden gates leading into the Tabriz barracks.

Youth steps inside into a huge area, the drill field for the troops, about the size of a football field surrounded by a two-story high wall on two sides. On two other sides are the barracks for the troops. Nobody is there now.

Youth walks toward the far corner of the drill field. The barracks sides of the field are divided into subdivisions consisting of high arches in the building covered with a wooden grid framing dusty windows. The noon sun provides bright light from the cloudless sky.

At the far corner of the field, Youth enters a dark shadowy archway leading into the barracks.

Exclaiming "My best-beloved!", Youth rushes down a dimly lit passageway toward the open door of a detention cell.

Looking stunned, Youth arrives at the open cell door, grasping each side of the threshold, in even dimmer lighting, "I saw his face," Youth says. He looks up.

He sees stars shine against the black sky, framed by the upper edge of the detention cell walls. In Youth's vision, the cell has no roof.

The sky has become cloudy. Illumination is reduced. Youth emerges from the dark archway to the drill field.

A Soldier swings a large mallet driving large iron stakes into a wide protruding square structural beam, one of those separating the windowed barracks quarters. In Youth's vision, he says, "The Bab then said to me, 'I shall choose no one except you to share with me the cup of martyrdom'."

Youth imagines five soldiers aim their rifles at the beam with iron stakes. They cock their rifles.

In this vision, Youth is suspended by rope around his wrists attached to each of two iron stakes above him. He hangs well above the ground. He is expressionless, as if nothing important were happening.

While suspended on the beam, Youth sees the five soldiers fire at him, with a puff of smoke from their muskets and a loud gunfire burst. Youth "floats" with his hands and feet dangling out from the wall, as if he were weightless. Youth's wrists now show no trace of the rope. Shreds of rope hang from the iron stakes in the building beam.

Youth imagines that he is no longer attached to the wall behind in any way. He is rising. Bullet holes have ripped his garment and covered his chest with blood right in the heart area, though Youth seems to direct attention to his weightless state. He rotates while rising to be facing and looking downward. He sees the barracks receding in the distance below him.

Note: Throughout, "rifles" are mostly barrel- or breach-loading, flint-lock musket types of the period, likely imported from Russia or England.

Zunuzi on one knee bends over Youth waking from a restless sleep. Youth lies on a rug before the wall where the new door had been in his dream. Something -- a crack in the wall, a table, a wall tapestry – makes this situation immediately recognizable.

Zunuzi, "Are you O.K.?"

Youth smiles, "Ah ... yes."

Zunuzi, "You know, I love you."

Youth, "I know. Let me tell you the vision I had while sleeping."

Babis March from Mashhad to Mazindaran

PLAIN OUTSIDE MASHHAD, KHURASAN
Northeast Persia
July, 1848

Dressed in white, Husayn chants, leading the noon prayer of over 200 Babis. On their knees, they touch their heads to the ground in unison. Their horses, loaded with provisions, frame the view on this rocky, flat near-desert plain. This group of Babis includes Husayn's Brother and Nephew, Banner, Baqir, Qambar and Thin. Unlike the others, Husayn wears no head piece. His hair blows in the wind.

Cannon hands a large sword to Husayn who straps it to his waist. Cannon announces, "I have offered to pay all of the expenses of Husayn and of all who choose to accompany him."

Cannon passes to Husayn the reins of a horse. Husayn mounts the horse. Cannon continues, "But Husayn accepted from me only a sword and a horse."

Husayn, "Muhammad, the Prophet of God, said, 'Should your eyes behold the Black Standards proceeding from Khurasan, hasten toward them, even if you have to crawl over the snow, because they proclaim the advent of the Promised One'."

Cannon opens a case, takes from it a green turban and hands it to Husayn who puts it on. The Babis mount their horses.

Cannon lifts from the case a manuscript, "I read from a message to Mulla Husayn from our Master, the Bab: 'Adorn your head with my green turban and, with the Black Standard unfurled before you, hasten to Mazindaran and lend your assistance to my beloved Quddus'."

From his horse, Banner, one of the Babis, lowers a pole to the case on the ground. Cannon attaches a large silk black flag to the pole. Banner raises it aloft, loudly proclaiming, "Ya Sahibu'z-Zaman!" (Oh, Lord of the Age).

Note: "Lord of the Age" was one of the titles of the Promised One (Qa'im) in Shi'ih Islam.

Husayn, "Without fear, we shall proclaim the New Day and invite the people to embrace its truth."
Husayn and Banner ride off with the Babis following leaving Cannon standing beside the case.

VILLAGE OF NISHAPUR

Nishapur: a dusty, mud-hut village on the plains of Khurasan near some of the world's richest turquoise mines.

The Babis water their horses as the well-dressed Turquoise (real name Haji 'Abdu'l-Majid), 25, leads his horse, loaded "front and aft" with bulging saddle bags. He approaches Husayn. Some ragged, local children surround Husayn, admiring him.
Turquoise opens one of the saddle bags. They are full of large polished turquoise stones, glittering in the sunlight, the wealth of this region of Persia, "From our turquoise mines." Turquoise hands a large stone to Husayn.
Husayn, "This is a gift?"
Husayn maintains his usual non-judgmental, stoic expression.
Turquoise, "Oh, yes."
Husayn, "Thank you. Then it is now mine to give?"
Turquoise nods "yes". Smiling. Husayn tosses the stone to the admiring children and mounts his horse.

HOWDAH

Something funny in their conversation prompts laughter from Tahirih and Quddus. They are inside a howdah, a cloth enclosed compartment for passengers mounted on the back of a camel. The howdah sways awkwardly as the camel walks. Tahirih is without her veil, but wears a scarf on her head.

Quddus, "You were marvelous ... infamous ... perfect!"

Tahirih, "So you think that we did indeed make the point clear enough?"

Quddus, "You ... were ... umm. Who could doubt that we are no longer Muslims!" The howdah motion stops. Quddus jumps out.

NEAR VILLAGE OF NIYALA

Many Babis gather to make camp in the late afternoon light. Hard at work are Sadiq, Dervish, Nose, Kid, Ali, Brows, Bread and Wool. Yes, Wool did survive and now wears a simple bandage around his neck. Quddus stands by the camel with the howdah and Street approaches. Tahirih jumps from the howdah. Quddus catches her elbows to balance and soften her descent. Tahirih greets Street, "Hi, there."

Gunshots, screams and jeers interrupt rooster calls at dawn. Startled camels grunt and horses whinny.

In the early morning light, Tahirih opens her eyes, awakened by the sudden disturbance.

A large heavy rock tumbles through the tree branches above her, deflecting through them downward. The rock hits the ground by her head with a sharp thud, "uhhh!"

Qanitih, bedding near Tahirih, jumps up, hysterical, "Tahirih!"

Most of the Babis had camped below a steep hill from which large rocks, some the size of little boulders, are raining down causing them to scatter in all directions.

On the side of the hill above, villager Niyali #1 holds a large stone with both hands above his head and shouts as he heaves the stone forward, "Heretics!"

Villagers jeer the Babis. Frightened shrieks. Rocks hit the earth. Some boulders roll down the hill.

The attacking villagers on the side of the hill throw heavy stones on the dispersed campsites below while Babis scatter running for cover away from the hill leaving their belongings behind.

Niyali #1, "Misfits!"

Tahirih runs out from under the tree toward the foot of the hill. Dervish coming to assist her is knocked out cold by one of the stones raining down on them.

Tahirih walks briskly toward the attackers on the hill gesturing wildly with her arms to attract their attention. Street runs after her carrying a sword. With her hands palms up, Tahirih shouts, "Stop it!"

Up on the hill, Niyali #2, mounted on his horse, appears to be a mulla cleric. He watches the scene with satisfaction.

With her gestures and exclamations, Tahirih continues, "What are you doing?" and "Stop it!"

Street grabs Tahirih's arm and tries to pull her to safety. Loud rifle shot. Hit in the side of the head, Street instantly falls limp and motionless to the ground at Tahirih's feet. Tahirih kneels over him bursting into tears. A villager shouts, "There's the whore of the lawless Babis!"

The mulla Niyali #2 speaks to himself, "Look how the well-bred poetess of Qazvin has revealed herself without shame to strange men."

SMALL ROOM, SARI

A candle on a small table illuminates an ink well and a paper with the beginning of a letter in Persian writing. Quddus' right hand dips a pen in the ink and writes. He softly chants in Persian the words he is writing, "To my beloved Husayn, the Babu'l-Bab."

Translated: To my beloved Husayn, the Gate of the Gate.

MAZINDARAN CAMPSITE

Quddus' soft chant of his letter to Husayn continues as the moonlit Mazindaran campsite of some of the Babis sleeping around a campfire comes into view. Husayn sits on a rock by the fire and reads the letter from Quddus, while Quddus' chant of the same text continues, "We shall meet but once more, for we both shall soon drink from the cup of martyrdom."

In the subdued light, Husayn's garments are clearly dusty and stained with dirt from travel.

VILLAGE OF MIYAMAY

Husayn and the Babis ride out of Miyamay on to a flat sandy plain. Viewed through the hot surface air, the image of the Black Standard carried by Banner and the riders shimmers. Husayn's white garments are now spotlessly clean. Walker is an old man from Miyamay and devoted to Husayn. He walks by Husayn's horse.

As Babis ride past, Baqir signals to Husayn. Both pull up and swing around their horses to look at Miyamay, "They listened to you! They are coming with us!"

An additional 30 riders, residents of Miyamay, emerge from the open gate in the village wall to join the Babis, who loudly exclaim, "Ya Sahibu'z-Zaman!

OFFICE OF PRIME MINISTER AQASI, TEHRAN
August, 1848

Aqasi's hand reaches down and pulls open the drawer that still contains the Bab's Epistle to Muhammad Shah that Husayn had delivered to Aqasi. He picks up his tobacco pouch and puts it and other personal effects from his desk in a travel bag. Aqasi looks up when Hujjat and Muscles enter.

Muscles tightly grips the upper arm of Hujjat as they scuffle entering the room. Muscles releases Hujjat who flexes the arm Muscles had gripped and rearranges his sleeve. Aqasi snaps to Muscles, "What in the hell is he doing here?"

Hujjat glares scornfully at Muscles. Hujjat turns to Aqasi and with a bright, wide grin, but disrespectful tone indicating sham sympathy, "How are you doing? Not so well, I guess, with the Shah so sick. I mean, with no him, there's no you."

With a quiet laugh, Aqasi sardonically describes Hujjat to Muscles, "My favorite Babi."

Aqasi turns a glass sand timer on his desk over. Sand starts falling to the lower compartment of the timer. Meanwhile, "Come. What is it? Quickly."

Hujjat says, "I have for you a message from the Bab himself, delivered from the remote prison you provided to him." Hujjat pulls out a three page manuscript. Aqasi steps forward and snatching the pages from Hujjat's hand.

Aqasi to Muscles, "Damn it! They didn't put that troublemaker to death?"

Aqasi begins to read, while Hujjat continues cheerfully, "It has to do with the treatment he received from your friends in Tabriz..."

Aqasi is indignant, "What does this say? Sermon of Wrath?"

Hujjat, "That's right. Your government has punished us for..."

Aqasi shrilly, "Shut up!" To Muscles, "Get him out of here!"

Aqasi paces back to his desk, places the message delivered by Hujjat in the drawer, still open, with the other Epistle to the Shah and closes the drawer.

He looks pensive as the last grains of sand fall in his timer. His time had elapsed.

HOUSE OF BAHA'U'LLAH, TEHRAN

Some distance from the front entrance of the house, Hujjat waits impatiently looking for someone to exit.

Hujjat sees Vahid emerge from the front entrance to the street. Hujjat says to himself, "It's about time."

Vahid spots Hujjat across the street and makes an obvious attempt to walk by ignoring him, as other pedestrians pass. But Hujjat catches Vahid, "Yahya, you must have news. You just walked out of the Tehran Babi headquarters."

Vahid, "That is right. I am known as a Babi, but you are under detention and should not be seen here."

During the above exchange, Vahid has led Hujjat to an area outside the house where flowers are in full bloom and out of the view of pedestrians.

Note: Vahid was highly respected by the Babis including Hujjat. Although the manners of expression of these two men are quite different, Hujjat is not intentionally flippant with Vahid as he was with Aqasi.

Inside, War sits and talks with Musa and Majid. War is solemn, tired and depressed, "The Prime Minister dismissed me from my post and sent me into exile. The British Legation has interceded with the Shah on my behalf. At great risk, I am in Tehran briefly." To Musa, "I have learned that your brother has been detained in Mazindaran on the Shah's order."

Musa, "We have heard but appreciate receiving your information."

War, "But did you know that the government plans to bring him to Tehran and put him to death?"

Musa and Majid are motionless at this news. Musa inhales deeply. Majid exclaims, "Jinab-i-Baha!"

War, "Is that what you call him?"

Back outside to Hujjat and Vahid strolling in a late summer, well kept garden.

Vahid, "Yes, new names have been given. Yours is Hujjat, meaning the 'Proof' because you have forcefully defended the Bab before the elite of the capital."

Hujjat, sham haughtiness, "I think they must be sorry they ever brought me here!"

Hujjat said it all, but Vahid contemplates the irony of it, "The Shah tried to decrease your influence, but the result was the opposite." They laugh. "The friends now call me Vahid."

Hujjat, "Vahid."

Back inside the house, War sits alone in the parlor. Musa leads Majid around a corner to the front door vestibule, "Make sure that this news is heard at the Russian Mission, so that the Ambassador will learn of it."

Majid, "Prince Dolgorukov has not been exactly..."

Musa, "Trust me."

CAMPSITE NEAR CHASHMIH-ALI, MAZINDARAN
September, 1848

Wind gusts. Disturbed horses vocalize. Men talking.

A windy moonlit night. A campfire glows near a large tree. The Babis settle in. Other fires of this large encampment dot the scene in the distance.

Nephew and Street sit leaning against the tree trunk staring at the dancing flames. The gusts of wind are loud enough that they speak loudly to be heard.

Although Street's clothes have been washed, the blood stain is still evident on the shoulder on the side of his head wound. Street shows Nephew his wound on the side where a bullet had grazed and knocked him out. He jerks his hand by the wound illustrating to Nephew the trajectory of the bullet, "Bang! Just like that!"

Dervish, Bread and Wool sit by Nephew and Street. Referring to the new arrivals, Street smiles in jest, "Next thing I knew, I was looking at those ugly faces!"

On the other side of the fire, other Babis sit, including Banner, Ali and Sadiq.

Just behind the fire, Baqir says to Husayn, "We are now organized in groups of ten men each for division of labor as you requested."

Husayn, "Good ... very good."

Husayn waits patiently for the Babis to quiet down. He stares into the flames before him. A gust of wind is brisk enough to scatter hot coals from the fire across the ground forcing some the Babis to jump to their feet. The wind blows forcefully and howls.

Husayn looks up at a huge branch extending well over him and the campfire. Its ugly form silhouetted in the moonlight appears threatening as it shakes violently in the wind over him. With each gust, the wood creaks and cracks. Husayn does not appear to be bothered.

The wind blows Nephew's turban off. He looks up to see the union of the branch and tree trunk swaying with louder creaking.

His garments flapping in the wind, Husayn shouts out to the men, "We stand at the parting of ways."

Husayn raises his arm toward the sky and the shaking branch above.

Husayn, "We shall await His decree as to which direction we should take."

With a howl, crunch and crash, the branch-tree union splits.

Gasping, Street and Nephew throw themselves sideways.

The branch, still hinged at the trunk end, crashes down in front of Husayn into the campfire, causing what looks like a mini-fireworks display as glowing embers fly everywhere with the impact.

Husayn steps forward over the huge fallen branch, "The tree of the sovereignty of Muhammad Shah has, by the will of God, been uprooted and hurled to the ground."

BRITISH LEGATION. TEHRAN

A crowd of elite Persian residents of the capital presses into the front patio of the British Legation. They seek the protection of the British Legation. Lots of people are talking and calling out in this commotion.

Farrant and War stand in the office main entrance. Many in the crowd call out to Farrant, who says, "They fear what the Prime Minister might do."

With the assistance of Russian, Dolgorukov emerges through the crowd before War and Farrant, saying, "People are seeking protection at our embassy, also."

Farrant to Dolgorukov, "Let us step inside."

Dolgorukov, Farrant and War move into the vestibule at the front entrance. Dolgorukov to Farrant, "The Prime Minister wishes to meet with the British and Russian envoys together. Will you come?"

Farrant, "I shall."

War shakes his head. His disapproval is evident to Dolgorukov and Farrant. As Farrant moves to close the door, Officer slips in and reports to Farrant, "It is confirmed by our own physician. The Shah is dead."

MOUNTAIN HIGHLANDS NEAR URIM, MAZINDARAN

Over 200 Babis march to the north in the wooded hills among the mountains of Mazindaran. The leaves of the trees and bushes of the forest are orange and yellow, many on the ground, reflecting the autumn season.

An incessant downpour of rain drenches everything. The trail is covered with mud and deep water-filled holes and puddles. Streams have overflowed and often flood the trail from the torrential rain.

The light is subdued under the continuous complete cloud cover. Strung out along this trail, the Babis plod along, about half on foot. The rest ride, some on mules, but most, often two at a time, on horses. They are drenched and weary, but look determined.

Meanwhile, parts of a forceful and passionate speech to Babis by Husayn are recalled, "Travel along this path is the greatest affirmation of faith in either the East or the West of the entire world today. From here on, enemies will attack and kill us."

Baqir and Banner, with the soaking Black Standard held aloft, ride their horses by along the trail, followed by Husayn and Ali on their horses. The old man, Walker, walks closely beside Husayn's horse.

Husayn's words continue, "This is the way that leads to our martyrdom. Whoever is not prepared, let him give up this journey and return to his home. You may leave us and no one will think badly of you."

Bread, Wool and Turquoise ride in the string of Babis along the trail. Bread tosses a sack of his belongings in a puddle by the trail. Turquoise lifts the saddlebags in front of him over the shoulders of his horse. He throws the bags to the ground. The flaps and some of the seams of the heavy bags burst open with the weight of the stones within and the force of the impact, scattering hundreds, maybe a thousand, large beautiful turquoise stones, worth a fortune, among the rocks and gravel. Rain water flows forcefully across the trail further scattering the stones while Babis walk past and over them.

Husayn's speech had told them, "Leave behind all your belongings and content yourself with only your steeds and swords, that all may see your renunciation of worldly things."

Dervish stares through the downpour at the turbulent, roaring flow in an overflowing stream by the trail, as Babis pass behind him.

Dervish tosses a sack of some belongings in the stream, grimaces in pain, doubling over gripping his abdomen in his arms and falls on his side into the mud and water, grunting in agony.

Nose and Sadiq kneel in the mud to assist lifting Dervish, who is retching, though not vomiting. His head thrusts back in pain, as he suffers opium withdrawal.

Kid sleeps on some leaves under trees by the trail as Babis plod past. Kid is protected from the rain by a cloth held by Street and Nephew.

Nose and Sadiq each hold one arm of Dervish over their shoulders to assist Dervish along the trail with other Babis near Kid, Street and Nephew. Street rustles Kid to wake him up, "Come on."

Kid, "When are we going to rest?"

Back To Wool, Bread and Turquoise who drops the rear saddle bags he had been carrying over the hips of his horse.

The shining turquoise stones scatter in the mud and puddles. Passing Babis step over them.

THE BAB'S FAMILY RESIDENCE, SHIRAZ

In bright sun light, Heckler, a rogue known to cause riots and revolts against the government of Khan, maneuvers the horse he rides to the closed doors in front of the residence, shouting sarcastically to those within, while he bangs his lance against the doors, "Hey, there! Any Babis home?"

Heckler rattles his lance in a hole in the wall producing a sharp clacking sound.

Inside, while placing a personal article in a small travel bag, Uncle hears Heckler.

Heckler continues rattling his lance in the wall aperture. He laughs, swings his horse around, waves his lance in the air and shouts toward the interior, "Rest in safety! Muhammad Shah has gone to hell!"

Heckler rides off.

In Uncle's parlor, the Bab's Mother stands in front of a window. She is weary and molested. She stares at Uncle arranging his bag on a small table. Meanwhile, the Bab's Wife sits on her knees on a rug between them. The Bab's Wife has obviously been crying, her eyes and cheeks wet with tears. She says to Uncle, "This harassment is never going to stop, you know."

Uncle, "After I visit the Bab in his confinement, I will see if our family can move from Shiraz to another city."

Almost speechless, a sniffle, not crying, the Bab's Wife to Uncle, "Ah,..."

Uncle responds to the Bab's Wife, "Don't worry, dear, I'll tell him everything." Wiping an eye dry, the Bab's Wife nods "yes" rhythmically to Uncle acknowledging that he had understood. Uncle softly repeats, "... everything."

Note: After the amazing escape of the Bab from execution in Shiraz by Royal decree, sadly, his wife never saw him again.

RESIDENCE OF KHAN, SHIRAZ

Khan is depressed, drunk and without hope slumped on a rug against the wall opposite the front entrance to the street.

Ferrier stands in the open entrance facing the street, next to Doorman sitting beside and playing cheerfully with his cane. Ferrier is also depressed and angry as well. He addresses Doorman impatiently, "It's been three weeks. How long will they keep us here?"

Ferrier looks out to the street, lined with armed Soldiers blocking the house off and staring contemptuously at Ferrier in the entrance.

Laughing like the mouse playing while the cat is away, Heckler rides up the street behind the Soldiers. He shouts into the residence, "Is the Prince Governor enjoying his captivity?"

Doorman rises to his feet by Ferrier and glances back toward Khan to see if he is looking. He isn't. Grinning, Doorman whispers to Ferrier with feigned alarm, "It could be for ever. The troops just want to be paid. But the governor is bankrupt." Doorman shakes his head, "...something these tribesmen just do not understand."

Ferrier, "Oh, God."

Doorman, "Worse, he has used all of his credit to send money to the capital to win the favor of the new Shah."

Behind Ferrier and Doorman, both disgusted in their own ways, Khan raises his head and with eyes half closed and slurred speech, "Joseph."

Ferrier shifts his eyes upon hearing his name, but does not even turn his head to acknowledge Khan.

Khan snickers pathetically, "You are not sorry, are you, Joseph, that I brought you from France to this place?"

Babis Attacked Again by Religious Fanatics

LARGE BARFURUSH MOSQUE, MAZINDARAN
October, 1848

Sa'idu'l-Ulama: Highest Islamic religious authority of Barfurush; avowed enemy of the Babis, particularly Quddus and Husayn; an old squint-eyed, tight-lipped villainous schemer.

It is standing room only. Hundreds have filled the mosque. Sa'idu'l-Ulama completes his ascent of the pulpit. He swings around glaring at the crowd, silencing them.

Acting hurt and outraged, Sa'idu'l-Ulama puts on a performance to incite maximum hate. Sneering loudly, "Bewail the plight of Islam!"

Sa'idu'l-Ulama feigns a stumble, shifting his feet, at the top of the narrow pulpit as he violently rips open his shirt tearing it down to the waist as if he himself were being desecrated, "Our enemies stand at our very doors, ready to wipe out Islam! This man, Husayn, leading

**SA'IDU'L-ULAMA
Islamic authority**

a savage band, will commit any crime, now that the protecting hand of Muhammad Shah has been withdrawn!"

Sa'idu'l-Ulama rips his turban off throwing it forcefully to the floor six feet below the pulpit platform, further shocking his listeners. With ugly hair dangling over his face, he shouts angrily, "Arm yourselves! Let all of you arise and exterminate them!"

OPENING IN WOODS NEAR BARFURUSH

As loud jeering shouts are heard under a partially overcast sky, Husayn and Banner, mounted on their horses, look ahead. Babis beside them, many also mounted, also gaze grimly ahead. They are in a grassy clearing surrounded by forests. Walker stands between the necks of the horses of Husayn and Banner.

Amid this uproar, Banner starts to draw his sword, but Husayn quickly grips his forearm, while maintaining his gaze ahead toward the jeering unruly crowd. Husayn says loudly, "Not yet! Not unless they attack and force us to defend ourselves."

About 50 yards ahead of Husayn and the Babis, a multitude of fully armed town people, Barfurushis, block Husayn's way into the town. If not with firearms, swords or knives, they carry any implement, axes, hoes, shovels, that could be used as a weapon. Some are mounted on horses. Others are dressed in military garb.

The some 230 Babis are dramatically out-numbered.

Without warning, a dozen of the Barfurushis, most dressed as soldiers, fire their rifles into the Babis. The rifle shots ring out amid the roar of the populace and cheers.

Hit by a bullet above an eye, Street falls limply, clearly dying instantly. Nose and Dervish kneel to look. Kid stares at his older brother Street. Several other Babis drop to the ground around him. Baqir cries to Husayn, "Allow us to defend ourselves! We cannot be disgraced!"

Husayn replies forcefully, "The time has not yet come!"

With another rifle shot, Walker falls mortally wounded.

Husayn sees Barfurushi, the one who killed Walker, rise from one knee with his rifle signaling the crowd of Barfurushis, who cheer his fatal shot at Walker. But Barfurushi is somewhat separated from the crowd and becomes worried when he notices Husayn glaring at him, unsheathing his large sword in his right hand.

Babis also ready their swords and bolt forward toward the Barfurushis, who at first respond in kind but then quickly begin to scatter.

Barfurushi, ignoring his sword, fumbles with his gunpowder bag in a doomed attempt to reload, as he scrambles for cover toward a small tree isolated in the grassland.

Husayn with sword held above his head, guides his horse in a gallop toward Barfurushi, who scampers behind the small tree, its branches and foliage beginning just above Barfurushi's head.

Realizing there is not time to reload, Barfurushi sees Husayn charging at maximum speed right at him. At nearly the same time, each acts. First, Husayn lowers his sword to a low horizontal position at his right side. Thus, Husayn's right arm extends down and away. Second, Barfurushi, horrified, presses his rifle, shoulder stock down, vertically against the tree trunk away from Husayn's approach. Preparing for the impact of Husayn's sword, he firmly grips the muzzle end of the rifle barrel with both hands at his eye level. He presses his knee against the shoulder stock of the rifle pressing it firmly against the tree trunk.

In the final moment before impact, Husayn drops the reins from his hand. He arches over to his right to grip the sword handle with both hands. He leans further off the horse's right side positioning the gleaming blade horizontally at Barfurushi's waist level.

In his final moment of terror, Barfurushi braces himself.

As Husayn's horse gallops past the tree, the top of the tree flies upward.

The tree stump severed at waist level has the lower half of Barfurushi on the grass beside it, along with the lower half of the rifle barrel, the end attached to the stock. A bit further along the path of Husayn's gallop the top of the tree and the top half of Barfurushi, 100 percent dead, are strewn. The muzzle end of the metal rifle barrel lies in the grass next to Barfurushi's lifeless hand.

At some distance, Husayn pulls up and swings around his horse to witness the result of his blow. He appears as startled as the others. "Who could believe such a thing could happen?" flashes in his mind.

Beyond this gruesome scene, all fighting had stopped instantly. The Barfurushis scatter in horror back into the village and into the forests. The Babis are stunned and mute, staring at the severed tree, rifle and Barfurushi.

Husayn gallops along the trail toward and through the dissipating crowd of frightened Barfurushis scampering back to their village. As he approaches and passes through them, many take aim and fire at him, but incredibly, neither Husayn or his horse are hit with a serious wound.

Dismayed by the gunfire and the sight of Husayn's arrival, Sa'idu'l-Ulama bolts his door.

Husayn rides his horse around the residence. Some blood runs down his right cheek from a surface wound by a grazing bullet. His shirt is torn from the gunfire -- enough to establish he is not wearing any sort of bullet-proof vest.

On the trail entering Barfurush, Qambar rides scared but bravely along the same path as Husayn through the crowd, but is not fired upon since most are reloading. However, some of the mounted Barfurushis follow him, but keep a respectful distance.

As Husayn circles Sa'idu'l-Ulama's compound, he repeatedly calls contemptuously to him, "Come on out here, coward!"

Pulling to a stop away from Husayn and the residence, Qambar is incredulous, "He's alive."

Cowering inside his residence, Sa'idu'l-Ulama hears Husayn beckoning, "Sa'idu'l-Ulama! Show yourself!"

Meanwhile, those Barfurushis that arrive form an arc at a cautious distance behind Qambar. They dismount, some kneeling by their horses, as the realization begins to form that one man alone, Husayn, had in effect defeated them all.

Adrenaline still pumping, Husayn angrily calls out once again, "You send your people out in holy war against us, while you hide in your house like a coward!"

Not a sound from the residence. Husayn then turns his exhortation toward the Barfurushis, approaching them to the extent of Qambar's position, "Why have you risen against us? What have we done? Consider. We faced your bullets."

Sword in his right hand, Husayn wipes blood off his cheek wound with the palm of his left hand, "Except for a scratch, you have been powerless to wound me or my horse."

Husayn reaches into a hole torn by the gunfire in his shirt and withdraws some bullets that had settled above the belt.

Husayn, "Here are some of your bullets."

He tosses them on the ground before his listeners, "God has protected me and willed to establish in your eyes the ascendancy of His Faith."

Around the severed tree, rifle and Barfurushi, the Babis gather staring at the scene. Clearly, they are still in shock at this sight and what they consider to be a miracle.

Note: Indeed they know that such an attempt would normally have spun a rider violently off his horse without significant damage even to the tree trunk. In addition, Husayn is not large or muscular nor is he trained in combat. By profession, he was a scholar and preacher.

Typical Caravanserai

Note: A caravanserai provides lodging to travelers. These stopping places are found along all major routes of Persia. This one, and most of them, were surrounded by walls to afford some protection at night. If there were any private rooms at all, the lodging was usually crude with few amenities. Most travelers pass the night in the courtyard, pitching tents or sleeping in a blanket, as they would elsewhere on their route. This particular caravanserai was near Barfurush.

Six bodies of dead men, including Walker, lie on their backs in a neat row shoulder to shoulder in the courtyard. Nose, Blade and Dervish place the body of Street in line with the others.

Kid, face blank, stares at his dead brother Street.

Around them, Babis and their horses fill the courtyard. Baqir and Banner, at the periphery, look at the dead, open the door to an inner room and enter it.

At the open gates, Bread signals to Wool to draw his attention to some hostile-looking Barfurushis. Rifles in hand, they gather inconspicuously among distant trees, about 50 yards away.

In a small caravanserai room, Husayn opens his eyes and turns toward Baqir and Banner waiting respectfully by the door.

Baqir, "Nothing. No one would sell us food or even allow us any water."

Banner, "Hostile forces surround us."

Husayn, "Before sunset, close the gates. The martyred friends will be buried without any visible signs of their graves."

In the courtyard, swords smooth the dirt. Additional soil is sprinkled over the gravesite to restore the surface to its original appearance near a corner of the caravanserai. Nose, Kid, Dervish and Sadiq stare at the spot.

Banner assists Bread and Wool to close the gates of the caravanserai.

In his bullet-torn shirt, Husayn walks among the Babis, over 250 of them. His cheek wound is moist red. The bleeding has stopped.

By the horses, Baqir tells Ali with Brother and Nephew, "Keep the horses saddled."

Husayn arrives at the corner where Nose, Kid, Dervish and Sadiq have finished the burials. Husayn embraces Nose, the bereaved father.

Outside, Barfurushi riflemen position themselves closer in the tall grass, some 20 yards from the caravanserai wall. The setting sun is low behind them.

Surrounded by seated Babis, Husayn speaks in subdued tones, "We marched through four days of rain without food or rest to this place. Then we were attacked without provocation. No words ... no argument can change the vial fanaticism of these people. Their riflemen have surrounded our position at close range. They think that we are infidels, but we can offer the call to evening prayer in the manner in which they are accustomed."

Adhan #1, a mid-teen Babi, starts to climb a ladder to the roof, looking up along the ladder.

Husayn looks at Adhan #1, "Anyone who does this will be renouncing his life."

While Husayn speaks, Adhan #1 hears every word, but continues climbing without even a glance toward Husayn or the others.

Adhan #1 mounts the roof from the ladder, stands erect with the courtyard filled with Babis below and behind him and chants loudly, "Allah-u-Akbar!" (God is the Most Great).

Multiple shots hit Adhan #1, killing him instantly and pushing him back off the roof into the courtyard.

No sooner had Adhan #1 hit the ground near the base of the ladder, another teenager, Adhan #2, begins to climb the same ladder toward the roof. Adhan #2 stands on the roof. He briskly paces toward the periphery and stares at the attacking Barfurushis, with the setting sun beyond.

He chants loudly in Persian, "I bear witness that Muhammad is the Apostle of God."

Hit by several rifle shots, Adhan #2 falls dead on the roof.

Husayn remains standing in the center of the Babis who are seated with the exception of some at the periphery. Baqir, Banner and Ali stand among the horses. Head bowed, staring at the ground, without any gesture, he continues, "These youths have not finished their prayer."

Blade mounts the ladder to the roof. No one in the courtyard moves.

Ali strokes the neck of a wide-eyed horse, jerking his head up, disturbed by the gunfire and pulling his tether tight.

Blade stands over the body of Adhan #2 on the roof. He chants in Persian, "There is no God but God."

No one moves, as Blade's prayer is heard. More shots ring out. Husayn turns to the gates, lifting an arm toward them, "Open the gates!"

Immediately, the Babis, fire in their eyes, jump to their feet. Qambar and Dervish work their way down the lines of horses in the stable area, one untethering their bridle reins, the other shooing the animals out into the Babis.

Swords drawn, Baqir and Banner are mounted at the open gate. The freed horses mix with the Babis who catch and mount them. Ali provides Husayn with his charger. Husayn mounts and gallops out of the caravanserai between Baqir and Banner, who spin around to follow. During sustained gunfire, Babis follow them.

Babi riders fan out from the gate exclaiming loudly, "Ya Sahibu'z-Zaman!"

The Barfurushis in the surrounding knee-high grass are caught by surprise that such a defensive counter-attack would be launched against them. They might also have thought that their one-shot muskets were superior weapons to the swords carried by the Babis.

Barfurushis stand, fire their rifles, then flee. Many fall under Babi swords.

Mounted on horses in the forest at a safe distance, Sa'idu'l-Ulama and General watch this skirmish. Sa'idu'l-Ulama opines, "You see how vicious they are?"

General, "But these people just shot three young men praying."

Sa'idu'l-Ulama, "They are infidels. They seek to establish a Babi state. I am glad that you came here to see this."

General, "This man, Husayn, seems invincible. The new Shah should know of this situation."

Sa'idu'l-Ulama, "Oh, I think so."

General: real name 'Abbas-Quli Khan; unsophisticated, rough; military general and chief of the nearby city of Amul; a friend of Sheil.

Later on the caravanserai roof just after sunset, Kid approaches the bodies of Afnan #2 and Blade. He sees that Blade had fallen over Afnan #2 with his head on the back of Afnan #2. The faces of these two dead boys face in the same direction and seem to wear slight smiles of satisfaction. Blade's eyes are not completely closed. Kid brushes them closed with his fingers.

Kid stands. Some bodies of Barfurushis lay in the grass outside the caravanserai.

In morning light in the caravanserai courtyard, Dervish sits against the wall among the Babis. He writes in his diary, "When they called for peace, that great one welcomed talks with chiefs of Mazindaran."

Note: Husayn has new clothes and his cheek wound is scabbed over, indicating passage of time.

Husayn hosts General and Mustafa Khan as the Babis look on, "Unlike the people of this town, we know how to receive the stranger in our midst."

Husayn motions for General and Mustafa Khan to sit on mats prepared for them and Nose serves them tea. Husayn continues, "We had no intention of staying in this place. Yet the local people attack us continually. But others have become our

MUSTAFA KHAN led besiegers of Babis

friends and have provided supplies."

Mustafa Khan, "The situation is a stalemate but could worsen."

General, "The religious authorities of the town have instigated these attacks. Let us provide an escort so that you may safely leave this region."

Later, Dervish records, "Though suspicious, that great one accepted this offer of safe passage."

Mustafa Khan: another swaggering pompous chief from nomadic Turkish stock.

Babi Defense at Tabarsi Shrine

TABARSI SHRINE

Note: The Shrine of Shaykh Tabarsi, containing his tomb, consisted of a rear tomb room, 10 paces by 9 paces and a front room, 10 paces by 11 paces, connected to a front porch facing east. It has a tiled roof inclining from the sides to the center. Outside, a small stone fence encloses a large grassy area situated in dense forest in a valley surrounded by hills about 14 miles southeast of Barfurush.

Tabarsi Shrine

Credit: Julio Savi

Note: Henceforth, the scar is seen on Husayn's cheek.

Alone, Husayn solemnly paces around the large tomb in the Tabarsi shrine rear room.

Husayn emerges from the tomb room to the front room, inspecting the site. Dervish's diary further recounts, "We were lead into the forest and ambushed. The friends overcame this assault, but not without losses. We were left defenseless near a small shrine in the forest."

Husayn meets Baqir at the front entrance and looks out at the Babis waiting outside.
Husayn addresses them, "We have arrived at our Karbala. This is our ultimate destination."

The Babis convert this location into a construction site.

At a point where the forest becomes dense, Baqir points outlining a perimeter to Banner, "These trees will be cleared up to here." Dervish uses his hatchet to chop at a tree. Others use axes and swords to trim branches off fallen trees. "As we fortified the shrine, our enemies launched surprise attacks from the forest," Dervish later wrote.

Babis clear trees to obtain wood in all directions. They dig a trench around the shrine, one meter deep and wide, enclosing an area about 60 paces N-S by 80 paces E-W. A heavy rain begins to fall. The Babis keep working.

Baqir and Banner walk toward the east side of the rectangular trench. They pass Brows guiding a horse pulling logs into the fort. Others guide horses pulling crude sleds fashioned from branches lashed together loaded with stones.

At the trench, Wool, Bread, Nose, Kid and others use bowls, shovels, axes and whatever to raise dirt and rock building up a mound on the inner side of the trench. On top of this mound, stone and mud are piled to create a wall. Rain water flows into the trench.

At the site of the future main gate of the fort, Sadiq and Ali ride horses past Baqir and Banner and toward the shrine. Baqir explains to Banner how he wants the construction of the fort to proceed, "The main gate will be here." He points to locations within the fort, "The friends should build shelters in this area and stables for the horses there."

As Baqir speaks, Babis use logs to reinforce the stones in the walls. Others carry stones to the top. Mud is used as mortar.

Sadiq and Ali dismount in front of the shrine, where Brother and Nephew appear to stand guard at the entrance.

Kid runs up to take their horses. Sadiq and Ali step up on the porch and enter the shrine. The Black Standard is now mounted above the front of the shrine.

Shrine of Shaykh Tabarsi by Edward Granville Browne

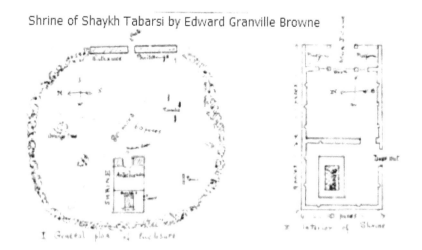

Lightning flashes strike the hills rising in the distance behind the shrine followed by loud thunderclaps.

Kid struggles to handle the two spooked horses. Nephew runs off the porch into the rain to help him.

Inside the shrine, Husayn is chanting a prayer. When Sadiq and Ali enter, he turns to recognize them. Sadiq asks, "During the rain, may we call in our patrols in the forest?"

More lightning flashes. Then a near thunder clap.

Husayn, "We should maintain our vigilance. The friends desire martyrdom, but they should not be subjected to any more unexpected attacks."

OFFICE OF PRIME MINISTER TAQI, TEHRAN
November, 1848

Note: This room was previously the office of Prime Minister Aqasi, but all of the decoration and furnishings, except his large European-style wooden desk, have been removed.

Workman carry into the room the wall map previously located in the Office of the Minister of War. They work on mounting the framed map on the wall by the desk.

Taqi supervises other workers unpacking chests of belongings to decorate the office. Dolgorukov appears in the open doorway, "Mister Prime Minister, may I come in?"

Taqi, "By all means, of course, I must apologize ... Soon, Nasiri'd-Din Shah will host a proper reception for the diplomatic community."

Dolgorukov enters, "I did not want to delay extending to you and the Shah my congratulations on the successful transfer of power."

Taqi, "Thank you. There are still rebellions in some districts, but these can be managed."

BRITISH LEGATION

By candle and lantern light, Dr. Cormick and Farrant share a quiet dinner in the parlor, "I was sorry to see that Taqi Khan assumed executive power. He is disliked by all classes. The young Shah is completely in his hands," Dr. Cormick says.

Farrant, "You missed the chaos before the Shah arrived from Tabriz. That bastard Aqasi tried to seize power and occupied the palace with 500 men. The presence of the Missions of England and Russia alone upheld the authority of the new Shah. Even so, several provinces may declare themselves independent."

PALACE OF THE SHAH

Nasiri'd-Din: now 17 years old and the Shah of Persia. He dresses in a mixture of European and Asiatic styles, with white pants and a pink silk frock coat, each button a large single diamond. His sword belt buckle is set with a large diamond and the belt holds a diamond-hilted dagger. Over the coat he wears a pink, gold-embroidered gown. His hat is the Astrakhan-style fur cap. His mustache is a bit longer and a stubble beard is forming. His practice was to clip it off, rather than shave; this resulted in a strange, disheveled appearance.

Nasiri'd-Din stands near a doorway to an inner room where Taqi sits on a carpet across from Mazindaran chiefs, General and Mustafa Khan. Nasiri'd-Din tells them, "You have wisely joined chiefs and princes from all of Persia who have vowed their loyalty to me. As your sovereign, I welcome and thank you."

Taqi addresses them, "Naturally, you will prove your loyalty and be rewarded in so doing. The Shah will..."

Taqi looks to the entrance where the Shah had stood.

Nothing. Nasiri'd-Din has left, "Ah ..." Taqi picks up papers, "Well, it is explained here. The Shah has ordered that you organize an offense against the Babis in Mazindaran. You are to seize them and bring them to the capital."

Taqi passes the paper, the order of Nasiri'd-Din, to General and stands up explaining, "The Sa'idu'l-Ulama of Islam in Barfurush has said that these irresponsible agitators challenge the authority of his Imperial Majesty."

General, "They are nothing but a handful of untrained and frail students and old men who are powerless to withstand our forces."

Mustafa khan, "My brother can raise a force of twelve thousand men along with the finances to pay them."

GARDEN OF MAYOR'S HOME, TEHRAN

In a small garden, rather bare at this time of year, by the main house, Mayor guides Vahid to a small house within the walls of this large residence.

Hujjat emerges from the small house to greet them, speaking cheerfully to Mayor, "If you are going to be a prisoner in the capital, be a prisoner of the Mayor himself!"

Mayor smirks showing disapproval of Hujjat's attitude. Vahid defuses this small bit of tension. To Mayor, "Thank you for your indulgence."

Mayor leaves, saying to Vahid, "A favor to you, not him."

Hujjat to Vahid, "That was a compliment."

Vahid, "Circumstances have changed with the new government. You are not safe now in Tehran."

Hujjat, "What about you?"

Vahid, "Listen carefully. You shall be smuggled out of Tehran and be on the road to Zanjan by morning light tomorrow."

Mayor: real name Mahmud Khan; served as Kalantar (Mayor) of Tehran and as Chief of Police; sections of his residence often served to confine prisoners, under varying degrees of restriction.

Tabarsi Fort 1.0

A hammer bangs a spike into wood.

The fort is essentially complete and looks lived in. The walls are about three feet high above the three foot high mounds with the total height from the exterior amplified by the trenches now filled with rain water forming a crude moat.

One of the gates is open. Dervish is the source of the banging sound. He stands high on a ladder and uses the mallet side of his hatchet to drive a spike into the gate timber on the outside. Wool passes to Dervish a head to hang from the spike by its knotted hair. This head joins about five others similarly hung from other spikes. Dervish snickers to Wool as he positions the final head, "When they see this, they are going to run like hell."

Inside the fort, except for areas immediately adjacent to the wall and in front of the shrine, there is a labyrinth of ramshackle dwellings made of mud and wood and thatched roofs, including a stable area for the horses. The Babis move about. Qambar and Thin prepare food.

Inside the Tabarsi shrine, Husayn speaks to his main lieutenants including Ali, Sadiq, Brother, Nephew, Baqir, Banner and Brows, "When Quddus arrives, you will show him a reverence such as you would feel prompted to show to the Bab himself. You must consider me as his lowly servant. You should not kiss his hands or feet, for he does not like such expressions of affection."

In the moonlight on a cloudless night, Husayn leads over 100 Babis from the open fort gates walking across a narrow scaffold over the trench moat. They carry lit candles and proceed chanting a joyful song in Persian. They walk away from the fort into the black forest.

The line of Babis led by Husayn becomes a string of flickering candles winding into the dense black woods.

This precession meets Quddus, arriving with several companions. Husayn smiles broadly holding up his candle to illuminate the faces of Quddus with several other riders, all mounted on horses.

Smiling broadly, Quddus dismounts and embraces Husayn, saying , "Allah-u-Abha" (God is most glorious).

The next day, all of the Babis, except Quddus, have assembled on grassland outside the fort.

Husayn stands at the entrance and starts counting, "One, two, three," etc, as the Babis enter the fort one by one. Baqir is first and remains standing by Husayn at the entrance to assist in the counting. Then, we see Ali, Brother, Nephew, Dervish, Sadiq, Brows, Nose, Kid, Wool, Bread, Banner, Qambar, Thin and so on.

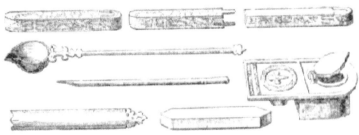

Persian writing instruments, The Penny Magazine, London, 1937

Later, Dervish sits against one of the shacks in the fort and pulls out his diary, ink and pen. He writes, "The believers in the new day came from all classes and professions ... students, priests, carpenters, tailors, merchants, blacksmiths and the like. Very few had any military training."

Inside the shrine, Husayn and Quddus sit on mats. Quddus has paper, ink and manuscripts spread out near him. He has been writing.

Husayn, "The friends within the fort number three hundred thirteen."

Quddus, "The friends should know that Muhammad said that there would be this exact number of the companions of the promised one. The people will recognize the fulfillment of this prophecy."

Husayn, "We have word the Mazindaran chiefs are bringing a force of twelve thousand men against us."

Quddus, "We will remain within these walls with the gates closed. We can have no more visitors."

December, 1848

Complete cloud cover obscures moon and star light. In almost complete darkness, during continuous sporadic gunfire, Nose and Dervish stand guard along a section of the stone wall. Each holds a captured rifle. Dervish wrote later, "We were under siege for one month. No food or water could be brought to the fort. Our supplies were gone."

Nose and Dervish survey the surrounding black forests and hills dotted with the campfires of the besieging forces.

On the other side of the fort, diffuse lanterns and candles dimly illuminate the area. Husayn addresses a small group of Babis including many familiar faces such as Brother, Nephew, Brows, Baqir and Banner. Amid intermittent gunfire, Quddus approaches them and Husayn speaks, "We entered Mazindaran with peaceful intentions. We were their guests. Look how they have treated us. They fire upon us day and night."

Baqir reports, "We have no more water."

Quddus, "God willing, this very night a downpour of rain, followed by a heavy snowfall, will refresh us and desolate the camps of our opponents."

Nose and Dervish peek over the wall. Rifle mussels flash producing loud gunshots. This gunfire originates from slots in barricades made of wood outside the fort erected by the besieging forces.

Distant campfires in the forests and on the surrounding hills flicker.

Suddenly, a pattern of brilliant lightning strikes several hill peaks in the panorama, dramatically illuminating the view for an instant. Nose and Dervish see the form of the surrounding hills and the positions of closer barricades outside the fort.

Seconds later, the crash, boom of thunderclaps arrive. A torrential rain pours down. Kneeling behind the wall, water drips on the faces of Nose and Dervish, who exchange looks, amazed and grinning, clothes drenched.

Dozens of Babis emerge, cheering, from their shelters, positioning containers to catch the water. Almost everyone is standing outside, looking up as the rain falls on them.

Nose and Dervish slowly rise to their feet in the rain, exposing their chests and heads over the wall, as they stare at the closest enemy barricade before them. The gunfire has stopped. But thunder and lightning continue along with loud cheers of "Allah-u-Akbar" amid the pounding fall of heavy rain.

Outside the Babi fort, behind a barricade, three Soldiers attempt to reload their rifles. They kneel in puddles and muddy soil. One of them picks up his powder bag. It is soaked and water comes out. He throws it down, "The ammunition is ruined!"

The Soldiers run from the barricade to the woods behind away from the fort.

To get a better view in the darkness, Nose and Dervish lean over the wall. Ecstatic and laughing, they grab each other in joy. With his free arm, Dervish waves his rifle in the air, shouting, "Run, you bastards!"

Through the dense rain, the distant campfires are extinguished as they disappear in a random fashion like light bulbs burning out, leaving the hills and forests black, except for occasional lightning.

Husayn and Quddus step on to the porch of the shrine, out of the rain. Lightning briefly illuminates Kid, standing by the roof of the shrine porch, catching water flowing from the roof into his mouth. Another lightning flash illuminates a nearby trench within the fort, into which water rapidly flows filling it.

As temperature drops during this December night, snowfall replaces the rain. By morning, the trench is now filled with water and covered with thin ice. Everything is covered with six inches of snow. After breaking some of the ice, Kid leads horses that are eager to drink.

Later in the morning, Quddus, Husayn, Baqir, Ali, Brows, Banner and Sadiq mount their horses in front of the shrine. They are armed with swords. Around them, the Babis, mostly armed with swords, some with rifles, are addressed by Quddus, "Our prayer has been answered. The rain and snow demoralized our attackers. But they will regroup. We are hopelessly outnumbered. At this moment, we will further scatter our assailants. Our purpose is to protect ourselves, not to cause unnecessary harm."

Quddus and Husayn, followed by Babis, ride down a passage between the shacks from the shrine toward the open fort gates. They proceed out on to the freshly fallen snow toward the forests and hills beyond.

In front of one of the wooden hovels lining the narrow street to the front gate, Kid, clutching a dagger, runs up to Nose. Babis file by as they leave the fort.

Kid, "I want to go this time."

Nose, "You're too young."

Nose grabs Kid's arm and leads him into the hovel through a tattered cloth covering its entrance.

Inside this wooden hovel, Dervish is sick and looks terrible. He is wrapped in blankets on the ground with beads of sweat on his face. He coughs repeatedly.

Kid is wide-eyed by Dervish's appearance, "My God."

Nose kneels by a small fire on the ground heating a small pot. Dervish is shivering. Thin puts a hand on his forehead and as if there remained some doubt, pronounces, "He's sick."

Kid lays down near Dervish's feet and pokes at the dirt with his dagger, while Thin helps Dervish to a sitting position. Meanwhile, Nose pours a small cup of the heated liquid from the pot and hands it to Dervish.

Grimacing, Dervish tries a sip from the cup. He spits it out, tossing the cup to the ground, "This is water! I'm starving, damn it!"

Sullen, Nose blows into his cupped hands to warm his fingers, "We're all starving, friend."

Kid looks up and flashes a brief meek grin, trying to cheer up the others, "Maybe they will bring back some food."

A log is thrown into the opening of a crude mud brick oven from which a raging fire burns and smokes from hot coals and wood. Bread pulls cooked loaves of bread from an upper compartment of the oven. His right forearm is covered with a bloodied bandage. His sleeves are rolled up. The heat of the oven warms him in spite of the snow and cold.

Bread's temple and cheek have been slashed by a battle wound as he grins pushing the hot loaves into a sack held by Thin. Meanwhile, Qambar appears supplying Bread with more kneaded dough to bake.

Inside the wooden hovel, Dervish bites a mouthful of freshly baked bread. The small fire crackles providing light. Laying on his stomach and propped up on his elbows, Dervish writes in his diary. He still suffers from fever, chills and shivering, "In 45 minutes, our little band overcame a trained army. The commander and 430 of his soldiers perished. 100 horses and 35 soldiers were captured."

Across from Dervish on the other side of the fire, Kid cleans a bullet wound in Nose's thigh. Kid uses a cloth moistened by hot water from a steaming pot. Nose is expressionless, as if he feels no pain. Dervish continues his account, "The rest were scattered. Quddus ordered that the prisoners be released. He said that we had already shown sufficient testimony to God's invincible power."

Note: Henceforth, Nose walks with a painful limp.

In front of the shrine porch, Brother, Nephew and Ali stand in the mud created by the rain and melting snow around a fire. They extend their hands to warm them. Meanwhile, Baqir passes toward the shrine entrance meeting Thin who scurries up with a sack of hot bread. To Thin, "We will not eat until everyone else has eaten."

Thin grins, "Then, eat!"

Thin passes loaves to Brother, Nephew and Ali, while Baqir takes some inside the shrine.

Note: Many show evidence of combat -- blood on garments, torn garments, various slash or bullet wounds, etc. However, Husayn, Quddus and most of the men are not wounded.

Passing bread to the others, Baqir sits with Husayn, Banner and Sadiq. Quddus stands nearby. Even inside, the coldness causes condensation of exhaled air.

Baqir reports, "Not one of the followers of the Bab lost his life in the encounter today."

Quddus, "Next time, we will receive cannon and mortar fire from the army of the Shah himself."

Tabarsi Fort 2.0

Kid follows tracks in the snow left by the Babis from their preemptive attack on the besiegers on the previous day. He bends and picks up some snow beside some tracks stained with globs of blood. He watches Bread, Wool and Brows push one of the many barricades around the fort over to carry it into the fort. Beyond, Babis hack at fallen trees to trim their branches off. Nephew leads a horse past pulling a sled filled with weapons, swords and rifles, left by the attackers. Chopping of wood, coughing, voices and horses grunting permeate the intense activity at the Tabarsi site.

Kid trots on logs placed parallel along part of a giant octagon shape marked in the snow and mud around the fort. Ahead of Kid, Baqir, Banner and Sadiq talk.

Kid approaches Baqir who instructs Banner and Sadiq at a nearby corner of the octagon, motioning with his arms, "The new walls will run like this. Here and in each of the eight corners, watch towers will be erected."

Meanwhile, more trees fall at the edge of the forest and horses are guided dragging cleaned logs placing them along the perimeter marked by Baqir, where other logs are already stacked. Kid stands nearby and says to Baqir, "Please ... sir." Baqir turns to Kid and affectionately, "Yes, son?"

Kid, "What should I do?"

Baqir grins and laughs, "What would you like to do?"

Kid, "Dig, sir."

Baqir winks at Banner and kneels on one knee with an arm around Kid's shoulder, "Well, son. Right now, we are standing on top of a big trench. Get the idea?"

Kid beams, "Yes, I understand, sir!"

CENTRAL SQUARE OF TEHRAN

Uncle and Vahid mix in the periphery of an agitated crowd gathered in the huge public square lightly covered with snow. The crowd presses around the entrance to the palace of the Shah.

Tehran: Crowd in front of the palace of the Shah.

"Not too close. I am barely tolerated here," Vahid says to Uncle.

Uncle cranes to look over the people. "Who is it?"

Vahid, "Mustafa Khan, a tribal chief."

Mustafa Khan stands at the center of the crowd at the base of the steps to the palace entrance. Two of the five tribal warriors with Mustafa Khan lower a body wrapped in a shroud from a pack horse to the ground.

By the other three warriors tending the horses of their group, Farrant pushes to the front of the crowd, followed by Wright. They stare at the corpse on the ground, a Barfurush leader named 'Abdu'llah Khan.

Taqi scurries down the palace steps. He is furious, eyeing the crowd, Mustafa Khan and the corpse at their feet, "What in the hell do you think you're doing!?"

Mustafa Khan is vexed and rests an elbow on another shrouded corpse. This corpse is one of two slung heads forward, feet aft, on either side of another pack horse. He points angrily at the corpse on the ground, "That's my brother, damn it!"

The two warriors open the top of the shroud to show the face of the dead man lying on his back.

The crowd reacts to this revelation. Embarrassed, Taqi smiles to the crowd and steps closer to Mustafa Khan, glancing down momentarily at the corpse, "So it is."

With seething rage, pulling out his dagger, Mustafa Khan exclaims loudly, "Twelve thousand men!"

He severs the rope over the hips of the pack horse causing the feet ends of the straight corpses to thud to the ground on each side of the horse. He points the blade at his dead brother, nearly screaming, "And a few miserable Babis got the commander!"

Taqi is extremely uneasy and visibly jolted by the louder thud as the full weight of the nearly frozen corpses hit the snow-covered ground after Mustafa Khan severs with one stroke the shoulder rope on the pack horse allowing the corpses to fall. Looking to the crowd on all sides, Mustafa Khan shouts out, "I also brought two princes of the royal family!"

Amid the louder buzz of the crowd reaction, Taqi raises an arm to attract attention and tries to make the best of the awkward situation. He nods "Yes" and loudly, "It was his brother!"

Taqi forcibly grabs the upper arm of Mustafa Khan and jerks him along with him up the steps away from the people, speaking to him in lower but angry tones, "Don't you ever speak to me like that again!"

Frowning, Mustafa Khan shakes his arm free and jerkily returns his dagger to its sheath. Taqi fumes, "It's your own damn fault. I offered the royal army to solve this problem and it was you who refused. Fool!"

Dervish and Nose sit on the dirt floor of their wooden hovel. They weave vines and straw into a crude rope. The raw materials and coils of the finished rope surround them.

Sadiq enters and picks up a coil of rope in each arm, "That was fast."

Dervish, incredulous to Sadiq, "You must be kidding." Snickering to Nose, "It goes this way when you work day and night."

On prolonged coughing by Dervish, Sadiq tells him sympathetically, "Hey, take it easy."

Note: Henceforth, Dervish is plagued by a cough.

Voices, movement and activity are everywhere along the construction of a new, higher wall around the Tabarsi fort. The Babis are weary, tattered and malnourished. The weather is cold, but the snow has gone.

Sadiq arrives with the two coils of rope fabricated by Dervish, adding them to supplies at hand.

Kid, Wool and others shovel dirt in the bottom of a trench. They throw the dirt up on to a mound on the inner side. Others position stacks of timber.

Further along the construction site, other crews place additional trimmed tree trunks into two parallel lines of vertical logs. They lash them together and to smaller cross pieces supporting the two rows of timber wall.

These two walls are separated by about six feet. On the nearby mound of loose dirt from the trench others scoop dirt into blankets and sacks which they carry into, and dump in, the space between the two timber walls.

Spaces between highly irregular vertical beams are filled with stones and mud mortar. Others perched twenty feet above the ground at the top of the two walls lash the tops of the poles together. They pull lines attached to an end of a long log below to raise it and add a new pole to the wall.

Between the walls, the dirt level rises as the workers carry dirt and stones upward where their cargo is dumped, thus entirely filling in the space between the walls. Finally, workers construct a watchtower at each of the corners of this massive octagonal earth-filled wall.

Familiar faces are featured: Ali, Banner, Thin, Qambar, Baqir, Bread, Brows, Brother and Nephew.

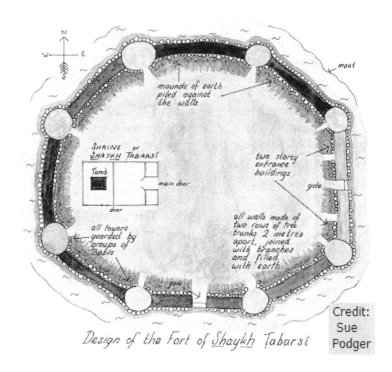

Design of the Fort of Shaykh Tabarsí

Credit: Sue Podger

PALACE OF THE SHAH, TEHRAN

Nasiri'd-Din, Taqi, Mustafa Khan and Prince sit around a rug enjoying refreshments. A sitar player provides music. Nasiri'd-Din and Prince are cheerful. Taqi and Mustafa Khan are tense and sullen.

Eating sherbet, Nasiri'd-Din comments to Mustafa Khan, "So. Mazindaran is unpacified." Then to Prince, "As the new governor, you will bring order to this province."

Prince is confident, "Consider me your servant."

Taqi to Prince, "We do not want to remain in doubt. You will be provided with three regiments of infantry, some of the best from the royal army. To this, we add several cavalry regiments with artillery."

Prince reflects, "That will add over 3,000 men to the forces already there."

Mustafa Khan asks Nasiri'd-Din, "Ah. May I speak?" He can. "Your highness ... the Babi chiefs are fearless. They lead their men right into rifle fire. Men scatter at the mere sight of the one named Husayn. Even here in Tehran they say, ah ... they say that he cannot be killed."

Taqi chuckles, "So Mulla Husayn is a legend."

Spry youth that he is, Nasiri'd-Din springs to his feet, surprising the older men around him.

A momentary glare and flick of a finger by Nasiri'd-Din toward the sitar player silences the music.

Having captured their attention, Nasiri'd-Din, with a hateful smirk, steps among the food on the rug and bends with a quivering clenched fist right in front of the face of Prince, who is mortified and motionless. Nasiri'd-Din sneers, "You shall erase them from the pages of history!"

Prince: Mihdi-Quli Mirza, son of Fath-'Ali Shah, uncle of Nasiri'd-Din Shah, appointed governor of Mazindaran in late November, 1848; led troops from the capital to reinforce the forces of the Mazindaran chiefs against the Babis.

TABARSI FORT
January, 1849

At the perimeter of the open area by the woods, Prince, with and escort of two soldiers, rides up to tents and boxes of supplies where Mustafa Khan observes the soldiers making preparations. Prince is confident and pompous, "I like what I see."

Mustafa Khan looks on skeptically, "I'm glad the Prince is happy."

Prince on his horse and Mustafa Khan on foot look at the east side of the fort with its main gates about 100 yards away. The cleared area is dotted with tree stumps. About 30 yards from the fort, some of the Prince's soldiers watch behind a new array of barricades.

"We are not ready to attack yet," Prince says. "Try to find out how many men and what arms they have."

In the shrine, Quddus hands Husayn a manuscript, which he puts in his coat, "Deliver this to the Prince."

Kid looks up from the ground within the fort.

Nose struggles up the cross-links between the watchtower support logs, something one would not even call a ladder. He reaches the platform some three meters up, "Uhhh!"

On the platform, Bread pulls Nose to his feet. Nose limps to Dervish. The three survey the view. Rifles are on the platform. Nose says quietly, "Good Lord! I see what you mean."

Hundreds of troops set up positions across the cleared area up to the forests and hills. Along the overlaying hills, military-issue tents go up everywhere. In the valley itself, more tents go up and soldiers mill about on the edge of the forests. Others boldly carry more barricades and boxes of ammunition closer to the Tabarsi fort wall. Cannon and mortars aim at the fort. "Lots of new company," Bread says.

Nose grins impishly, "Well, I can't run now. I can hardly walk."

Dervish starts a laugh that becomes a hacking cough.

Mustafa Khan stands just beyond the scattered barricades in full view in front of the fort. He cups his hands around his mouth and shouts, "I want to see the man you call the Babu'l-Bab!"

Nose sees Husayn, holding a sword aloft with a white cloth tied near its tip, scamper down and up the trench toward Mustafa Khan.

Dervish stoops to grab a rifle, as Bread grabs his upper arms from behind, saying fearfully, "Don't even move."

Within the fort at the partially open gate, Baqir and Ali watch Husayn march toward the barricades and Mustafa Khan.

Husayn walks briskly toward Mustafa Khan. Further away, Prince watches. Husayn tosses the sword in the grass and passes soldiers, who cock their rifles behind barricades. But the soldiers do not know what to do, startled by Husayn's bravado.

Husayn crosses the brown grass passing tree stumps, approaching Mustafa Khan, who nervously looks about and back at Prince.

Finally, Husayn and Mustafa Khan stand face to face. Husayn passes to him the manuscript given to him by Quddus. Mustafa Khan trembles and appears awe-struck, though he is actually a larger, taller man than Husayn.

Husayn, "I ask that you deliver this to your Prince. Tell him that we disclaim any intention of subverting the monarchy of Nasiri'd-Din Shah. Our cause concerns the revelation of the promised one of this age."

As Husayn speaks, Mustafa Khan is relieved by what he hears.

Mustafa khan, "Then, what are we to do?"

Husayn, "Let your Prince arrange for us to meet with the mullas and doctors of Islamic law. We shall prove our claims and the Prince may be the judge."

Mustafa Khan is now disgusted with his own role in this situation and looks off at the gathering royal troops, "What are we doing here?" He looks at Husayn, "You people are innocent."

HOUSE OF BAHA'U'LLAH, TEHRAN

Musa accompanies Uncle and Sayyah out to the street. Amused by Uncle's appearance, Vahid observes from the doorway. Uncle's dress is completely changed. He is disguised as a dervish in dress similar to Sayyah's.

Uncle, "How do I look?"

Sayyah, "A genuine wandering dervish and Sufi mystic!"

Uncle, "Anything but a Babi, eh?"

Musa, "It is impossible to help our friends in Mazindaran. They are completely surrounded. Many of us, including my brother, have been imprisoned and whipped by the besiegers for trying to reach the fort."

Uncle, "My original plan was to visit the prison of our Master."

Musa, "Stay off the main routes. Sayyah carries sensitive documents." To Sayyah, "Take good care of him."

Sayyah: Literally "courier", early 20s, small, looks tough, walked vast distances carrying messages between the Bab and his friends. In these times, to be caught with these letters might mean execution of both their recipients and the messenger.

RESIDENCE OF DOLGORUKOV, TEHRAN

Three Persian musicians provide traditional Persian music featuring the sitar.

Farrant and Wright sit around a carpet joining War, sitting at the head of the dinner setting on the floor. On this cool evening, Dolgorukov hosts his guests Persian-style. Servants serve tea. Dolgorukov is the last to sit.

Traditional Persian lunch. L'Univers La Perse, 1841.

War looks concerned to the point of displeasure as he eyes the stranger, Wright. Dolgorukov introduces War to Wright, "The distinguished Mirza Aqa Khan, previously Minister of War."

Farrant to Wright, "Prince Dimitri Dolgorukov, the envoy for Russia."

Wright, "My pleasure, gentlemen."

Farrant, "This is Austin Wright. He is an American missionary."

War, "Interesting."

Wright, "Christianity in Persia..."

War, "I know of your religion. I meant ... America is interesting."

Dolgorukov notices War's discomfort with Wright. To Wright, "Reverend, um, the Mirza is keeping a low profile since the government has changed."

War to Wright, "He means that you have not seen me here, ... understand?"

Wright had not expected this sort of situation, "Oh."

Farrant, "There's no problem with that, is there, reverend?"

Wright, "Not at all, no."

Dolgorukov sighs happily, "Well, the accession to the throne of the young Shah, did you see it?"

Wright, "Yes! The celebrations, the pageantry, magnificent."

For Farrant, now everything is politics, "Indeed. But north-east of the capital, the disciples of a fanatic have assembled in Mazindaran."

Dolgorukov, "A fanatic?"

Wright, "It's the Babis. They have fierce quarrels with the orthodox Muslim clergy."

War grabs the role of "expert" for these foreigners, "What you call a 'quarrel' is something rooted in Islam, the basis of present government. The Shah rules in the absence of a certain heir of the prophet Muhammad."

Wright, "A descendent of Muhammad?"

War, "Yes, he was martyred over 1,000 years ago in Karbala. But the people believe he will return and claim all authority of the state again. The Babis say this 'return' has occurred. Now, you cannot expect our young king and all of our doctors of religion to simply step aside, can you?"

Spellbound by this explanation, Wright is visibly somber, flush with a rush of mixed emotion, "I hadn't seen it ... that way."

Dolgorukov, "Thus, military force against them is inevitable."

War immediately confirms, "Oh, they know that."

TABARSI

From a watchtower at dusk, Nose and Bread see through falling snow three cannon some 50 yards from the fort fire in rapid succession, emitting bright flashes and clouds of smoke. They dive to the platform facing toward the fort interior.

Most of the cannon fire hits the walls of the fort causing little damage or simply overshoots the fort due to poor positioning of the artillery.

Inside a wooden hovel, Kid and Dervish lie on their stomachs side by side. Kid watches Dervish write in his tattered diary. A cannon ball crashes through the roof and wall. The shelter collapses on them.

Nose run-limps by the shacks to the wreckage. Covered with dust, Kid crawls out as Nose appears and passionately embrasses Kid. "Hey, it was nothing," Kid says.

Meanwhile, Wool and Banner lift debris and Sadiq lifts Dervish, coughing loudly in the dust, to his feet. Without his spectacles, squinting, Dervish sums up the situation, "A man can get hurt."

Sadiq, "We're going out tonight." Stooping to find his hatchet, Dervish is ready, "Well, let's go."

Banner, "Later, well after midnight."

Without his spectacles, Dervish looks into the wreckage, reflecting, "I'm going to have to see."

In the shrine building, Quddus instructs Husayn, Baqir and Ali while he wraps his forearms with strips of wool blanket in the fashion of a protective bandage. Subdued, very serious, "There will be no light, not even a single candle, in this fort tonight." More cannon blasts.

Quddus, "The friends should sleep now."

224

Babis Target Munitions to Disable Besiegers

After more intense snowfall and some warmer air, snow collects and melts into slush forming mud in the walk ways between the shacks and hovels.

At the front gates, Quddus and Husayn head some 90 Babi riders extending in all directions in the open areas along the walls and down to the shrine. Their swords are not drawn. They face the gates.

Quddus looks up at the adjacent watchtower where Bread signals to Quddus with a horizontal outward movement of his arms meaning "Nothing, all clear".

Responding to a hand signal from Quddus, Dervish and Nose on one side and Wool and Brows on the other pull the gates open.

Some 90 riders and about 112 on foot quietly move out of the fort. About 100 remain in the fort.

At the edge of the woods surrounding the fort, the Babis pass a group of tents, their black color now completely covered with a coat of snow.

Babis form a trail of slush and mud. Nose rides by Dervish who walks among the others, looking about alertly lest the government troops might be awakened. "Quietly, we marched toward the stronghold of the Prince, his base of operations," he later wrote in his diary.

Husayn and Quddus lead the men along a trail in the woods through the snowfall. Their weapons are not drawn. Encampments, tents, artillery, stacked boxes of munitions and campfires surround them in every direction.

As Dervish later wrote, "At this late hour, the Shah's troops were asleep ... Well, not all of them."

Along the string of marching Babis, Nose and Dervish grin widely, nodding and waving "Hello" into the forest.

Two government soldiers crouched near a campfire grin and wave back at Nose and Dervish.

Nose holds Dervish up on the side of his horse as they pass through a two-foot deep, ten-foot wide stream without a bridge along the trail. They move among Babis crossing the stream. As described in the diary, "We marched for two hours over six miles to the core of the government troops."

As the Babis progress along the trail, small groups of them sneak off the trail quietly disappearing into the dark forest. The size of the main group on the trail led by Quddus gradually decreases.

VILLAGE OF VAS-KAS

Note: The Prince and his commanders were stationed here at a high point above the valley containing the Tabarsi fort.

Quddus, Husayn and Baqir abruptly pull their horses to a stop.

Holding rifles, three soldiers of the Prince stand blocking the trail. Dim campfire light originates behind the Babis. They appear as dark silhouettes to the soldiers. Fearful, pointing a rifle, one calls out, "Shadows! ... Who are you?"

Husayn, "We just arrived..."

Baqir, "...to meet the Prince." The soldiers step to the side of the trail. Barely visible through the falling snow, the small village of Vas-Kas is just a row of mud-brick dwellings, with one larger Main House, in a clearing beyond.

It seems that the three soldiers guarding the trail entering the village assume that the Babis are additional reinforcements loyal to the Prince. One points the way,

"Well, it's the Main House, there. But you will have to wait until morning."

A sword slashes a rope tied around a tree. Horses grunt in reaction to this sudden activity. Dervish's hatchet severs another rope around a tree.

Holding his hatchet, Dervish jerks his arms in the air and Nose rides among about 20 now untethered horses. They quietly disperse the animals among the trees.

By the light of a torch, Banner arranges a fuse in an open box of gunpowder placed at the front door of the Main House.

Back on the trail, one of the soldiers spots the torch light at the Main House. Looking perplexed, he calls his two companion soldiers to attention, "Hey!?"

Several unsaddled horses, their tethers dangling, wander on the trail in front of them.

Suddenly, loud explosions startle them.

In the Vas-Kas Main House, the explosions cause Prince to jump up in fright from his blankets and pillows on his sleeping mat. Long underwear only, he looks in panic.

Startled and confused, the soldiers on the trail try to grab the horse tethers. A series of additional very loud violent explosions emit brilliant flashes of light and fire around them throughout the woods. Most of the horses run off.

A torch lights the fuse leading into the wooden box of gunpowder placed at the front door of the Main House.

Horrified, the soldiers on the trail turn toward another series of explosions that suddenly light up sites on distant hill sides. Backing away, one falls to the ground.

By daring stealth, some 200 Babis had maneuvered through thousands of government troops encamped in a huge, several kilometer area. The Babis had spread throughout this area and targeted gunpowder and weapons supplies to disable and demoralize the hostile troops. Many ran from the scene and never returned.

In the midst of this well-crafted commando-style raid, Husayn, Baqir, Ali, Banner, Bread and Wool stand a distance from the front of the Main House. They are suddenly illuminated as the box of gunpowder at the door of the Main House explodes blowing the door in and a good part of the front wall around it down.

Swords drawn, Baqir, Banner, Bread and Wool charge into the Main House.

With a wool blanket over his shoulders, Prince hears screams of agony from the front room of the Main House. He frantically opens the shudders of a rear window, jumps out and runs off into the snow and darkness behind the Main House, illuminated by a nearby blazing thatched mud hut.

Waving his sword in the air, Nose rides by the three soldiers of the Prince guarding the trail. Nose screams, "The Prince is dead! Run!"

The three soldiers drop everything and run for cover.

A torch lights another fuse leading into a powder box on the snow in the woods.

In front of the Main House, Quddus, Sadiq, Ali and Husayn with other Babis have mounted their horses. A group of partially dressed soldiers with rifles gather at the edge of the village clearing.

In the woods, Dervish carrying a torch and his hatchet runs up to a snow-covered tent and slashes the support lines collapsing it. Soldiers crawl out in their long underwear and run, as more powder boxes nearby explode and Dervish shouts, "Your Prince is dead!"

With the Prince's sword, Baqir runs from the Main House to Husayn, Quddus and other riders. Taking the sword, Husayn says to Baqir, "Let's go! Where are the others?"

Baqir looks around back at the Main House, "You better get going!"

Quddus to Baqir, "We'll wait. Get the others!"

Illuminated by burning furniture in the front room of the Main House, Wool and Bread stuff their pockets with coins from a chest filled with a fortune of gold and silver coins used to pay the troops. Around them, six or so government commanders lie dead, either from the blast at the door or from sword wounds. "So this is how they pay 'em," Bread says.

As Baqir enters, Banner shouts at Bread and Wool, "We are not to touch their possessions!"

Baqir, "Out! We should have been long gone by now!"

Dervish rides double with Nose. They join the Babi riders outside the Main House. Soldiers gathered nearby open fire at the riders.

From the trail by which they entered the village, behind them, another group of partially dressed soldiers open fire.

Ali, "We're surrounded!"

Quddus, "Let's take this side!"

Waving swords, Quddus, Ali, Sadiq and others ride toward one group of soldiers as some are reloading.

Husayn, Brother, Nephew and others mount a similar charge in the other direction.

Quddus is shot in the mouth and flipped off his horse.

Amid further gunfire, Quddus applies pressure with his hands to limit profuse bleeding. He faces downward, spits and coughs to clear his airway. When he lowers one hand, it contains bloody teeth and bone fragments.

TABARSI SHRINE

Prince's sword lays on a mat. Quddus and Husayn sit on the floor on either side. Quddus holds a bloody cloth to his mouth-cheek area with his left hand, writing on a paper with his right hand. As the Dervish diary later recorded, "Unable to speak, Quddus wrote instructions for the friends."

Quddus hands the paper to Husayn. Baqir stands at the front door, "The friends suffer from hunger and thirst."

Quddus nods to Baqir and writes another note. The Dervish diary states, "Many of us had already drunk from the cup of martyrdom."

OFFICE OF PRIME MINISTER TAQI, TEHRAN

Taqi leans over a large paper on his desk containing a sketch of the octagonal Tabarsi fort and surrounding valley. Loud, indignant rage, "The Prince has allowed a handful of students and old men to defeat the army of the Shah ... again!?"

A Royal Soldier across from Taqi has no immediate answer. The British Officer observes, standing by the window. Taqi continues, "What if I had sent the Prince against both the Russians and the Turks!?"

Royal Soldier, nervous, "The Prince says..."

Taqi snaps back with loud disdain, "The Prince?" Then to Officer, "What do you think?"

HALLWAY IN THE PALACE OF THE SHAH

Seated on chairs outside Taqi's office, Russian speaks softly to Dolgorukov, "The state of Mazindaran has become serious."

Dolgorukov, "This brings too many Persian troops near our borders."

Russian, "The Babi chief, Husayn, is cunning and efficient. If he escapes, we have to think of the Babis in our territory."

Officer walks out of Taqi's office nodding respectfully to Dolgorukov, "On the Shah's order, the Prime Minister is sending General Abbas-Quli Khan against the Babis."

BACK TO OFFICE OF PRIME MINISTER TAQI

Trembling, the Royal Soldier places a dirty bundled blanket on top of the Tabarsi fort sketch on Taqi's desk. Taqi fumes. Royal Soldier opens the blanket and picks up the two pieces of the rifle cut in two by Husayn. One rifle piece in each hand, Royal Soldier raises the heavy pieces between his and Taqi's eyes. Voice cracking with emotion, he says, "The Prince sends this evidence of the strength of a man who cut into six pieces a tree, this musket and its holder, with a single stroke of his sword."

As Royal Soldier places the rifle pieces back on the desk, Taqi laughs and grabs the heaviest sword from a wall display. Raising the sword with two hands, Taqi crashes it down with full force on the rifle barrel.

With a hollow clang, the sword deflects leaving only a scratch.

Fifteen Minutes of Fame for a General

TABARSI
February, 1849

General's tent is at the edge of the woods outside the Babi fort. It is big, square-shaped and striped, clearly distinguishing it from the black, triangular tents of the troops.

Amid occasional cannon blasts, General meets Warrior, on foot, and Prince, on horseback.

Warrior, "Same thing last night. No light or sound from the fort."

General, "They may all be dead by now."

Prince, "We should storm the fort."

General smiles, "Tomorrow."

Sadiq dumps a sack of horse bones into a pit filled with the picked bones of several horses and Brows and Wool shovel dirt burying them. As horses died from wounds, the Babis ate them to remain alive.

Sadiq passes Thin and Qambar drawing water from a newly excavated well in the fort. Some Babis wash their clothes.

Where the watchtower was now remains only the stumps of the large beams that once supported it. Sadiq joins a group sitting listening to Husayn. The group is Ali, Bread, Kid, Nose, Brother, Nephew and Dervish.

Dervish writes trying to capture every word in his diary. Husayn sits on a box and is relaxed and reflective. His dress is completely different. Instead of the fur hat seen previously, he again wears the green fez-shaped turban of the Bab. Instead of white, he wears a navy blue coat and gloves. They sit in the shadow of the wall below a watchtower.

Husayn's delivery is soft, warm and inspired, "Meet the All-Powerful clean from the dust of this earth. Take the embrace of the Beloved with pure joy. Die now, before death comes."

Husayn glances up at the sound of a cannon blast, "Do not harbor vague hopes of defeating them. Whoever desires martyrdom, let them come with me tonight. Before dawn we shall scatter the foe who blocks our path."

Husayn touches Dervish's writing hand. Dervish stops writing and looks up at Husayn, who says, "Recording the names is not necessary."

In the darkness before dawn, Husayn, Baqir, Brother, Sadiq, and other Babis, most on horses, have quietly positioned by the edge of the woods among the tents and barricades of the government troops.

Husayn raises his sword toward the stars and moon above. The silence is shattered by a loud cry, "Ya Sahibu'z-Zaman!" The Babis charge off in all directions.

Breathing heavily, General runs in fright from his tent. His jacket is unbuttoned. A rifle is strapped over his shoulder. He is illuminated by stroboscopic cannon blast flashes. Hastily fastening his pants, he climbs up a nearby tree. Below the tree, horses are tethered along lines from the tree to stakes in the ground nearby.

Hatchet in right hand, Dervish runs toward the tree and tent.

Husayn slows his horse from a gallop, arriving between the tent and tree. An entry in the Dervish diary reads, "He moved faster than the bullets."

Baqir and Brother arrive from different directions at another location outside the fort. They pull their horses to a stop meeting each other in front of tents and woods. On foot, Babis and government troops run in every direction. The black woods lights up with dozens of flashes from rifle fire at them. As a Babi falls by them, Baqir and Brother charge at the spot from which the rifle fire originates.

Near General's tent, Nose limps toward Dervish as the explosives at a barricade behind them detonate. The barricade and dry long grass around it burst into bright raging fire illuminating the tent area almost as if it were day.

Among the spooked horses tethered to the nearby tree, Husayn tries to maneuver his horse, but its legs are tangled in the ropes of the horse tethers. With Husayn immobilized below him, General shoots Husayn in the back from close range above in the tree.

Husayn slumps to one side from his horse. Dervish is there to catch and lower him to the ground among the legs of the horses.

Kneeling over Husayn, Dervish draws his left hand toward his mouth in horror. The hand is bleeding. Husayn looks at this hand wound and faintly, "Brother, what happened to you?"

For the first time, Dervish sees the blood on his hand and realizes that he is wounded, "They cut my hand."

SHRINE IN TABARSI FORT

Note: Henceforth, Quddus' mouth wound appears as a scar on his mouth, cheek and throat. He speaks with difficulty in a muffled, gagged, hoarse tone.

The dark room is suddenly dimly lit as a lantern is ignited. Eyes closed, Husayn lies limply on his back on a mat. Quddus kneels over him. "Leave me alone with him," he says. Baqir, Brows, Sadiq, Ali, Nose and Dervish slowly back away out the door. They close the front doors.

With a hand on each shoulder of Husayn, Quddus helps him rise to a sitting position. Husayn opens his eyes. Quddus beckons, "Speak with me."

The sky brightens near dawn. Baqir and Brother stand facing away from the closed front doors of the shrine. At a side, Sadiq observes Dervish peek into the interior through a slit in the doors. In his diary, "They spoke until dawn."
Babis wait surrounding the shrine entrance.

DOLGORUKOV RESIDENCE

Dolgorukov writes a dispatch, "The news from Mazindaran is even more fearful than before. The Babis have routed General Abbas-Quli Khan, killing hundreds of his men."

BACK TO TABARSI FORT

Quddus emerges from the shrine to greet the waiting Babis. Sadiq narrates, "Ninety friends were wounded. One third of them and that master, Husayn, tasted the sweet wine of martyrdom."

PARLOR OF VILLAGE HOME
March, 1849

General has relocated his temporary headquarters in a village away from the Tabarsi fort from which he had retreated after his defeat by the Babis. General is not aware that the man he shot was Husayn.

Sa'idu'l-Ulama, "You can't do this."
General, "My men are afraid to sleep at night!"
Sa'idu'l-Ulama, "You've pulled back from the Babi position. What if they escape?"

236

General, "Impossible. We're still all around them ... Why don't you stick to religion?"

Sa'idu'l-Ulama, "This is a holy war."

General, "Tell that to my soldiers. They fear Babis will descend on them in the night. They say Husayn is more than a man. It is unreal. When they tell me that his every blow causes a mortal wound, how do you fight that?"

Sa'idu'l-Ulama, "You are close to victory."

General, "I'm pulling out."

Sa'idu'l-Ulama, "Do you want the Prince to claim the victory? Think of the rewards. The property of the Babis. The favor of our sovereign."

BACK TO TABARSI SHRINE

Wasted by hunger, the Babis are weak. Quddus' ability to speak has improved but is still clearly impaired.

Quddus addresses the Babis, "Whoever feels the desire, let him stay. Whoever feels the least hesitation or fear, let him freely leave while there is chance to escape."

PARLOR OF VILLAGE HOME

Interrupting General's morning tea, Warrior pushes Traitor to the floor, "This man was captured trying to escape the Babi fort."

Immediately interested, General stands and draws his sword from its sheath from where it was placed on a table.

"Escape? I come to help you," the fearful Traitor says.

General, "Leave us alone." Warrior leaves. "A traitor ... or a spy."

As Traitor speaks, General closes in pressing the sword to Traitor's chest, "The Babis are starving and miserable. Without Husayn, they can be easily defeated."

General, "What?"

Traitor, "They have no food."

General, "Husayn?"

Traitor, "Husayn is dead."

Realizing the importance of this intelligence, General repeats the word with delight, "Dead."

Grinning, lost in thought, without the slightest expression of aggression, General suddenly thrusts his sword in and out of the chest of Traitor, who falls back with a barely audible grunt. General kneels by the lifeless body of Traitor, lying on his back and lovingly places Traitor's hands on his chest as if he was respectfully arranging the corpse for burial. He says softly with a note of irony, "You were very helpful." He chuckles, "Now your help is mine alone."

General turns toward the door and shouts out loudly, "This man attacked me!"

TABARSI SHRINE

With a bloody bandage on his wounded left hand, Dervish stands and entertains some seated Babis: Baqir, Quddus, Ali, Brows, Banner, Thin, Bread, Wool, Nose, Kid, Sadiq, Brother and Nephew. He speaks with dramatic gestures and wild, silly expressions. Amid the giggles and laughter of his little audience, the words from Dervish are not heard.

Instead, Sadiq narrates, "The siege was renewed with fresh vigor. After a time, sensations of hunger left us."

And Dolgorukov narrates, "In a political report I cannot paint a more gloomy picture."

OUTSIDE TABARSI FORT

In a flashback to an earlier event, nineteen Babis with swords raised storm out the fort gate on horses. This sortie is led by Baqir and includes Banner, Thin, Sadiq, Brother, Nephew, Brows, Bread, Wool and Nose. They fan out in all directions.

Dolgorukov narrates, "The Prime Minister estimates over 100,000 Babis in Persia as news of their exploits reaches every province. He is quite worried."

The nineteen Babis call out, "Ya Sahibu'z-Zaman!"

As some soldiers fire rifles at them, General rides out of the woods behind them. He is immediately recognizable with his distinctive appearance and military jacket, decorated and embroidered with golden thread.

The Dolgorukov narration continues, "All attacks by the generals have failed to subdue them."

Spinning their horses around in the middle of the clearing between the fort and the woods, Ali points toward the woods and shouts to Baqir amid the gunfire, "There he is!"

Ali and Baqir charge the riflemen and General. Terrorized, General turns right back into the forest.

The Dolgorukov account continues, "In spite of their numerical inferiority, those fanatics continue to repulse their attackers."

Alone in the woods, Ali and Baqir look about and at General's sweating horse. General is nowhere in sight. Ali snickers, "Looks like the general fell off his horse."

One of General's boots is still stuck in one of his horse's stirrups. "Hey, look at this," Baqir says to Ali.

BACK TO TABARSI SHRINE

Back to mirth and laughter in what one might call "the Dervish show".

A besieger cannon blasts outside as Dervish says, "Here's another one."

A cannon ball crashes through the roof of the tomb room in the shrine. The Babis see through a doorway part of the roof fall into the tomb room. After a short pause, smiles reappear with more giggles and muffled laughing. They prompt Dervish, "Go on."

"OK, there was this small Babi," Dervish says pointing to Kid, "about your size, standing on the crest of a hill."

Dervish spreads his legs, puts his hands on his hips and glares downward, looking tough, acting the part of the small Babi.

"A regiment of troops ride by and the general sends 100 cavalry charging up the hill at the Babi. They disappear over the hill and the battle rages. Finally, the little Babi, his clothes tattered, reappears at the top of the hill. Enraged, the general orders 100 more men to charge at him. As they storm up the hill, one of the wounded soldiers, crawls desperately to the hill crest, screaming, 'Go back! It's a trap! He's not alone! There's two of them!'"

With his listeners pressed by hunger and seemingly intoxicated with their mirth, the Dervish story punch-line is greeted with hearty laughter, as some of the Babis slap hands and roll on their sides.

TABARSI SHRINE
April, 1849

Cool moonlight through gaping holes in the shrine roof illuminates rubble on the floor. In one corner, under a captured barricade of the besiegers, propped from the floor to a wall, Quddus sits alone writing by warm candlelight. As he chants his verses, Sadiq narrates, "We lived on the melody of verses in praise of the Bab, written by Quddus."

TABARSI FORT

Outside the fort, Nose and Kid eye campfires by the edge of the woods, as they creep through the green spring grass growth. They stuff their shirts with clumps of grass. Sadiq narrates, "That most holy one urged us to try to retain our physical strength."

Back inside the fort, Nose feeds the remaining horses with bundles of grass.

Kid puts green grass in boiling soup pots managed by Thin.

Wool and Brows dig up and remove horse bones that had been buried previously.

Sadiq chops saddles into little pieces with a sword and Kid gathers the bits of leather into a bowl. Dervish uses his club to break the horse bones into little pieces on a flat rock. Kid brushes some bone fragments into his bowl and adds its contents to Thin's soup pot.

At another soup pot, Bread dishes out a bowl full to Baqir.

Near some shacks, Brother and Nephew sit on the ground holding their soup bowls. Nephew sucks on a bone fragment and sips the liquid while Brother fishes a piece of leather from his bowl to chew on.

In the debris strewn shrine room, Quddus sits on a mat. Baqir places a bowl of "soup" by Quddus, "Thank you."

Outside the fort, another cannon blasts. Quddus jumps up. He and Baqir run up to the front door. The cannonball crashes on wooden shacks in the fort. At the front doorway, Quddus and Baqir look to the impact site. Quddus to Baqir, "See if anyone's hurt."

Baqir finds Brother and Nephew lying stunned by a shack that is now collapsed in rubble.

Meanwhile, at the top of a ladder, Quddus rises to survey four very high towers built in the clearing around the fort.

Tabarsi Fort 3.0

During preparation of the troops by the woods, Royal Soldier and Prince observe the new towers built around the fort. Smoke from raging fires rises from within the fort's walls.

Royal Soldier, "Sulayman Khan brought mortars with explosive charges. No need to fire into the fort any more. We can see in from the towers. There's nothing in there."

Prince, "We'll go over the walls tomorrow. Maybe we can find some skulls to show the Shah."

Inside the fort, the place looks empty. Some walls of the shrine still stand. The shacks are gone replaced by potholes, ash, smoking, smoldering wood and piles of dirt. A section of the timber on the inner side of the wall burns. Not a soul in sight. The fort interior is wasted, empty.

Kid enters the fort through a crack in the front gate and dashes behind a huge mound of dirt to the entrance to a network of underground tunnels.

Beaming with pride, Kid reports to Quddus in a tunnel under the fort, "I saw the Prince by the woods."

By candle and lantern light, the remaining Babis look on in tunnels connecting to a larger underground room, the walls and ceilings shored up with timber taken from the shacks. Everybody is muddy. The Babis are starving but determined

Quddus, "Let's do it now."

Looking up at Quddus, Kid grins as Dervish and Bread rush off in response to Quddus' order. When anybody moves, sloshing water is heard. Seepage from the tunnel walls has collected several inches deep on the floor.

Sadiq and Nose light torches as Baqir, Brother and Ali lead unsaddled horses out by the tattered Black Standard mounted on the tunnel wall.

Almost too weak to move, Brows and Wool crawl out of the mud of a low, narrow connecting tunnel.

With a sword, Nose slashes free a bundle of dried grass attached to a ceiling beam of the tunnel.

Outside the fort, a man with a knife cuts a choice piece of meat from a pig roasting on a fire. Placed on a plate, this meat is then placed in front of Prince, wearing a bib and sipping from a tea cup. Prince sits across from Royal Soldier. Food is in abundance on the mat on the ground. Prince drops his tea cup when a loud cry of "Ya Sahibu'z-Zaman!" fills the campsite.

Prince runs to his horse. Beyond, torches carried by a dozen or so Babis riders move in the distance around the bases of the towers surrounding the fort.

Riding his horse bareback, Baqir throws a bale of dry grass under the tower. He swings around and tosses the lighted torch igniting the grass.

Perched above, a soldier fires his rifle down at Baqir.

Dervish runs up on foot throwing more bales of hay under the tower creating a blazing fire. Behind, another blazing tower 50 yards away blows up as the gunpowder supply on top of it detonates.

TABARSI FORT
May, 1849

The walls of the fort not far behind, Nose and Kid again crawl in the green grass. Kid starts to pull up a clump of grass, but Nose catches his hand and embraces Kid from behind, pointing ahead, "Do you see that gap there?"

Beyond them is a gap in the campfire lights in the woods leading up the hills, "Uh-huh."

Nose, "You remember that big house in Tehran."

Eyes watering, Kid turns to Nose, "Where Jinab-i-Baha lives?"

Nose, "That's right. Now, go through that gap and go to that house."

Frowning, with a sniffle, blink and tear, "But they stopped the cannons."

Nose presses Kid to his chest in a tight embrace, "Do what your father says."

Babis Betrayed and Massacred at Tabarsi

In the desolated interior of the fort, weak and starving, Nose, Sadiq, Brows and Wool languish on the side of a mound of excavated dirt.

At the demolished water well, Thin draws out a pail of water as Ali and Baqir wash mud from their face from a water bowl and Quddus walks by with a large Qur'an in hand.

Sitting and lying about everywhere, the Babis watch Quddus. He holds aloft the Qur'an with its front cover open exposing a hand written message, "A solemn vow from the Prince himself, written on the holy book of Islam."

Quddus lowers the Qur'an to glance at the Prince's message, "He promises our lives and liberty if we leave this position and surrender our arms ... Sworn on the Qur'an. He affixes his seal ... We shall respond to their pledge to enable them to demonstrate the sincerity of their intentions."

Sadiq comments sarcastically to Nose, "What the tongue of the Prince professes, his heart does not believe."

Quddus heard Sadiq's skeptical comment. He closes the Qur'an and looks up at Sadiq. Tragically, Quddus appears to agree with Sadiq.

MAYOR'S HOUSE, TEHRAN

Note: Mayor's Wife and Mayor are in their 50s.

Wearing head scarfs and face veils, Mayor's Wife and Tahirih descend a stairway toward the main parlor, "I love you, Tahirih. If you would just be a good Muslim, my husband would not have to keep you confined here."

Reaching the bottom of the stairs, they look up.

Standing in the middle of the parlor, Nasiri'd-Din looks at Mayor, by a doorway to an inner hall. Mayor signals to Mayor's Wife with a downward brush of his hand over his mouth.

Mayor's Wife removes Tahirih's veil whispering to her, "I'm sorry."

Tahirih softly, "It's all right."

Mayor clearly disapproves of this meeting between Nasiri'd-Din and his prisoner, Tahirih. Half Tahirih's age, Nasiri'd-Din is Shah, but still an awkward teenager. Mayor impatiently beckons Mayor's Wife and they both quickly exit the parlor. Nasiri'd-Din stares at Tahirih's beautiful face and steps back a pace as Tahirih confidently meets him at the center of the room.

Nasiri'd-Din, "You ... received my request?"

Tahirih, "I did. I read it."

Nasiri'd-Din, "I ... like your looks. You would be my wife and have a high position in the palace ... and abandon the Babi cause."

Tahirih, "Wealth and power be for thee. Prison and death be for me."

Appearing embarrassed, Nasiri'd-Din turns away stepping to the front door, conniving to flatter Tahirih, "So far history has not shown us such a woman as you."

Nasiri'd-Din turns back to Tahirih to see the effect of his remark, but Tahirih is indignant, "How could you dream that I would be your wife when you are exterminating my friends!"

Looking about as if he were innocent of this accusation, "It is the Prime Minister who deals with the Babi chiefs."

Tahirih, "Chiefs? They are heroes of God."

Now Nasiri'd-Din is indignant and disdainful, "The surface of this earth will be purified of their presence."

OUTSIDE TABARSI FORT

A series of explosions wakes Kid up and he cautiously crawls out from under some bushes. He squints as the rising morning sun shines into his face. Some long poles are stuck in the ground in front of him.

At the edge of the bushes, Kid looks through these poles to see in the distance that one side of the fort wall has been demolished to piles of dirt. Explosives set by government troops detonate bringing more of the fort wall down. Kid grabs a pole for support as he stands up to witness this destruction.

The pole falls in front of Kid, horrified to see Nose's head stuck on the end of the fallen pole. Whining like a scared puppy, Kid looks up and to the side.

Soldiers rolling up their tents to break camp look up.

Kid looks up to see that the tops of the poles all have heads of Babis. Kid runs in terror into the woods behind.

Tears streaming, aghast, Kid runs through the forest and falls, curling up on the ground, when loud sustained barrages of rifle fire are heard in the distance.

RESIDENCE OF SA'IDU'L-ULAMA - DUSK

Emaciated, bound in heavy chains around neck, wrists and legs, Quddus sits in the dirt under the watchful eye of Royal Soldier in front of the residence. Some Barfurushis look on. Sa'idu'l-Ulama and Prince bargain, "We shall reward your service to Islam. You can leave this man with us."

Prince, "By royal order, he should be taken before the Shah."

Sa'idu'l-Ulama, "A substantial reward. I am not going to eat or sleep until we agree."

Prince looks at Quddus, "Then you know who he is."

Quddus glares defiantly at them.

"He led a few Babis to resist an army for over six months."

GRASSY CLEARING IN TABARSI WOODS

The only living being in sight is Kid. He walks among the bodies of dead Babis strewn in the grass.

Kid is expressionless, in shock, no more tears.

Weapons and anything of value, any jewelry, etc, are gone.

Kid kneels by Dervish dead on his back, a little dried blood on his shirt. Looking around, Kid picks up the diary by Dervish. Meanwhile, the voice of Dervish reads from this diary, "This affliction is the jewel of our treasures. We do not bestow jewels on everyone."

Note: 200 Babis remained when the Prince betrayed them.

HOUSE OF BAHA'U'LLAH, TEHRAN

By lantern light, Musa continues reading the diary of Dervish, "I long to depart this life and return to my God."

Kid, all cleaned up in new clothes, sits before Musa, who looks up at Majid, saying. "That ... that was the last entry."

Musa's Wife enters and caresses Kid, "Come on. You're going to bed."

Kid and Musa's Wife head for the parlor doorway.

Musa to Majid, "The boy walked for two weeks."

Kid pauses at the doorway, before his exit with Musa's Wife, "Oh. Quddus wasn't there ... among the martyrs, I mean."

Majid to Musa, "He doesn't know. I just heard myself. Quddus ... Candles in his flesh, Quddus was stripped and attacked by a mob."

Musa's left hand holds the diary on his lap. His right hand closes it and rests on it, while Majid continues, "They, like wolves, they cut him apart in a hundred pieces which they cast into a fire.

Babi Numbers Increase Throughout Persia

VILLAGE STREET, CHIHRIQ
Summer, 1849

Ruins of Chihriq fortress

Sitting in a doorway, Wright, dusty from travel, wipes sweat from his neck with his handkerchief. He intently watches the entrance to Shaykh's house, a bit down the narrow street of this small village.

Rising beyond, in the distance, the rugged rock mountain with the prison fortress confining the Bab, protrudes above the hills.

Note: At Dolgorukov's insistence, the Bab had been moved from Mah-Ku near the Russian border to confinement in Chihriq, further to the south. Coincidence or not, Chihriq is near Wright's home base – the Christian Mission in Urumiyyih.

SHAYKH'S REAR ROOM

Shaykh is busy copying a page of a manuscript in Persian. Uncle and Sayyah sit with Shaykh in his workshop, a small cramped room filled with books, stacks of manuscripts and a large, trunk-type chest.

Looking through some letters, Uncle says, "These letters have no names."

Sayyah touches his forehead, "It's all up here."

Shaykh with admiration, "Show him."

Sayyah looks at the first letter Uncle holds, "That is to Hujjat in Zanjan." Next letter, "Ah ... to Mirza Ahmad in Qazvin." Next letter, "Jinab-i-Baha in Tehran."

Shaykh says playfully, "He doesn't look that smart, does he?" Sayyah directs a mock leer at Shaykh, who continues in a serious tone, "If Sayyah is arrested, these letters cannot be used to implicate others ... you know what can happen."

BACK TO VILLAGE STREET, CHIHRIQ

Eyes appears walking toward the entrance to Shaykh's place from the direction of the mountain fortress.

Wright intensifies his surveillance.

Not noticing Wright, Eyes enters Shaykh's house.

Wright stands up, a slight smile, "That's the place."

BACK TO SHAYKH'S REAR ROOM

Looking glum, Eyes pulls out some manuscripts hidden in his shirt and puts them on a table, "This is from last week."

Shaykh to Sayyah, "Lock the door." While Sayyah locks the door bolt, to Eyes, "What is it?"

Eyes, "With news of the slaughter at Tabarsi ... I can't tell you how despondent the Bab is."

Several sharp knocks on the door jolts them into apprehensive action. Sayyah holds the door as if to prevent someone from barging in. Shaykh opens a secret compartment behind a wall rug. Meanwhile, Eyes and Uncle franticly gather up loose papers and manuscripts.

With more sharp knocks on the door, Shaykh crosses to the door, signaling to Uncle that the papers should go into the secret compartment. Having peeked through a slit in the door, Sayyah whispers to Shaykh, "A foreigner."

There is a bookcase and a table with paper and other materials used by scribes and copyists in the front room. Trying to act casual, Shakyh, suspicious and tense, slips out into the front room to greet Wright. Shaykh eyes a piece of paper in Wright's hand, "Yes, sir?"

Wright, "I hope you don't mind. The front door was not fully closed."

Shaykh, "I understand ... what service may I be?"

Wright hands the sheet of paper to Shaykh. With a noticeable reaction, Shaykh sees that it contains three lines of Persian script in the center.

Shaykh immediately steps to the entrance of the front room, drawing Wright away from the door to the rear room.

Wright, "Could you make a copy of that?"

Shaykh holds the paper up in the direct sunlight, glancing out to the street to see if anyone is there. The street is empty. "This is a prayer," he says.

Wright, "I can't read it, but I think it is by the Siyyid-i-Bab."

Shaykh, "Oh?"

Wright, "I got it from a dervish, but he was a rogue, so I can't be sure. You have many books. I would love to obtain some of the Babi sacred writings."

Shaykh, "I'm afraid I can't help there."

Wright examines a beautiful page of Persian calligraphy with colorful border illumination, placed on Shaykh's work table, "This is a work of art. Could you do something like this with that prayer?"

Frankly, their behavior looks contrived. With open books in their hands as if they were calmly reading, Eyes and Uncle sit on the floor. Sayyah sits on the chest. Shaykh enters, hands to Eyes the paper from Wright and to Sayyah, "Follow him."

Sayyah promptly exits. Pensive and worried, Shaykh bolts the door. "Who was he?" Eyes asks.

Shaykh, "I don't know ... a Christian." Uncle takes this as good news, "Sounded like an American."

Eyes hands the paper to Uncle, "Look at this."

Shaykh, "He was asking questions. I sent him away."

Uncle, "Their minds are more open."

Shaykh is defensive, "What would that man be doing way out here?"

Uncle, "Maybe he is a seeker."

Eyes opens the chest to show Uncle that it contains stacks of manuscripts, thousands of pages. To Uncle, "But we had this in plain view. The original of our holy book."

Shakyh, "We could not take the risk."

Note: Shaykh's concern about Wright is based on the plight of the Babis and the fact that it was not unknown that foreigners might be employed as agents of the government even though the ruling classes generally mistrusted them.

After completing his mission to see again his nephew, the Bab, Uncle returned to Tehran, accompanied by Sayyah.

Turmoil and Death in the Capital

BRITISH LEGATION, TEHRAN
December, 1849

The parlor is decorated for Christmas. Sharing an evening with Sheil, upon his return from London, selected members of the diplomatic community brief him on events in his absence. The Babis now concern everyone.

Dolgorukov says, "The army lost almost 4,000 men but the expedition against the Babis in Mazindaran has put an end to the worries of the Prime Minister."

Farrant, "They were intent on rebellion."

Dolgorukov, "The Prince offered a truce, then massacred them."

Sheil, "My God."

Dolgorukov, "This success is more worthy of pity than a defeat. The indignation it aroused has excited a spirit of a new and even more dangerous resistance."

Ferrier, "It stimulated, rather than halted, the progress of Babism. Now they have numerous adherents in every province."

Sheil, "The Shah dead. Persia went to hell while I was in London."

Dolgorukov, apologetically, "The news is not cheerful."

Sheil, "Please, I want to hear it."

Farrant, "There may be thousands of Babis in the capital alone."

Ferrier, "Discontent pervades all classes."

Farrant, "The new King is a mere boy who does little in his government."

Dolgorukov is resentful, "He does preside over executions." Dolgorukov describes an incident at the palace.

FLASHBACK AT PALACE OF THE SHAH

It is July. Dolgorukov uses his handkerchief to wipe sweat from his forehead and neck and to cover his mouth as if he might vomit, "I was about to meet the Shah one day, when eight criminals were strangled right there in front of us."

Dolgorukov is aghast. Nasiri'd-Din stands on the platform reserved for the Shah. He observes with satisfaction as an attendant drags away one of the bodies fallen in a heap in front of the platform. Nasiri'd-Din wears a fire red jacket and the dead "criminals" wear shabby clothes of the poor.

Nasiri'd-Din to Dolgorukov, "Please excuse the delay."

Dolgorukov with choking cough, "Your Majesty ..." He is indignant, "This barbaric custom should be abolished at once." Forcefully, "Every European nation is horrified by this savagery."

BACK TO BRITISH LEGATION

Dolgorukov finishes his account of his story and looks disgusted. Sheil and Farrant watch in silence. Ferrier shrugs, "This has always been the normal practice in Persia."

Leonora, "Justin?" Leonora curtsies at the parlor entrance, "Good evening, gentlemen."

Sheil struts with pride toward Leonora, "May I present my lovely wife."

Leonora: 35, new wife of Sheil, brought back from London; intelligent, sweet, upper-class, but not very pretty.

HOUSE OF BAHA'U'LLAH, TEHRAN

Servant holds the reins of a horse which Vahid mounts in front of the house. Musa looks up. With glad resignation, Vahid bids farewell, "This is my last journey. You will see me no more."

Inside the house, Kid and Sayyah watch Nabil take notes interviewing Uncle, who says, "I was guardian of the Bab."

Nabil, "What year was that?"

Uncle, "Well, the father of the Bab died when he was very young. I tried to put him in school."

Musa enters and to Uncle, "Sir, I urge you to leave Tehran." And to Nabil, "You, too."

Uncle, "Why fear for my safety?"

Kid with youthful impetuosity, "You better do it."

Nabil to shut up Kid, "OK."

Karim enters and to Musa, "I'm going to the sanctuary in Qum."

Musa, "You will be safe from arrest."

As Karim and Musa talk, Uncle and Nabil continue. "What was it?" Uncle asks.

Nabil, "The school, sir. Could you elaborate on that."

Nabil: 19, Babi poet, a bit conceited at this age, compiled a history of the Babis completed in about 1888.

OFFICE OF PRIME MINISTER TAQI
January, 1850

Sitting on a chair across from Taqi at his desk, Sheil presents an official communication, "The Foreign Ministry of Her Majesty's government in London supports the position of Prince Dolgorukov."

Taqi curtly places the letter aside. He can't read English. Sheil continues, "The Persian translation will be delivered."

Taqi, "Just what are we talking about?"

Sheil, "The revolting practice of executing criminals in the Royal presence should be abandoned."

Taqi, "I see."

Sheil, "This is no longer done even in the most savage nations."

Taqi is quiet, but hostile, "Quite a statement to make, Mr. Ambassador."

Sheil is unperturbed, "We prefer a public execution. It is unworthy of a sovereign to preside over such an act."

TABARSI SHRINE

It is cold at dusk. The floor is still strewn with debris fallen from the collapsed roof. Snow falls in the shrine ruins and has collected on the floor and debris.

Shivering, overwhelmed with emotion to have arrived at the spot where so many martyrs beloved to him suffered, Sayyah slowly crosses to the corner where Quddus had once sat writing. Kneeling at that spot, Sayyah picks up a fragment of paper. Most of it had been burned and there is no writing on it. Sayyah lowers his head to the floor and starts a chant of an evening prayer.

PALACE OF THE SHAH, TEHRAN
February, 1850

Mayor and Taqi emerge from Taqi's Office and pace briskly down the hallway. Mayor seeks Taqi's favor, "I arrested them. We have seven Babis."

Taqi, "How do you know?"

Mayor, "A confidential source."

Taqi, "Are you trying to insult me? Who identified them as Babis?"

Officer approaches them in the opposite direction and greets Taqi, "Your Excellency."

Taqi replies sweetly to Officer, "I'm glad you came." Then in a bitter tone, "You will observe something."

Note: Nasiri'd-Din Shah again wears his bright red coat. It was his custom to wear it when he was passing judgment. The seven prisoners, suspected Babis, are bound in heavy chains. Throughout "in chains" means the usual heavy chain linking neck, wrist and leg cuffs. The seven Babis include Uncle and six faces not seen previously. They are all very well dressed representing the higher merchant, ecclesiastical and government classes. One of them is a well-kept dervish.

Seven suspected Babis in chains sit on the floor before Nasiri'd-Din Shah, who sits with a casual posture on his platform.

Prime Minister Mirza Taqi Khan

Uncle stares stoically up at Nasiri'd-Din. Two soldiers stand holding rifles on either side.

Taqi, Mayor and Officer arrive. Taqi nods to Nasiri'd-Din who then addresses the prisoners in a depressed tone, "We make no real demand on you. You may go free once you have denounced the Bab." He pauses to sip tea. The Babis are silent. "Not a single word?"

Mayor points to one of the Babis and says, "This one has stood mute, but he has no speech impediment."

Nasiri'd-Din looks at Officer and perfunctorily, "The Grand Vizier will have to exercise his authority."

Taqi addresses Uncle, "There are offers to pay the ransom for each of you." Uncle ignores Taqi. "In times of distress like this one may gain his freedom in this way without any shame. Everyone understands this. What do you say, gentlemen?"

Uncle replies resolutely, "To deny the Siyyid-i-Bab is to deny Muhammad, Jesus, Moses and all prophets of the past."

Nasiri'd-Din concludes with feigned sympathy, "I am sorry to hear that."

BRITISH LEGATION, TEHRAN

The British Legation is close to the central square. The exclamations of a multitude is heard as if we were not far from a sports stadium.

Sitting on a divan in the parlor reviewing dispatches, Sheil receives with calm satisfaction the report of Officer who stands, flush with emotion, before him, "They executed seven Babis in the central square, sir."

Sheil stands, "Was the Shah present?"

Officer, "No, sir. The Prime Minister supervised the affair."

Sheil, "Excellent." He looks out the window and then somewhat molested asks, "What is that?"

Officer, "The public is in a frenzy. They, ah, are heaping waste on the bodies, you know, human filth."

Sheil, "Good Lord."

Sitting with a book in a chair, Leonora appears to be struck and intensely interested in this talk.

Sheil advises Officer, "Perhaps we should discuss this in the office."

Leonora, "This interests me, Justin."

Sheil pours some tea, saying, "Islamic people can be merciless to Muslims gone astray. Was there any incident or disorder during the proceeding?"

Officer, "No, not really."

Sheil offers some tea, "Would you like a cup?"

Officer, "No thank you, sir."

Sheil is satisfied, "Well, it seems that public executions are feasible here."

With a loud door slam, Farrant arrives in a rage, extending his arm pointing at Sheil and loudly, "Did you know those people were murdered for their beliefs?"

Sheil, mixing his tea, "Calm yourself!"

Farrant is about to attack Sheil. Officer steps forward but not fully between them. "We are not to blame here," he says.

Raising a brow, Leonora looks to Sheil, who is composed.

Very angry, Farrant continues, "Oh, sure. Who wanted to see public executions?"

Sheil stands with his tea cup, "You were the one who hinted at a Babi conspiracy! And on what evidence was that based?"

Farrant slumps on the divan. Officer is startled by his outburst, but sympathetic to Farrant, having also seen the executions. Seated next to the divan, Leonora puts her book aside.

Farrant is incredulous, "Doctors of law, scholars, noted merchants. All innocent."

Officer, "I'm sorry, Frank."

A sudden sob, then with a faint smile of admiration, "One of them laughed, waved at the crowd and said, 'Yes, I am a Babi, I am going to die for you'."

Still by the window, Sheil is unmoved, even stern, "If they were innocent, we shall make note of that, but you better get hold of yourself."

Officer comments to Leonora, "One man said that he was so happy, that he would not know if he was throwing his hat or his head at the feet of his beloved."

CENTRAL SQUARE OF TEHRAN

With a handkerchief held over his mouth and nose, Farrant walks among the seven dead Babis. They were beheaded. The corpse of Uncle is recognizable by his distinctive jacket.

A few pedestrians cross the square walking among the scattered corpses. A woman dumps refuse on one of them.

Looking bewildered, 30 Babi prisoners in chains sit in front of the palace. They are poor villagers.

Unidentified prisoners

Officer speaks with one of several soldiers armed with rifles guarding the prisoners, then steps away to meet Farrant, saying, "The captain is upset. His unit came 350 kilometers with these prisoners."

Dolgorukov and Russian ride up on horseback, "Good day."

Farrant, a bit dysfunctional, looks at Dolgorukov, saying in a molested tone, "These corpses have been out here for three days." He continues in a bitter monotone, "Their way to humiliate them."

Dolgorukov, "One can only regret the blindness of the Shah's authorities. Who are these prisoners?"

Officer responds, glancing nervously at Farrant anticipating a reaction, "Babis from Zanjan, sir."

Farrant in another outburst, "Well, I'll be damned!"

Farrant storms off toward the prisoners, while Dolgorukov apparently mistakes Farrant's frustration for disapproval of the Babis, "Quite so. They threaten to disrupt public order.

OFFICE OF PRIME MINISTER TAQI, TEHRAN
Spring, 1850

Prime Minister Taqi and General talk in front of the wall map. General is polite but not beholden to Taqi and not interested in becoming engaged against the Babis again. Taqi speaks methodically, but under stress, "Some 3,000 Babis led by Hujjat are spreading ideas inciting unrest in Zanjan."

General, "Such is Persia today."

Using the wall map, Taqi illustrates for General the sites and route of which he speaks, "Zanjan is strategic on the trade route between Tehran and Tabriz. And the governor of Zanjan threatens to flee the city."

General, "That would be unthinkable at this point. What could the Shah do if governors start fleeing their posts?"

Taqi, "The governor demanded that troops be sent to Zanjan."

General, "Surprise. He has a brain."

Taqi, "Your experience with the Babi problem in Mazindaran can help us. He wants to provoke an incident to justify an attack on the Babis."

General knows that Taqi may be overlooking some of the humiliating defeats that he had suffered from a few hundred Babis in Mazindaran. He turns away.

Taqi, "Well?"

General, "Have reinforcements ready."

SHAYKH'S REAR ROOM

Shaykh is packing up papers pertaining to the writings of the Bab. Messenger and Eyes set a wooden baggage trunk down. The trunk is locked, different from the chest that is still there and also locked.

Eyes says to Messenger, "You need a mule to carry this."

Shaykh spreads out a map on the trunk, a sketch showing the positions of Chihriq, the large lake between Chihriq and Tabriz, Zanjan, Qazvin, Tehran and Qum. Shaykh shows Messenger the route to take from Chihriq to Qum, south of the lake, Zanjan and Qazvin, "OK, you're going far south of Zanjan. We have problems there." Pointing to the sketch, "Then from here to Qum."

Eyes, "It was unthinkable ... he said this was the last springtime that he would be with us."

Messenger: named Mulla Baqir, mid-20s, scholarly-type, was Islamic cleric (mulla), now a Babi.

Nasiri'd-Din Shah Qajar witn royal troops.

Siege of Zanjan Babis by the Shah's Troops

GOVERNMENT HOUSE, ZANJAN

Zanjani #1 and #2, guards of the governor, armed with rifles, are posted at the entrance of Government House. They see Hujjat standing along the narrow street with his hand casually propped on a sword, as if it were a cane. "Let's arrest him," Zanjani #1 says.

Hujjat points up at the top of the building across the street, brings his finger to his mouth and to Zanjani #1, "Shhhh!"

Looking up, Zanjani #2 grabs #1 before he does something foolish. On the top of that building a small group of Babis aim rifles at them.

Affecting complete confidence, Hujjat manipulates the sword as one would a walking cane and strolls past Zanjani #1 and #2, greeting them pleasantly as he enters Government House, "Good day."

Note: These Babis, Zanjani #1 and #2 and the Babi prisoners previously seen in Tehran dress as typical of the tribes of this region. Though Hujjat's style is still bold and stinging, he now appears calmer and hardly raises his voice.

Greasy: 40s, repulsively fat, another cruel pillager of Persia's people; Governor of Zanjan; titled Majdu'd-Dawlih, maternal uncle of Nasiri'd-Din Shah; known to loath Hujjat.

With a horizontal blow, Hujjat's sword shatters an attractive vase, one about the size of a human head.

Startled, Greasy, the Zanjan governor, and several women serving him refreshments look up at Hujjat. Greasy sits on a rug, at the head of it. As the women run off, Greasy braces himself and Hujjat steps forward, "That could have been your head, don't you agree? Do I look upset? I am upset."

In contrast to his words, Hujjat holds the sword limply at his side in a non-threatening manner. Greasy grunts, moving to rise to his feet, "Uuuuhh."

Hujjat, "Oh, don't get up."

He doesn't. Greasy, "What are you going to do?"

Hujjat, "It's what you do."

Greasy regains his usual domineering manner, "I'm not going to grovel before an infidel, or let you usurp my authority."

Shifting his grip of the sword to hold it loosely as a cane, "When people freely choose to change their beliefs, you call it rebellion because your authority remains only in your head. You have no authority that anyone would want, parasite that you are."

Greasy, "Don't lecture me. Get to the point."

Hujjat, "You have freely chosen to arrest a mere child of our people, then to kidnap them and now to assemble an army to intimidate us."

Though Hujjat has the upper hand at the moment, Greasy spits in Hujjat's direction and defiantly, "I also ordered your arrest and detention in Tehran."

Hujjat, "No matter ... But if my companions are attacked, I will take steps to defend their lives." Hujjat walks out.

LARGE ROOM, ZANJAN

Amid sporadic rifle fire, through smoke and dust in the air, Zaynab scurries down a narrow stairway lined with women passing a series of rifles both up and down the stairway.

In a later dispatch to St. Petersburg, Dolgorukov would write, "Troops have attacked the Babis in Zanjan. But the governor and all authorities of the Shah have been driven from the city, which was then put under siege."

Zanjan province military camp.

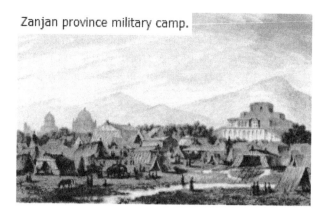

At the base of the stairs, Zaynab walks briskly through a large room where more women and girls are reloading the rifles to pass them back upstairs.

She enters a small room, closing the door behind her.

Hujjat's Wife holds her newborn baby, crying loudly, disturbed by the rifle fire.

Zaynab concludes her report to Hujjat, "That's my report, sir."

Hujjat sits near Hujjat's Wife, with Zaynab, clearly beholden, sitting in front of him. Looking closely at Zaynab's dirt-stained face, Hujjat asks, "What is your name, son?"

Zaynab is really a 15 year old girl dressed as a boy and is suddenly frustrated and unable to lie, "Zaynab, sir."

Suspecting as much, Hujjat removes her hat and lovely hair falls to her shoulders, as she appears crushed by disappointment, "That's a girl's name."

Zaynab, "I can fight them. I have been."

Hujjat looks at Hujjat's Wife, who shows no disapproval.

"They're killing our babies, sir," Zaynab continues.

Reflecting, Hujjat hands back to Zaynab her boy's hat, "Then you need a boy's name. ... Ali?"

Gratified, Zaynab pops up to restore her disguise as a boy with the hat preparing to leave.

Meanwhile, Hujjat's Wife says to Hujjat, "Hundreds of the youth could not celebrate their weddings since the siege began. We should perform their marriages. We don't know for how long, or if ... their lives are just beginning."

OFFICE OF PRIME MINISTER TAQI
Summer, 1850

Sheil and Dolgorukov sit together on a divan, with Ferrier seated on a nearby chair. General is seated at Taqi's desk. They listen to Taqi, standing in front of the wall map, conduct a briefing. He indicates the map positions of Shiraz and Nayriz.

"In the south, a regiment and two cannon have been sent from Shiraz to Nayriz to end an uprising led by Siyyid Yahya."

Sheil and Dolgorukov speak quietly to each other, "Isn't he the famous scholar?"

Dolgorukov, "Yes. We met him. He turned Babi."

Taqi adds his hostile opinion, "A very dangerous man. In the north, 400 horsemen and a battery of artillery have been sent to Zanjan in response to a Babi insurrection." War enters and watches. Taqi continues, "Hujjat and his conspirators there control a large part of the city."

War chides Taqi, "Another holy war?"

Taqi doesn't care who might see that he loathes War. Taqi is vexed and barks to War, "How dare you speak! How dare you barge in here!"

War sits on a rug away from the group and chuckles, "Mahd-i-Ulya told me to sit in."

Ferrier turns to Sheil with that "Who?" look. Sheil responds with an expression suggestive of the absurdity of the situation, whispering to Ferrier, "The mother of the Shah."

Taqi eyes War, "End of meeting."

Sheil, "Excellency, Christians and Jews live in Persia. Has His Majesty's government made effort to negotiate an accord with the Babis?"

Skillfully, Taqi tries to manipulate the outlook of the foreign diplomats. He gruffly states, "You can't be serious, at a time when revolution and the threat of rebellion sweeps through Europe."

BACK TO LARGE ROOM, ZANJAN

Removing their scarfs and pulling out long hair, women and girls line up to have one of them shear the hair off. The removed hair is placed in a pile. Meanwhile, vibration from the nearby impacts outside of cannon balls shot by government troops causes ceiling plaster and dust to fall on them.

A Sheil dispatch to London later recorded, "The duration of the siege of Zanjan is inexplicable."

From this pile, other women take hair and quickly twist and roll it into cords which others, further down this assembly line, weave into rope. In turn, this rope is efficiently wrapped and bound around boards of hard wood to form an object something like a long, very narrow barrel.

The Sheil dispatch continues, "The women cut their hair to make rope to bind wood to form cannons."

After another cannon blast, a cannon ball suddenly crashes through the ceiling behind the women near the door to the small room. Amid the dust and the women's screams, Hujjat runs out of the small room. Though no one is seriously hurt, one girl fell under the rubble and lies, dazed, on the floor by the cannon ball. She scrambles up and away.

Hujjat picks up the cannon ball and passes it to a man who had run down the stairs into the large room. Without delay, this man lugs the cannon ball back up the stairs.

A later Dolgorukov dispatch recorded, "The army is unable to force the Babis to submit voluntarily."

The Sheil dispatch: "As fast as artillery fire is shot upon them, they pick up the balls and return them to the army out of wooden cannon."

Just as a woman finishes tying the last knot binding the "barrel" or "wooden cannon", Hujjat and another man carry it away and up the stairs. The women immediately position other boards to form another wooden cannon.

A report by Ferrier to Paris further reveals the international attention that this awesome episode in Zanjan received. Ferrier wrote, "The Babis run up and down the rooftops with makeshift cannon in their arms."

The Sheil report concluded, "Contrary to all rational expectation, the Shah's troops cannot expel them from this nearly defenseless city."

WRIGHT'S STUDY

At his table, Wright admires the copy of the Bab's prayer that he had left with Shaykh. Shaykh had rendered this stylized, illuminated version, in Persian script. It is framed on the wall next to a similarly framed stylized English rendering of the Lord's Prayer from the Bible. Wright narrates, "The Babis passed through the historic phases of all the great religions."

CHRISTIAN MISSION, URUMIYYIH

Wright emerges, descends the steps and walks down the slope toward the lone tree under which he teaches his classes, weather permitting. Now he has no students. Nobody else is in sight on this cloudy day. He and the mission building are alone and isolated. Wright narrates his thoughts, "When they again took the Bab to Tabriz, all the missionaries watched with great interest. They saw him pass by ... yet Christendom remains ignorant of this great event, as if it had taken place on the moon, or among the inhabitants of another planet."

ROOM IN SANCTUARY MOSQUE, QUM

Karim bolts the door. Messenger and Nabil set the heavy trunk down, treating it as a sacred object.

Qum: S G W Benjamin, Persia and the Persians, 1887

"The Prime Minister plans to reduce Zanjan to dust and authorize a general massacre," Karim says.

This news produces a pensive moodiness and a feeling of excitement among the men. Messenger hands the trunk key to Karim, saying, "Personal effects of the Bab."

Nabil, "Let's open it!"

Karim frowns and hesitates. Nabil enthusiastically eggs him on, "Come on. Just a second."

Nabil obtains the key from Karim's hand and hastily unlocks the trunk. He lifts its lid to reveal a very long scroll of light blue paper on top of manuscripts, pieces of clothing, prayer beads, etc. Meanwhile, Karim insists, "I shall take it to Jinab-i-Baha in Tehran. I leave tonight. The Bab should be in Tabriz by now."

In the lantern light, Messenger holds the paper as Nabil unrolls the scroll revealing a large perfect shape of a five-pointed star on the large page, perhaps four feet long. The shape of the star is actually formed by very intricate, fine calligraphy. The men are awe-struck by the beauty of the Bab's work. Nabil gasps and whispers softly, "My God, countless derivatives of the word 'Baha'!"

The Bab's Star Tablet in the British Library

Martyrdom of the Bab

ZUNUZI'S HOUSE, TABRIZ

Rubbing his hands together and about to say something, Zunuzi enters the front parlor from an interior hallway. But he sees that no one is there. His hands fall limply to his side. Disappointed, he notices that the front door has been left slightly open. His son Youth is gone.

Tabriz: NW Persia

GATE OF TABRIZ BARRACKS

Colonel leads Eyes, Hasan and the Bab through a loud jeering crowd toward the entrance and courtyard of the barracks. The hostile onlookers press in close. As soon as Colonel passes, the crowd spits and sneers at them.

Suddenly, Youth, barefoot, hatless, disheveled and overcome with emotion, leaps from the crowd to the ground at the feet of the Bab, "Wherever you go, Master, let me follow!"

Colonel turns and impatiently beckons them to keep moving. The Bab assures Youth, "You will always be with me."

Colonel: Col. Sam Khan, a Christian and Armenian, was commander of 750 Armenian troops (the Armenians); charged with guarding the Bab at the "arsenal" (the Barracks).

Note: Eyes and Hasan now appear worn and their clothes are dirty and ragged. Their normal headwear is gone and they have improvised scarfs from rag cloth.

RUSSIAN CONSULAR OFFICE, TABRIZ

Russian runs in. A Persian clerk mans the front desk. Russian asks frantically, "Where is the Russian Consul?"

The clerk hardly looks up pointing limply behind Russian.

Russian turns toward Anitchkov, who pensively taps a pen in his palm. "The Bab is detained in the arsenal," Russian says.

Anitchkov, "The order from the Shah is to put him to death. The governor has disassociated himself from this act. He fears a miracle."

Now the clerk is clearly interested and looks up.

Anitchkov: Russian Consul at Tabriz, an important post since this large city in NW Persia was a major trade center.

TABRIZ BARRACKS

Youth, Hasan and Eyes sit against the wall opposite the door of a detention cell. Eyes sorts out a handful of manuscript pages into several piles on his scarf spread on the dirt floor. Several candles stuck in the dirt provide dim light.

The Bab says, "Tomorrow will be the day of my martyrdom. If one of you would now arise and end my life, I prefer to be slain by the hand of a friend than by a stranger."

Hasan and Eyes are paralyzed, aghast at the thought. Youth, almost as if he were in a trance, slowly rises unraveling his belt with his hands, tears raining from his eyes. Bursting into sobs themselves, Eyes and Hasan jump up grabbing Youth pulling him to the floor. The Bab tells them, "This youth who has risen to comply with my wish will, with me, suffer martyrdom."

To Eyes and Hasan, the Bab says, "You will not confess your faith so you may live to tell the truth."

Suddenly, Zunuzi is shouting. Colonel swings open the creaky detention cell door. Zunuzi demands, "Let go of me!"

Youth springs to his feet while Colonel steps forward into the cell doorway pointing at him, "You. Get out here."

In light from a wall lantern, Zunuzi holds a one year old baby in a blanket and struggles with two of Colonel's men, Armenians, who hold Zunuzi back in the narrow passageway.

Youth steps out into the passageway with Colonel and looks at his stepfather Zunuzi, then at Colonel's palm, as he opens it revealing a gold coin.

Colonel to Youth, "He paid to see you."

Youth lunges forward toward Zunuzi. Colonel instantly extends an arm blocking the way.

Zunuzi is held back about six feet away. He extends the baby toward Youth and desperately, "Think of your child ... and your wife!"

Zunuzi draws the baby back to one arm and extends the other opening his palm to reveal two more gold coins, while shifting his gaze to Colonel, "I have more!"

Colonel to Youth, "Go with him. I will say you just changed your mind."

HOUSE OF BAHA'U'LLAH, TEHRAN

At the open front door, Karim arrives with the heavy trunk containing manuscripts and certain effects of the Bab. Karim and Servant inch the trunk into the dimly lit interior vestibule. Servant and Musa are in night clothes.

Musa takes Servant's place handling the trunk, saying to Servant, "Put the lights out."

Looking outside, Musa asks Karim, "Were you seen?"

TABRIZ BARRACKS

In the detention cell, Hasan sits by Eyes who tries to keep writing on a paper placed on his scarf as a floor mat. But Farrash literally lifts Eyes to his feet. His pen falls on the paper, which is only half full of writing.

As Eyes is pulled away by Farrash, Hasan bows to pray.

Meanwhile, the Bab addresses Farrash. His tone is that of a general statement, rather than something directed specifically at Farrash, "Until I have completed my last message, no earthly power can silence me. All the world is powerless to deter me from fulfilling, to the last word, my intention."

RUSSIAN CONSULAR OFFICE, TABRIZ

Farrash shoves Eyes, now without his scarf, to the floor, but Eyes stumbles and maintains his footing. He withdraws a folded manuscript from his shirt and manages to place it before Anitchkov, who sits behind his desk.

The one-eyed Mamaqani lurches toward Anitchkov. He tries to grab the manuscript. Glaring indignantly at Mamaqani, Anitchkov calmly and deftly snatches up the manuscript. Manaqani pauses. Standing by the window, Russian instantly scrambles to Anitchkov's side and loudly and firmly tells Mamaqani, "That document is now in the possession of the Russian Consul!"

Mamaqani is enraged, "I consented that this prisoner be brought here!"

Smiling triumphantly at Mamaqani, Eyes steps back and sits on a Persian rug.

Anitchkov opens the folded manuscript. A slip of paper with some writing in Persian on it slips out of the manuscript. Anitchkov passes it to Russian.

Ugly as ever, Mamaqani tries to see the paper and hear what Russian says near Anitchkov's ear. Russian whispers to Anitchkov, "It says he cannot speak openly at this moment."

Anitchkov looks at Eyes and announces rhetorically, "The personal secretary of the Bab."

Mamaqani adds proudly, "I signed the death warrant of the Bab with joy." And scornful of Eyes, "But you can't believe a word that this man says. He served at his feet for six years."

Eyes touches a spot of light dancing on the rug from a small hole in the window curtain, flapping in the breeze. He recalls the day in 1843 when he and Shaykh sat around a similar light ray dancing on floor tiles in the courtyard of Siyyid Kazim in Karbala.

Manaqani laughs disdainfully, "But look at him now!"

Eyes further recalls that Mamaqani in Siyyid Kazim's courtyard looked with displeasure toward the light ray.

Manaqani concludes, "Now he denies any faith in the Bab!"

Eyes straightens his back, bites his lip, raises his arm pointing at Mamaqani's face, glaring at him and exclaims forcefully, "When Siyyid Kazim died, this man had the nerve to declare that he himself was the promised one! How ridiculous he is!"

TABRIZ BARRACKS

High up on a ladder in the drill field, an Armenian swings a large mallet driving two large iron stakes into the plastered surface of the structural beam featured previously in Youth's dream. These stakes are about 10 feet above the ground. On roofs around the barracks drill field about 16 feet up, an agitated, massive 10,000 spectators observe.

Under the hot mid-day sun, Armenian soldiers are assembling in the drill field. They load their rifles.

Note: The Armenian soldiers dress differently than the Tabriz soldiers in Youth's dream described above. Spectators are a cross section of the Tabriz population, all ages from young children to the old, men and women.

HOUSE OF BAHA'U'LLAH, TEHRAN

Kid sits on the divan between Musa and Musa's Wife. They look up.

Majid arrives at the parlor entrance. Panting, he reports blankly in a serious but not sad tone, as if it were a foregone conclusion, "Vahid was martyred in Nayriz." He catches his breath, "They're taking Babi heads on bayonets to Shiraz."

NARROW TABRIZ STREET

At an isolated spot with no one else in sight along a non-descript walled street, Shaykh hands to Eyes a new headpiece and the reins of a horse, "Put this on and get going."

TABRIZ BARRACKS

Youth rises to his feet by Farrash, who leads him toward the door of the detention cell. Colonel nervously speaks to the Bab, "I am a Christian ... I have nothing against you. I do not want to shed your blood..." He is painfully trapped, "but I have been ordered!"

Farrash leads Youth out. The Bab replies to Colonel, "Follow your instructions. If your intention is sincere, God is able to remove your fears."

Colonel turns around. Having returned, Farrash waits in the doorway.

On the roof of the barracks on the beam-side of the field, Russian looks about. He pushes through the throng of spectators, as a mother by him holds a small child up to see better. "Ten thousand spectators," he notes.

Without shoes or hat, Youth looks around as two Armenians, one on each wrist, complete loop knots in ropes already tied to Youth's wrists.

An Armenian pulls the loop knot tight in one of these ropes, inches from Youth's wrist.

Shaykh is on the roof of the barracks adjacent to Russian's position. He can see the beam in the distance below with Youth and an Armenian starting up a ladder. Above them, spectators begin to move back realizing that they are in a dangerous position if the firing squad will be firing in their direction.

At Russian's position, Youth, the beam and ladder cannot be seen. However, Russian can see the Armenians below starting to form a pattern, grouping in three long curved lines in arcs around the beam position. Russian makes further mental notes, "My God! ... Sam Khan has 750 men in his firing squad."

With Youth and the Armenian half way up the ladder, panic breaks out in the spectators above them. They scatter.

Russian is pushed over by spectators rushing back.

Tabriz: Barrack-square where the Bab was executed. Pillar marked X is where he was suspended and shot.

At the top of the ladder, the Armenian puts the loop on one of Youth's wrists on a stake. He places the loop attached to Youth's other wrist on the second stake.

Farrash, Colonel and the Bab emerge on to the drill field. Spectators shout out, "There he is!"

The Armenian gives Youth a little shove from the ladder and Youth dangles by his wrists from the stakes.

Youth shouts to the Armenian, "Put him behind me ... please!" The Armenian responds by trying to fish Youth back on to the ladder.

Farrash loudly reproves the Armenian, "You don't take orders from him!"

Colonel shouts at them, "Do what he said! Put the Bab behind him!"

The front line of Armenians lie on their stomachs, positioning their rifles. The second row begins to kneel on one knee. The third row remains standing to fire over them.

Russian regains his footing and sees this firing squad formation.

Instead of fleeing the city, Eyes arrives at the drill field main gate. Wearing the hat Shaykh gave him, he slips inside, hoping that nobody recognizes him. He moves along the barracks wall among spectators viewing from the edge of the drill field.

Finally, Colonel plants his feet at one flank of the Armenians, ready to fire on Youth and the Bab. Some in the crowd shout out, "Now he will rise to heaven!"

Colonel looks down as he raises his fist aloft, screaming, "Ready!"

Armenians cock rifles, as the crowd hushes.

A child grips the nearby hand of an adult.

Colonel screams, "Aim!"

Colonel closes his eyes grimacing.

In the spectators, a mother holding a two year old puts her hand over its eyes turning the child away.

In near silence, Colonel thrusts his fist down, screaming, "Fire!"

In a very loud gunfire volley, flashes and smoke burst forth from the rifles.

Inside the barracks directly behind the beam holding the suspended prisoners outside about 8 feet above the floor, a circular area with a 5 foot radius of the small rectangular window panes on both sides of the beam bursts inward, shattered by so many bullets that the fragments are very small. The wooden frames of the window panes are shattered to splinters by the tremendous force of the impact.

Viewed from the drill field outside, the gunfire volley reduced the ropes suspending Youth and the Bab to threads. The plaster was blown off the beam leaving the iron stakes stuck in bare mud-bricks.

Moments later, in the room behind the beam, dense smoke from the gunpowder blasts gusts inward through the gaping semi-circular holes on each side of the beam.

Spectators in hysteria around him, Shaykh peers through his watery eyes and the smoke. The bright sunlight is obscured. A cloud of dense smoke from the rifle volley darkens the area.

Shaykh pushes forward among the spectators and screams of hysterical women. But his view is nearly non-existent since a huge cloud of powder smoke has completely filled the drill field.

From all sides, crowd members shout out hysterically, "He has disappeared!"

Youth lies on the ground at the base of the beam. He sits up rubbing his temple with one hand and picking up one of the many ball-shaped bullets lying about. The ropes tied to his wrists dangle, but a few inches of length remain. The rope ends are frayed.

The smoke cloud begins to rise. Farrash grabs Youth's forearm. Youth looks up at Farrash. Both are bewildered. "Am I dead?" Youth asks.

During the activity outside, Eyes has make his way back to the detention cell. It is much darker inside than before. He frantically gathers up papers that had been left on the cell floor. He is nervous and breathes heavily. Amid the uproar outside, Eyes hears a closer sound and looks up startled.

Visibility in the drill field increases as the cloud of smoke begins to clear. The Armenian riflemen have all stood up and look around and at each other.

The spectator uproar has now turned ugly and the authorities are being jeered, "Where is he?", "He rose to heaven", "A miracle", "The Bab has returned to God" and the like. Hysterical screaming and wailing continues. Colonel examines the wrists of Youth as Farrash looks up at the increasingly hostile spectators. The Bab is nowhere to be seen and Youth is not even scratched. Youth looks around dazed and grinning.

Some Armenians cautiously approach Youth and Colonel. Farrash loudly barks out orders, "Close the gates! Search the grounds! Find him!"

Armenians and others in the drill field below run in all directions in and out of the barracks and arsenal quarters adjoining the field.

Farrash grabs Youth's arm again and parades him out in plain view of the spectators, still in hysterical uproar. Farrash thrusts Youth's arm in the air and points with a dramatic jerking motion with his other hand at the rope on the upraised wrist of Youth, shouting, "Look! The bullets cut the ropes! Look! They just cut the ropes! That's all! No more! This is no miracle!"

It was the Bab that Eyes had heard at the detention cell doorway. The Bab sits and chants the words of his last message, as he had promised would be done. Eyes sits calmly writing to record every word of the Bab.

Farrash enters the cell, looks at the Bab and gasps, "Unhurt!"

The Bab calmly addresses Farrash, "I have finished my instructions. Now you may proceed to fulfil your intention."

In the room behind the beam, direct sunlight now casts the shadows of the beam and of the remaining window frames on the floor. Splinters of wood from the shattered frames and fragments of glass, much of it almost a powder, glistens in the sunlight. The gaping semi-circular holes in the windows indicate the concentrated distribution of bullet impact points centered about half way up the two-story brick beam. At the periphery, some of the remaining dusty window panes are partially broken from stray bullets.

A piece of glass hangs precariously from one of these frames at the border of the open hole. It falls.

The glass hits the floor and the debris on it and breaks into several pieces with a mild tingle sound.

Postscript

The exact words of the Bab are recorded in his writings and history books. This true story continues to this day.

The man in charge of the execution of the Bab interrupted the Bab's last message. The Bab made an astounding statement that he would complete his last message. And he did finish that message to his followers.

750 large musket balls bombarded the Bab and his young companion, severing the ropes suspending them but not even scratching either one of them.

The reported events appear to defy the law of probability. The rifles used in those days were not very accurate. There was no smokeless powder either. A huge cloud of smoke brought darkness at noontime.

The Christian commander of the Armenian regiment (Colonel) begged to be relieved of his duty. He refused to make another attempt on the life of the Bab. He took his men from the scene, praising the Bab to his dying day.

Some claim that the failure of the Christian regiment to execute the Bab fulfilled a belief among Shi'ih Muslims that the "promised one" could not be harmed by non-Muslims. Indeed, the Christian regiment was probably chosen for the execution to discredit the claim of the Bab and his followers.

Another regiment was brought in composed of Muslim soldiers. And now the Bab had completed his last message as promised and had said that his time had come.

The Youth and the Bab were suspended on the same beam in the drill field and shot to death.

The Russian Consul Anitchkov ordered that a sketch be made of their remains. Their bodies were smashed together by the impact of the bullets. They were literally joined into one mass. But their faces were strangely free of marks from the bullets. The young companion in martyrdom of the Bab had begged to be with him always.

The inseparable frames of the Bab and that youth were thrown into the dry city moat to be eaten by dogs. Another Muslim belief is said to be that animals cannot harm the body of the true promised one. But some Babis risked their lives to recover these remains, lending further support for the truth of the Bab's claim.

What happened next is a whole other story. But about 60 years later, these remains were brought to Haifa and interred in 1909 at the Baha'i World Center.

The faith initiated by the Bab quickly spread around the world to people in well over 100,000 localities and some 150 countries and independent territories. People who today call themselves "Baha'is."

Between then and now, many thousands of people gave their lives as martyrs rather than deny their beliefs. Even today in some areas of the world, Baha'is are still persecuted simply because of their beliefs.

Clearly, the message of the Babis was not suppressed. They were the Dawn-Breakers.

Made in the USA
Coppell, TX
21 February 2022

73881982R00164